BLOODY LONDON

R.G MORGAN

Prologue

During my time as the chronicler of Sherlock Holmes, I was on several occasions compelled to explain that my accounts of his exploits were selective rather than exhaustive. There were often enquires from those with intimate knowledge of cases which failed to make the printed page as to why I had omitted them from my published reports.

The answer was either that the matter was of such delicacy that it could not be relayed to the public without the greatest risk to national security, or else that my friend brought so swift a conclusion to the matter that to record it in an entertaining fashion was rendered quite impossible.

Yet there is one case which provides so glaring an omission from my accounts of Holmes' more illustrious adventures, that it must have long seemed quite inexplicable.

It was in the year 1888 that Sherlock Holmes was engaged in what seems destined to forever remain the most remarkable and infamous of his many cases. Over thirty years after events, the murders committed in Whitechapel by the man known as Jack the Ripper have never expunged themselves from the collective consciousness of this country. For many years, I have remained silent on the part played by my friend in the pursuit of his most celebrated opponent.

So extraordinary were the events of 'The Autumn of Terror', which tested Sherlock Holmes like no other case, it seemed itself a crime that they were never conveyed to a wider audience. Holmes insisted that I never reveal his part in the matter, and for many years I kept my silence on the matter.

What follows is my own account of the Whitechapel murders, which I was forced to promise Holmes that I would never commit to paper. Although ignoring his wishes weighs heavily upon me, I have long felt that failing to record the true story of Jack the Ripper carries an even greater burden.

Posterity has been kind to the name of Sherlock Holmes. His reputation seems only to have risen since those distant days when his rooms in Baker Street seemed to be the hub of all crime detection. The name of Jack the Ripper has equally endured: his deeds as infamous now as when they were commanding headlines around the world.

The events I recall on the following pages, as both my memory and notes allow, are of the battle that passed between these two immortal figures in those dark days of 1888.

Dr John H. Watson

March 1919

1.

An outrage at George Yard

It was the afternoon following the Bank Holiday that found Holmes and I lounging about our sitting room, solemnly reading the newspapers. It had thus far proved to be a miserable summer and from the overcast sky, a thin rain persisted which tapped incessantly against our windows.

'I see that The Times was very impressed with Professor Baldwin,' I said.

'A triumph of entertainment over accomplishment,' replied Holmes without looking up from his paper. 'A crowd-pleasing exercise, I'll grant you, Watson. But one utterly devoid of any scientific merit, I am sorry to say.'

'You are quite insufferable at times, Holmes,' I said. 'Why, the man attained a thousand feet in his balloon.'

'Really, Watson, you disappoint me,' said Holmes, putting down his paper and eyeing me contemptuously. 'I would have thought that a man of science such as yourself would have wished to take in a more worthy spectacle as a means of entertainment on a dreary Bank Holiday. At least they had organ recitals at Crystal Palace.'

'I only suggested it to relieve you from the tedium of Baker Street. I am aware you've had no new cases in weeks.'

'Forgive me, my dear Watson. I know you had my best interests at heart. I confess to finding the damp air curiously invigorating. But I need work, my dear fellow! A challenge! London doesn't produce the criminals that it once did.'

Before I could respond, Mrs Hudson knocked upon the sitting room door.

'Inspector Lestrade to see you, Mr Holmes,' said our landlady, as the figure of that same man emerged from behind her.

'Thank you, Mrs Hudson,' said Holmes as he surveyed the Inspector's harried appearance. 'Lestrade! Pray sit down. Why, you look positively washed out.'

The Inspector took a seat as instructed. From the light crimson of his cheeks and faltering breath, it was clear that he had arrived here in some hurry.

'Something terrible has occurred, Holmes,' he blustered.

'Evidently,' said Holmes drily. 'And what is it that has brought you here in so crumpled a state?'

'Murder, Mr Holmes. The most brutal I have ever seen.'

'I see,' said Holmes with perfect equanimity. 'And where did this outrage take place?'

'George Yard, just off Whitechapel High Street. The body was found a little before five o'clock this morning. It has made The Star already.'

'Forgive me, Lestrade,' said Holmes, leafing through his collection of newspapers until he had found a copy of The Star. 'But we were a little late in rising today and I am somewhat behind with my morning reading. At Watson's insistence, we spent an exhausting Bank Holiday traipsing across London in the name of entertainment.'

My friend cast me a withering look and Lestrade's eyes darted between us in perplexed fashion.

'The story is on page two,' said the Inspector.

'Ah, I see. Watson, if you would be so kind,' said Holmes, handing me the folded-up paper.

'Certainly, Holmes.' I proceeded to read the short account of the murder, which ran as follows:

'"A Whitechapel Horror. A woman, now lying unidentified at the mortuary, Whitechapel, was ferociously stabbed to death this morning, between two and four o'clock, on the landing of a stone staircase in George's-buildings, Whitechapel.
George's-buildings are tenements occupied by the poor labouring class. A lodger going to his work found the body. Another lodger says the murder had not been committed when he returned home about two o'clock. The woman was stabbed in no less than twenty places. No weapon was found near her, and her murderer has left no trace. She is of middle age and height, has black hair and a large, round face and apparently belonged to the lowest class.'"

'You see, Mr Holmes? It really was a most savage attack,' said Lestrade when I had finished reading.

'Evidently, Lestrade.'

'Twenty times!' I exclaimed. 'What on earth possesses a man to strike so repeatedly? Robbery, perhaps?'

'But the poor woman had nothing to steal,' replied Lestrade. 'And there were no cries or shouts heard by anyone in the building.'

'Revenge, then?' I offered. Holmes shook his head.

'No, no, my dear fellow. If there were no cries heard, then this was not the result of an argument or revenge attack. No, the woman was led to her death quite willingly, her assailant attacking her with quite sudden and unbridled ferocity.'

'We think she may have led her murderer there, in point of fact,' said Lestrade, with the casual air of superiority which so often infuriated Holmes. 'We believe her to have been an unfortunate.'

'Well that point is suggested from the hour of her death upon the landing of such a building,' said Holmes testily. 'He was evidently a client of hers.'

'That is what we believe.'

'A most singular case. Any there any other details of note?'

'Well, the fellow who discovered the body, a labourer by the name of Reeves, noticed that her hands were clenched and her skirts had been pulled up to the waist.'

'I see. Clenched hands, of course, are a classic trait of strangulation. I should think that the woman was dead before her killer commenced his frenzied attack.'

'So, what are we dealing with?' asked Lestrade. 'A madman?'

'A madman does not kill so silently and leave no clue as to his identity,' said Holmes, shaking his head. 'I fear you may have entered rather murky waters, Lestrade.'

'And your advice?'

'Is to complete your enquires and return here with the facts. I require more data before I can reach any conclusion.'

'Right you are, Mr Holmes. I shall inform you of any developments.'

Lestrade departed with a rather dejected air as Holmes strolled over to the window, lighting a cigarette as he followed the Inspector's path along a drizzly Baker Street.

'I do not think that we have heard the last of this pretty puzzle, Watson,' he said, before lounging back upon the sofa in a heap of newspapers. There he remained in quiet contemplation for the rest of the afternoon.

Sherlock Holmes was proved correct on Lestrade's returning to Baker Street, although it was over a week before we heard from him again regarding the murder at George Yard. Holmes had been engaged in one or two minor cases which did little to pique his professional interest but necessitated some time away from Baker Street. Thus, I had seen little of him for several days when he returned home on a Wednesday evening, during which time the George Yard victim had been identified.

'It is a lamentable fact of the profession of Consulting Detective,' he said wearily as he poured himself a whisky and soda. 'That to deduct and theorize is seldom enough to conclude even the most mundane of cases. One must prove one's theories correct even when the solution is obvious from the first. I have just spent a tiresome few days proving the innocence of a Mr Thackeray from Maidenhead, when I was certain that he was entirely blameless in the matter even before I had left the confines of Baker Street.'

Holmes sipped on his whisky, his eyes glazed with exhaustion as he sat down heavily in his chair. His thoughts, whatever they may have been, were interrupted by the appearance of Inspector Lestrade in our doorway.

'Good evening, Lestrade,' said Holmes brightly. 'Why, you look in dire need of a whisky, my dear fellow. Please, sit down.'

'Thank you, Mr Holmes,' said Lestrade, taking a seat. 'Good evening, Doctor Watson. I thought I would call in on my way to the Yard.'

'How very kind of you, Lestrade. I see that you left for work far earlier than usual this morning upon receiving a telegram summoning you as a matter of urgency,' said Holmes, as he poured the Inspector's drink. 'You were then compelled to return home in a hurry before reaching your destination.'

'Why, yes!' he exclaimed. 'How the devil did you know that?'

'My dear Lestrade, the merest glance at the fresh wound to your right jaw line tells me that you cut yourself shaving this morning.'

'I see. Well that is quite correct, Holmes.'

'You are a man of meticulous personal habits, Inspector. Such a blemish tells me that you were compelled to shave in a hurry. As I know you to be as particular with regards to your punctuality as you are to your appearance, it is evident that you were compelled to rush your morning routine. It is obvious that only an urgent call to the Yard could provide such an emergency.

'The earliness of the hour is confirmed by the left side of your face being noticeably bristlier than the other, indicating that you were compelled to shave by candlelight. You have consequently failed to shave evenly, as the candle was placed to your right, denying you a full view of the opposite side.'

'Splendid!' I observed.

'You do have a way of observing these little things,' conceded Lestrade. 'I've never denied that. But how do you deduce I returned home?'

'Your shirt collar is clean. There is no corresponding blood stain which should provide evidence of your abrasion. You clearly returned home soon after leaving in order to replace your shirt with a fresh one. You did this in a hurry, for there is still a smear of blood on your right forefinger, indicating that you did not even pause long enough to properly wash your hands.'

'A very workmanlike series of deductions, admittedly,' said Lestrade as Holmes handed him a whisky.

'I assume you are here regarding the Tabram murder?'

'You have been following the case, then?'

'I have read the newspaper accounts while engaged in one or two petty trifles, Lestrade,' said Holmes.

'I thought it would interest you. Yes, Martha Tabram was her name. A wretched life if ever there was one.'

'I understand from the papers that some soldiers were suspected?' I said. Lestrade sighed.

'Yes, they were, Dr Watson,' he said. 'We had hoped we were about to solve the case. A PC Barrett stated that he saw a soldier loitering outside George Yard on the night of the murder. But he was then unable to point him out in an identity parade. We were also given the run around by a friend of the deceased by the name of Mary Ann Connelly. She failed again today to identify anyone who couldn't provide a cast iron alibi.'

'You have had quite the time of it,' observed Holmes wryly.

'The injuries alone were enough to give me fits,' sighed Lestrade. 'A total of thirty-nine stab wounds, it's now been confirmed. All but one was made by an ordinary penknife. The was made by a bayonet, or so the doctor thought.'

'As I recall, Lestrade, it was a weapon very much like a bayonet, not necessarily that precise weapon. You have read the reports, Watson. What do you make of it?'

'I can only say as a medical man that as soft tissues compress and wounds can stretch after death, it is not easy to have more than a fair idea of knife size in such an attack.'

'Thank you, Watson. Consider, Lestrade, that a bayonet is hardly the easiest of weapons to conceal. Is it likely the murderer would choose such an instrument and then use it just the once?'

'You think the soldier enquires without prospect, then?'

'I do.'

Lestrade appeared exasperated as he studied Holmes.

'Well, I must be leaving in any case,' said he, finishing the remainder of his whisky and rising from his chair. 'I am needed back at the Yard. Goodnight, Holmes. Dr Watson.'

'There is something I do not like about this business, Watson,' said Holmes, as soon as we had bidden Lestrade farewell and watched him hurry out of the room.

'The lack of motive?'

'Precisely, Watson. I have never known a crime without a purpose, yet this murder has none. There was apparently no argument, and the poor woman's position in life makes it impossible that robbery was our man's intention.'

'Did she have something that the killer wanted back? Some personal effect, perhaps?'

'I do not think so,' said Holmes with a shake of his head. 'Surely if he had desired an item in her possession, there would have been a quarrel before he resorted to murder? And why then proceed to stab the woman no less than thirty-nine times, instead of simply taking his spoils and making good his escape? The strangulation itself would have been enough to render her quite helpless. No, whoever murdered this woman brought her to George Yard for the sole purpose of inflicting those gruesome injuries. And until we know his purpose, I am not sure we have heard the last of this killer.'

'You think he will strike again?' I gasped.

'I believe he will, Watson. Although I hope to God that I am wrong.'

2.

A mystery at Buck's Row

Despite his indefatigable nature when in the midst of a case, which at times bordered on the inhuman, Sherlock Holmes had never been an early riser. Although seemingly impervious to lack of sleep when on the scent of a solution, at other times it was impossible to stir him from his bed at a decent hour without receiving the most rigorous protestations in defence of slumber. It was therefore something of a surprise to be awoken from a fitful sleep at eight o'clock on a Saturday morning by Holmes' shrill cry emanating from our sitting room. I opened my bedroom door to the sight of Holmes reading a telegram, a marked frown upon his sharp features.

'Ah, Watson!' said he as I entered the room. 'Read this.' He thrust the telegram into my hands. It read as follows:

Another murder. This one in Buck's Row, Whitechapel. For God's sake come immediately. Lestrade.

'Goodness, Holmes! Another murder, just as you predicted!' I exclaimed.

'It would appear so, Watson. Can you be ready in five minutes?'

'Most certainly.'

Within minutes, I was rushing down our staircase, still completing my dress as I emerged onto a quiet, chilly Baker Street to see Holmes hailing a cab.

'Do you think this attack was by the same hand as the last?' I asked, as we clattered east towards Whitechapel in a hansom.

'It is impossible to be certain until we are in possession of the facts, but I suspect so.'

'How can you tell?'

'Come, Watson. The use of the phrase 'another murder' surely suggests that there are features of this latest atrocity which place it above the common and force comparison with the George Yard outrage. I fear that something quite ghastly awaits us at Buck's Row.'

We approached our destination along Whitechapel Road, merging with the trams, omnibuses, cabs and carts which seemed to fill every foot of its vast expanse. The great rush of humanity which swept past us seemed like a microcosm of the great city itself. On either side of the road were tall, decrepit buildings, stained by smog and ravaged by age and ill-repair. They housed every manner of shops, from fishmongers to a seller of caged birds, whose noisy offerings were stacked precariously outside his premises. The gutters trickled with blood from the slaughterhouses, the mud-caked pavements stinking with the odour of rotten fruit. Above the clatter of the road elderly hawkers, clad in their long, filthy coats barked their wares, competing with the newspaper boys for the attention of passers-by.

The murder site was a narrow, cobbled road just north of Whitechapel Road and the London Hospital. At its western point was a board school where the road widened out into a larger thoroughfare. Holmes called our driver to halt and we alighted just where the road began to narrow and grow darker.

We saw the agitated figure of Lestrade talking to another officer outside a row of shabby, two-storied cottages. Word of the murder had evidently spread, for further up the road was a rabble of early morning sightseers standing restlessly outside a warehouse and gossiping in low voices.

At the sound of our footsteps, Lestrade turned sharply, a look of relief sweeping across his features as he saw Holmes and I approach.

'Mr Holmes,' he cried, striding towards us. 'And Dr Watson. Thank God you've arrived.'

'We came as quickly as we could,' I assured him.

'I owe you both a debt of thanks and that's the truth,' said the vexed Inspector, rubbing his hands together in the cold morning air. 'Another murder, even more brutal than the last one.'

Holmes surveyed the row of cottages, whose walls were just catching the first rays of morning sunlight.

'Committed just here, I presume?' said Holmes, as he walked over to the stable yard at the end of the cottages.

'Why yes, Holmes. It was just there. How did you know that?'

'On a cold morning such as this, Lestrade, soaked cobblestones will stay wet for some time. I do not imagine the stable owner is in the habit of washing down his yard at such an ungodly hour. I take it that the blood stains have been washed away?'

Lestrade nodded.

'The lad who lives next door. He works at the stable, so I'm told. He washed the blood away before Inspector Spratling arrived.'

'Dear, dear, Lestrade. You really do not make it easy for me to formulate any conclusions.'

Holmes returned to his examination of the yard gate.

'I cannot see what can possibly be deduced by mere bloodstains, in any case,' replied Lestrade defensively.

'Which is why I fear that you will never rise to the top of your profession.'

'And is there any clue to be found here?' asked Lestrade, appearing to ignore Holmes' remark.

'None, Lestrade,' he replied, studying the ground around the yard. 'The owner of the stable has an elderly dog which is never kept on a lead. The man was ambitious once, but in recent years has had less interest in his work. But I can tell you nothing of what transpired here this morning.'

'You can see nothing which aids the enquiry?' asked Lestrade.

'There is no clue to be gathered here as I see it now. What may have existed before I arrived and has been carelessly washed away, I cannot say.'

'It was not my command to wash any evidence away, Holmes!' protested Lestrade, his wiry frame knotted with rage.

'Well you can at least assist me now. The facts, Lestrade! I cannot work blind!'

Lestrade eyed Holmes sulkily before reaching into his breast pocket for his notebook.

'We don't know her name yet, but we think she was an unfortunate, just like Tabram. She was found by the stable door, just as you said. She was on her back, her head facing east and her left hand touching the gate. She was found at about three-forty by two carmen on their way to work. While they went in search of a policeman, PC Neil

13

passed here on his beat and came upon the body. He saw by the light of his lantern that the throat had been savagely cut.

'Dr Llewellyn was summoned, and the body removed to the mortuary. There was very little blood at the scene and the Doctor was uncertain whether she had been murdered where she was found. The neighbours were questioned. Mrs Green, whose son washed the blood away, lives on the first floor. She's a light sleeper and yet was undisturbed throughout the night. A Mr Purkis, who manages the Essex Wharf just opposite the stable, lives with his wife on the second floor at the front of the house. The wife says she was awake most of the night, yet the first she knew of anything was when they were awoken by a Constable telling them that a murder had been committed.'

'It is most certainly an interesting case,' said Holmes. 'And there is the decided want of a clue as to the culprit.'

'But I haven't told you the worst part,' said Lestrade, his voice quietening as he drew closer to us. 'When Inspector Spratling examined the body at the mortuary, he found that her stomach had been dreadfully mutilated.'

'Dear God, Holmes!' I exclaimed.

'Can you take us to the mortuary, Lestrade?' asked my friend earnestly.

'Certainly, Holmes. Inspector Helson has already been there. The body will have been washed by now, but we can go at once if you think it may help.'

'In the absence of any other clues, I consider it essential.'

'Very well. I shall leave instructions and we can be on our way,' said Lestrade. He hurried over to a Constable stood just opposite the stable yard.

'Well, this business certainly grows darker, Watson,' said Holmes. 'I'm not sure I can recall a case like it.'

'Have you any theory at all?' I asked.

'I have several. But I cannot yet be certain that any are correct. I can, however, state with some degree of certainty that this poor woman was murdered where she was found. If Lestrade's summary of events proves correct, I would wager that this was not the result of a quarrel, but something far more sinister.'

14

'If you gentlemen are ready, we can make our way to the mortuary,' said Lestrade, as he rejoined us. 'I hope you won't object to a walk, but it is only a couple of minutes away.'

'On the contrary, Lestrade, it shall allow me time to digest the information with which you have furnished me. Please lead the way.'

'Holmes,' I said, as we turned along Baker's Row. 'Perhaps I am failing to see the obvious, but how on earth could you deduce so much about the owner of the stable?'

'Ah, Watson!' said Holmes, with a mischievous grin. 'I could see that my deductions had baffled you. The presence of a dog was apparent from the scratches along the front of the gate. The scratches were evidently made in excitement while his master opened the gate. The distance between the scratches and the gate prohibit the possibility that the dog was on a lead while the gate was being unlocked. The older scratches were somewhat higher than the more recent, suggesting a gradual decline in vitality and thus an elderly canine. The gate lock, you observed, was extremely old. One could see numerous scratches upon it. These were evidently caused by someone attempting to insert the key in the dark when opening or closing the stable. Since all the scratches were old, it seems clear that the stable owner has ceased to work the hours which he once did.'

'Why, I might have studied that gate all day and not noticed that!' I exclaimed. Holmes gave a shrill laugh, his foggy breath visible in the cold air.

We passed onto Old Montague street, which was already coming to life as the many shopkeepers prepared for the day's trade.

Lestrade directed us into a thoroughfare next to a costermonger's, at the farthest end of which was little more than a shed, now much dilapidated with age and decay. This we discovered from the makeshift sign upon the door, itself rather the worse for wear, was the Workhouse Infirmary Mortuary.

The mortuary, if one could call it such, was a cramped room of about ten feet square. On one side of the wall were shelves holding a clutter of jars and bottles. In the centre of the room, on a rickety mortuary table, the poor woman laid covered by a white cloth.

A middle-aged man dressed in filthy shirt and trousers was sat in one corner on a wooden chair. He nodded in acknowledgement at Lestrade as we entered, but otherwise ignored our presence.

'I warn you, Holmes, the injuries are awful,' said Lestrade. 'Dr Llewellyn said he'd never seen such a brutal affair.'

'Watson, perhaps you would do the honours?' said Holmes.

'Certainly, Holmes,' I replied. I peeled back the cloth to examine the corpse.

During my time in Afghanistan, I was witness to many appalling wounds and observed the extent to which a human may cause injury to another. I have also assisted in numerous operations and post-mortems. But I confess that despite Lestrade's warning, I was quite unprepared for the sight which met my eyes. Before me lay the body of a woman, perhaps in her late thirties, with greying hair and delicate features. I am sure that she must have once been pretty; before the corrosive life that had led her to her death had dulled any vestige of beauty. Yet my eyes were drawn in the first instance to her throat, which had been fearfully slashed in two distinct cuts from ear to ear. The poor woman had also been subject to an attack upon her abdomen, performed with a ferocity I could scarcely have imagined.

'What can you tell us, Watson?' asked Holmes, his features quite ashen as he surveyed the horrific spectacle.

'The throat has been savagely cut back to the vertebrae. I'm not sure I have seen anything quite like it. The abdomen has been mutilated from just below the breastbone to its lower part, laying open a portion of the belly. It is appalling, Holmes.'

'That it is, Watson,' said Holmes. 'Lestrade, I must warn you that in the compass of my experience, I have never encountered a case that presented so much by way of intrigue while offering so little in the prospect of clues. I fear we shall find that these events may herald a chapter in the annals of crime that remain quite their own.'

'You are certain that these two murders are linked?'

'Watson asked me that very question before we arrived at Buck's Row. I have seen nothing there nor before me now which dissuades me that my response to him was incorrect. I am quite certain that they are.'

16

'That was our initial thought,' said Lestrade. 'I had hoped you would find something which led you to another conclusion.'

'If I am correct, then you at least have only one murderer to find rather than two.'

'But what's his game, Holmes?' asked Lestrade.

'That is the most worrying aspect of all,' said Holmes, as he glanced again at the poor woman's remains. 'I haven't yet the least notion.'

Our journey back to Baker Street was memorable only for the silence of my companion. Sherlock Holmes, with his arms folded and long frame arched stiffly into the seat of a hansom, seemed to be the very picture of contemplation. My experiences of such instances informed my decision to dare not interject my own thoughts on the matter. Although he often requested my opinion- I flatter myself that on occasion he valued such contributions- at other times Holmes was to be left to his own thoughts. I confess that the murders, such was their unbridled and apparently motiveless ferocity, occupied my own mind as we rattled west through the more salubrious environs of the capital.

Holmes refused breakfast upon our return to Baker Street, disappearing into his bedroom the instant he had persuaded Mrs Hudson that sustenance was unnecessary. It was not until late morning that he emerged into our sitting room, appearing as though he had just awoken from the most invigorating sleep.

'Ah, Watson!' said he. 'I had half expected to find you already out for the day. Am I to take it you are not meeting a certain Miss Morstan?'

Ever since my betrothal, Holmes had taken it upon himself to subject me to well-meaning jibes regarding my impending marriage to Miss Mary Morstan. To the detached sensibilities of Sherlock Holmes, the pursuit of a wife was an unfathomable endeavour, dependent as it was on that most illogical of human impulses: love.

'I am not, Holmes. I quite fear I would be poor company if I were. This morning's business has rattled me somewhat.'

'As it has I, Watson. I have never seen so vile a spectacle.'

'Have you considered the case further?'

17

'I have done little else since the moment I cast eyes upon the poor woman's remains.'

'And have you formulated any conclusions?'

'None, save for the fact that only further enquires in the correct places may provide us with any clue to the matter.'

'And which places might these be?'

'They are my very next port of call, Watson!'

'Can I be of any assistance, Holmes?' I asked, as he made his way to the door.

'Absolutely, Watson. Please inform Mrs Hudson that I shall not be returning for dinner. It would also be of inestimable assistance were you to procure that information concerning this second atrocity not already furnished us by Lestrade.'

'Of course, Holmes.'

'Splendid! I shall send word of my own progress as soon as my enquires throw any light upon this sorry affair.'

Sherlock Holmes was absent that evening and the following morning had still not returned to Baker Street. Knowing my friend's methods as I did, I was not perturbed by his absence and more than a little curious as to where his enquires had taken him. Endeavouring to fulfil my promise to Holmes, I made my way to Scotland Yard in search of Lestrade. The name of Sherlock Holmes was enough to allow my passage up a staircase and into Lestrade's office. The Inspector was sat at his desk, barely visible above a mountain of files and so engrossed by the papers in his hands that he scarcely noticed my arrival.

'Good Heavens! Dr Watson!' he exclaimed, when he saw me approaching his desk. He stood up and shook my hand, motioning for me to take a seat. 'Please excuse the mess. This place has become bedlam in the last few weeks. I presume that your visit relates to yesterday's events?'

I nodded.

'Holmes has asked me to make enquires regarding any new information that might be of interest.'

'Well there is certainly plenty of that, Doctor,' said the Inspector, gesturing to the stacks of papers that occupied almost his entire desk. 'But none which has provided the slightest lead in finding the culprit.'

'Are there any facts of which you feel Holmes would be interested?'

'I can you give you her name if you like. She was Mary Ann Nichols; known to many as Polly. A friend of hers from the workhouse identified her yesterday evening. She'd just turned forty-three and had been separated from her husband for some years. She made her living on the streets. The last person to see her alive was a friend who saw her drunk on a street corner. That was about an hour before she was found murdered.'

'And of the murder itself? Is there anything you can tell me?'

'Dr Llewellyn is performing the post-mortem this morning in preparation for the inquest. Perhaps I could arrange a meeting with him for later this evening?'

'That would be splendid,' I said.

'And might I enquire where Holmes is?'

'In truth, I haven't a clue, Inspector. He is pursuing his own course of action and asked me to make investigations on his behalf.'

'Hum! Devil knows what goes on in the mind of Mr Sherlock Holmes. Still, if he can shake anything out of this one, I'll be amazed. Our finest detectives haven't yet found the slightest clue.'

'I am sure Holmes will uncover something soon, Inspector.'

'That remains to be seen, Doctor,' said Lestrade. 'I shall see you out.'

That evening, I visited upon Dr Llewellyn at his surgery on Whitechapel Road. It was situated just along from the Working Lads Institute, where Mary Nichols' inquest was being held. I arrived promptly at the given address; a narrow, three-storied building with a whitewashed front. Upon ringing the bell, I was greeted by a shy-looking maid, who could scarcely have been aged more than sixteen. She showed me into the back parlour and announced my arrival to a man who rose from his chair opposite Lestrade to greet me.

'Ah, Dr Watson!' said the man, shaking me warmly by the hand. 'I am Dr Llewellyn. Please sit down.' He indicated an armchair next to Lestrade, who greeted me warmly as I took my seat.

Dr Llewellyn appeared to be aged about forty, of middle height and stout build. A neat beard gave him a distinguished air, while his ruddy complexion and keen gaze hinted at a formidable nature.

'Inspector Lestrade told me of your interest in the Nichols case,' said Dr Llewellyn as he drew up his chair.

'The Inspector contacted my friend, Mr Sherlock Holmes, following the Tabram murder,' I explained. 'Holmes has followed events closely ever since.'

'I have long been an admirer of your friend's cases from your excellent series of chronicles. How may I be of assistance?'

'Anything you think may provide a clue as to the murderer would be of immense help, Dr Llewellyn. I understand you completed the post-mortem this morning?'

'Yes. A most disagreeable task.'

'Dr Watson viewed the body himself early yesterday morning,' said Lestrade.

'Really? And what did you make of it as a medical man?'

'I'm afraid I did not examine the poor woman properly. Yet I could not help being struck by the sheer calculated brutality of the attack. I rather hoped you might be able to furnish me with further details of her injuries.'

'Certainly. I can give you a copy of my post-mortem report. It was a most brutal attack. With regards to clues, I thought the knife must have been strong-bladed, moderately sharp and used with great violence. All the wounds were performed using the same knife and might have been executed within five minutes. I felt the murderer showed some rough anatomical knowledge, as he seemed to have attacked all the vital parts.'

'You saw some suggestions of surgical knowledge in so frenzied attack?' I asked incredulously.

'I myself thought it the result of some apoplectic rage. Yet a more thorough examination persuaded me that the killer evinced no mean degree of skill. It seemed to me that no-one with at least a serviceable regard of anatomy could have made those incisions.'

'Extraordinary!' I exclaimed.

'Do you mean to say it was a Doctor or surgeon that killed these poor women?' asked Lestrade, appearing equally astonished at this intelligence.

'I could see no medical purpose to the cuts I saw, Inspector. I certainly thought them not beyond a butcher or slaughterman.'

'And there are certainly plenty of those in Whitechapel,' said Lestrade wearily.

'It does narrow down the field appreciably, however,' I observed, certain that Holmes would be delighted with this information.

'It does give us a line of enquiry, I'll grant you, Doctor. But I'd still preferred it if our man had left a clue behind. As it is, I don't know whether to look for him at Barts or Smithfield Market.'

'I am sorry I cannot be of any more assistance, Inspector,' said Dr Llewellyn.

'I apologise if I sounded ungrateful, Dr Llewellyn. But as you will have noted at this afternoon's inquest, we have precious few clues and a public screaming for an arrest.'

'I quite understand your position, Inspector,' said Dr Llewellyn. 'Perhaps Mr Sherlock Holmes is at this moment discovering a clue.'

'I wouldn't count on it,' said Lestrade stuffily.

'You will concede that Holmes has proved himself correct on many occasions in the past,' I said in defence of my friend.

'He has put us on the right track once or twice, Dr Watson. I'll not deny that. But I fear that this time he has met his match.'

I politely declined the offer of tea and drew the interview to a close when it became clear that there was little else Dr Llewellyn could add to his account of the injuries. Although it had done little to brighten Lestrade's hopes of capturing the murderer, I was certain that Holmes would greet knowledge of the killer's anatomical skill with great interest.

3.

The Blue Coat Boy

Despite my many years as both his companion and chronicler, Sherlock Holmes never failed to astound me with his tenacity when in pursuit of a criminal. Thus, several days following my visit to Dr Llewellyn, I had still received no word from him. It was far from uncommon for Holmes to withhold the results of his investigations until he had the case firmly in his grasp. I therefore did not take his lack of communication as a sign that his efforts had thus far proved unsuccessful.

After spending the morning at my practice, I returned home to Baker Street, my mind occupied by the murder of Polly Nichols and the question of whether Holmes was any nearer to finding the culprit. By late afternoon, I had given up all hope of hearing from Holmes that day. Yet at four o'clock a telegram arrived, the contents of which sent me rushing for my coat and hat:

Watson. Please meet me at once at the Blue Coat Boy, Dorset Street, Spitalfields. This business is proving rather more interesting than I imagined. SH

I was in a cab within minutes, bound east into the great unknown. My knowledge of the lower portions of London was scarcely that of Holmes, and I confess to possessing only the vaguest of impressions as to the exact location of Dorset Street. I had certainly never heard of The Blue Coat Boy, which I imagined to be a hostelry or beer shop.

During the journey, I wondered what it was that had caused Holmes to request my presence. It was not beyond my friend to send such an enigmatic summons halfway across London, merely to announce that he had solved the case. With two poor women dead and Holmes certain that the killer could strike again, nothing would have given me greater pleasure than to arrive at my destination to discover that he had confounded Lestrade's expectations and identified the murderer.

Dorset Street was a narrow thoroughfare just off Commercial Street. I departed the headlong rush of carts and omnibuses of the main road and turned into as desperate and squalid a street as I was certain could be found in the whole of this great city. The tall buildings on either side hinted at a former prosperity, but were now much decayed and crumbling, drowning the filthy road in their yawning shadows. Men lounged in ancient doorways while gangs of women, some holding babies, stood outside lodging houses in their ragged clothes and battered bonnets. Almost every other house had the familiar box-shaped sign suspended above the doorway, signalling it as a common lodging house. My driver announced that we had reached my destination and drew to a halt outside one such establishment, much to the interest of some burly locals.

The Blue Coat Boy was a beer shop, outside which were standing perhaps a dozen men drinking tankards of ale which were served through a large front window. A couple of women, one with a child in a rickety pram, stood to the left of the window gossiping. Holmes was not amongst the noisy rabble, so I ventured inside. It was a cramped affair, filled with what I took to be tradesmen or market workers, who were either standing around wooden barrels or sat in the few seats tucked in the corner.

'Drink, Sir?' asked a large man with coarse whiskers as I cast my eye around in search of Holmes.

'Beer, thank you,' I said hastily. Without another word, the man filled a small tankard from a jug by the window and handed it to me, wiping his hands in his filthy apron.

'Three farthings,' he said huskily. I gave him a penny and he nodded in gratitude when I told him to keep the change.

I walked to the back of the shop, ignoring the inquisitive-I might say hostile- stares of the men I passed, but Holmes was nowhere to be seen. An old gentleman with a great white beard caught my gaze and gestured with his cane for me to sit opposite him in the furthest corner.

'A rarely see a fine gent such as yourself in here,' he rasped as smoke billowed from his clay pipe.

'I am looking for someone,' I replied, glancing about me.

'I'm not sure you will find him here, Sir. Do I know his name?'

'You may in fact have read it,' I said, pointing at the man's crumpled newspaper. 'I am looking for Mr Sherlock Holmes.'

'Sherlock Holmes? Yes, a name that is familiar to me. Such a great detective. Such a fine brain. Such a faculty for deduction. And he is coming here, you say?'

'I expected to find that he had already arrived.'

'He is on a case, then?'

'It is really more than I can say,'

I turned away from the man and peered eagerly at the door, hoping to see Holmes emerge at any second.

'But it must be something important to bring him here?' the man persisted.

'I'm afraid I won't know that until I speak to him.'

'I should think such a man as your Mr Holmes must be involved in something interesting, would you not agree?'

'On the contrary, I am sure it is no matter at all,' I replied, half-ignoring the man as I scouted for Holmes emerging through the rabble of drinkers.

'Come, Watson. Surely the murder of two women is of some consequence.'

I spun around at the familiar tones to see Sherlock Holmes with an enormous grin beneath the beard he had now pulled down below his chin.

'Holmes!' I exclaimed in wonder.

'Please, Watson!' said Holmes good-humouredly as he adjusted his beard.

I glanced around, but my ejaculation had barely been noticed amongst the raucous laughter and shouted oaths.

'I am sorry, Holmes. But I had no idea it was you. Your theatrical skills never cease to amaze me.'

'Think nothing of it, my dear fellow,' said Holmes in a low voice as he leant across the table. 'But it would be advantageous were my identity to remain between ourselves.'

'Of course, Holmes,' I half-whispered. 'Do you anticipate danger?'

'I am pleased to say that I do not. How long that remains the case, I cannot be sure.'

'You have made progress then?'

'I believe so, although I do not flatter myself that I am in any way able to offer a solution. Have you discovered anything of interest?'

'I saw Dr Llewellyn yesterday afternoon. He thinks the murderer of Polly Nichols had some anatomical knowledge.'

Even beneath his expert disguise, I could detect the sudden alertness in Holmes' face.

'This is a development of the first order,' said he. 'And Llewellyn is certain of this?'

Holmes nodded in rapt interest as I informed him of Dr Llewellyn's findings.

'Interesting, Watson,' he said thoughtfully. 'This could yet prove decisive in capturing the foul miscreant.'

'I am glad to hear you say so,' I said, observing his wry smile. 'I must say, you seem in good spirits.'

'Shortly before you arrived, I completed an extremely interesting conversation with a young gentleman of the press.'

'Here?'

'Where else, my dear Watson? One can learn more gossip upon the murders from half an hour in such an establishment as from a week of knocking upon front doors in Whitechapel. It is here that you shall find London's cleverer journalists.'

'I take it that this relates to your telegram? What have you discovered?'

'There is a man known as Leather Apron who roams about Whitechapel, terrorising the local women. My acquaintance informs me that this mysterious figure often threatens them while brandishing a large knife.'

'Good Heavens! Do you believe it?'

'The facts, if indeed they are facts, do not support your intelligence, Watson. Leather Apron is no slaughterman. Our man, however, is apparently a slipper maker, so would be well acquainted with knives.'

'And what is our next move?'

26

'Back home to Baker Street, my dear Watson! I fear I am in quite desperate need of a bath and a good dinner. Now Watson, be a good chap and assist an elderly gentleman to his feet, would you?'

Sherlock Holmes was laid upon the sofa in our sitting room, having just devoured some of Mrs Hudson's excellent cooking and appearing as satisfied as I had seen him for some time. I was aware that he possessed a number of boltholes across the city, although their location remained a mystery to me. What comforts these dens afforded him, I could not say. But to judge from his voracious appetite and eager indulgence in his many vices upon his return to Baker Street, it was evident that Holmes denied himself of certain luxuries during his time at these mysterious abodes.

'I must confess, Watson, that after several days absence, Baker Street does possess an undeniable charm,' said Holmes, a contented smile playing across his face. 'I find that one can only go so long without contact with a hot bath.'

'The deprivations to which you subject yourself during enquires is commendable, Holmes.'

'And my meagre sacrifices have not been in vain. Bates has proved to be a most interesting contact.'

'Bates?'

'My apologies, Watson. I refer to Mr Benjamin Bates. He is the journalist fellow whom I met at The Blue Coat Boy.'

'Of course. He has been of some use, I take it?'

'I would go as far as to say invaluable, Watson. He seems a most enterprising young chap, if a little over enthusiastic at times. He has recently been appointed as a reporter on The Star.'

'The new evening paper?'

'The most sensationalist evening paper in London, Watson. They have written more on the recent murders than any other paper, all in the most provocative language imaginable. I believe young Bates to be personally responsible for half of it.'

'And how is it that he came to your attention?' I asked.

'In truth, I believe I came to his. At least in the first instance, that is.'

Holmes saw my quizzical expression and gave me a short laugh.

'Do not imagine, Watson, that when someone endeavours to find me about London, that it is in anyway conceivable I should not hear of it.'

'He was following you?' I asked. Holmes shook his head.

'I was made aware by various agents that a certain young journalist had made discreet enquires regarding where I might be found. I take it that you were not troubled by such a visitor?'

'Absolutely not, or else I'd have told you at once.'

'I thought as much. As I guessed, Mr Bates was remarkably well informed regarding my habits, having sought me out at a number of haunts which are unknown to all save a small number of my most trusted associates. I knew at once that this was a most ambitious and resolute young fellow.'

'Yet you do not suspect his motives to be sinister, I take it?'

'I do not. He seems, in truth, rather an agreeable chap, possessed of an unusual faculty for transforming the merest hint of intrigue into something wonderfully salacious. He also has a decided talent for unearthing the gossip which is presently sweeping through Whitechapel.'

'And why did he want to meet you?' I asked, growing more intrigued by the mysterious Benjamin Bates. Holmes leaned towards me and his face opened into a wide grin.

'Why, he wishes to help me, Watson.'

4.

Dark Annie

'Help you?' I exclaimed in astonishment. 'But whatever for?'

'He got wind of the fact that I was assisting Lestrade and wished to compare notes, as it were. His proposal is that he will provide me with whatever information he can glean from the denizens of Whitechapel. I assure you, Watson, that Mr Bates' methods put even my own to shame.'

'And what does he wish from you in return, Holmes?'

'Naturally, that was my immediate question. In exchange for this intelligence, he requests regular updates on my own progress and, by extension, that of the police.'

'And you have agreed to this?' I cried in astonishment.

'I have, Watson. At least in principle. I believe this is to be an absolutely unique arrangement in the whole of my career.'

'But why on earth should you assist a member of the press, Holmes? You might jeopardise the entire investigation.'

Holmes appeared agitated at this accusation and rose to his feet with a malevolent expression across his features. He then sighed, his face easing into a thin smile.

'Because, my dear Watson, what is also unique is the challenge that I feel awaits me in my pursuit of this killer. Any assistance that presents itself, whatever the arrangement may be, I feel it wise to engage. Let me assure you that I do not intend to reveal any details to Bates which I consider might in any way compromise the capture of the man we are seeking. On the contrary, having an ambitious journalist print whatever it is I tell him, be it fact or fiction, while sharing with me his own results would appear to be an extremely prudent strategy, would you not agree, Watson?'

'You mean to play him to your advantage?'

'Precisely!' said Holmes. Without another word he marched past me into his room, from which I could hear the strains of his violin until long after I had retired to bed.

Sherlock Holmes was correct regarding the talents of Benjamin Bates. Over the next few days, The Star ran a series of long and lurid articles on the emergence of the new suspect called Leather Apron. The first of which began:

'LEATHER APRON.'

THE ONLY NAME LINKED WITH THE
WHITECHAPEL MURDERS

A NOISELESS MIDNIGHT TERROR

The Strange Character who Prowls About
Whitechapel After Midnight- Universal
Fear Among the Women- Slippered Feet
And a sharp Leather-knife.

What followed this most provocative of headlines was a lengthy piece by Mr Bates gleaned, it appeared, from all manner of tittle-tattle and cobbled together from his many excursions into the lower quarters of Whitechapel. Leather Apron was a Jewish slipper maker of singularly unpleasant appearance whose moniker derived from the apron which he was often observed wearing.

Although his present whereabouts were unknown, Leather Apron's reign of terror allegedly spanned several years. The story was described by Bates in the most colourful prose and lacking only for the least substantiation.

'This Leather Apron business shows no sign of abating, does it not, Watson?' said Holmes on the Friday morning, as we were reading the morning papers.

'I see that the man now has a name, Holmes,' I said, without looking up from my paper. 'Jack Pizer.'

'Ah, yes,' said Holmes, leafing through his own newspaper. 'Although I see they are still yet to run him to ground.'

'Do you think he may be our man?' I asked.

'I cannot be sure,' said Holmes thoughtfully. 'The wild speculation of the press makes it impossible for me to form any realistic opinion until this Pizer chap is found.'

'That shouldn't be very long,' I observed. 'There can be no-one in London who does not know his name or description.'

'That is if he exists at all, Watson. I fear that Jack Pizer may be a creation of both local gossip and the newspapers' desire to make as much of these crimes as possible.'

'Our friend Benjamin Bates, you mean?'

'He is perhaps the principal rather than sole offender,' said Holmes, brandishing a copy of The Star in his hand. 'To read The Star's columns, you would think poor Pizer had already been found guilty.'

Mrs Hudson opened the door at that moment, bringing both our breakfast and a telegram for Holmes. As I assisted her in preparing the table, Holmes impatiently read his correspondence whilst muttering loudly to himself.

'It is from Lestrade,' he announced, tossing it wearily amongst the scattered newspapers. 'He wishes my attendance at Scotland Yard. It seems this Leather Apron business is stretching him rather thin. Could you perhaps accompany me?'

'I should be delighted, Holmes. Have we time to eat first?'

'My dear Watson, things are not quite so urgent just yet that I would send you on your way without sufficient nourishment. We shall of course leave after breakfast.'

We found Lestrade lost in a veritable sea of papers and files and bemoaning his lack of any progress whatsoever upon the murders. His disposition was in no way improved by Holmes' news that he had made little or no progress in his own investigations. Holmes neglected to mention his acquaintance with Benjamin Bates. Yet beyond this glaring omission, he painted an entirely truthful summary of his enquires which I was aware had uncovered precious little information. The efforts of Scotland Yard had yielded results of a similarly desultory nature.

The emergence of Leather Apron had merely exacerbated Lestrade's cause, faced as he was now with a suspect whom no-one could find, while at the same time hunting for the murderer of Martha

Tabram and Polly Nichols. The weight of such a tortuous enquiry told in the gaunt aspect of the Inspector, his pinched features appearing to have thinned noticeably since I had last seen him.

Before our departure, Holmes assured Lestrade of several potential routes of enquiry and his resultant hope of solving the murders. I was unsure whether Benjamin Bates had given Holmes genuine belief that the murderer was about to be caught, or if my friend merely wished to bolster the spirits of the weary Inspector.

The following morning, Saturday 8th September, I was stirred awake by an appalling commotion emanating from the hallway. Someone was knocking loudly on the front door and hollering for all they were worth. I made my way gingerly down the staircase and opened the door to see a wild-eyed man staring at me, his face so ravaged by fear and shock that my first concern was for his well-being. The man immediately gripped me by the shoulders, as if in the throes of some apoplexy.

'Sherlock Holmes?' he cried, as if his very life was dependent upon his finding that man.

'What on earth is all this about?' I asked in astonishment. 'Do you require medical assistance?'

'Are you Sherlock Holmes?' he repeated desperately.

'I am Dr John Watson. Mr Sherlock Holmes lives here. What is this about?'

'I need to see Sherlock Holmes!' he cried impatiently as he struggled to get past me.

'For God's sake!' I cried angrily. 'What is the matter?'

'Another woman ripped to pieces!' he bellowed. I froze at the words, standing in astonishment for several seconds until I heard footsteps behind me. I turned to see Holmes emerge at the top of the landing, both his eyes and aspect telling me that he too had been torn from his sleep by our mercurial visitor.

'Watson? What has happened?' he asked, walking sleepily down the staircase with the cord of his dressing gown trailing behind him.

'There has been another murder, Holmes,'

'Where?' he asked sharply, gripping the bannister as though in fear of reeling from this intelligence.

'Anbury Street,' bellowed our visitor, before I could respond. 'Thank God I've found you, Mr Holmes. Can you come with me? I've a cab waiting.'

'Of course. Watson, I fear we will have to forgo breakfast this morning. Now, hurry!' he barked.

'But Holmes, we do not even know who this man is,' I protested, following him breathlessly up the stairs.

'It matters not, Watson! Please hurry!'

Such was the command of Holmes' voice that I gave no dissent and rushed back to my room to dress. Within moments, we were dashing out onto Baker Street. Our visitor had already taken his place in the hansom, shouting for the driver to depart just as Holmes and I were alighting.

'I am sorry, gentlemen, if I have caused you some alarm. But the matter is of great urgency,' said the man, appearing somewhat calmer now that he had secured his quarry.

'That much is evident,' said Holmes. 'But might I enquire as to who I must thank for the remarkable speed with which this intelligence has reached me?'

'My name is Henry Holland. Mr Benjamin Bates sent me,' said he. 'Said you was to be told immediately and brought to 'Anbury street without delay; roused from your beds if needs be.'

'I see, Mr Holland. Well, I shall certainly express my gratitude to Mr Bates for his consideration. Can you tell me anything of what has happened?'

'It was awful, Mr Holmes,' he said in a low voice.

'You have seen the body?' asked Holmes in surprise.

'Yes, Mr Holmes. I am a box maker. I was passing along 'Anbury Street on my way to work when a man burst out into the street screaming that another woman had been done in. I went into the yard and saw her lying there. I never saw nothing like it in my life.'

'A yard you say?' said Holmes. 'The murder was committed inside a yard?'

'It was indeed, Mr Holmes.'

'Well, Watson, this is certainly intriguing. Can I ask, Mr Holland, what you did after viewing so grizzly a spectacle?'

'I and a few other lads in the street ran off to find a policeman. I found one by the market, but he was on fixed duty, so I went back to the yard. Mr Bates said he'd make it worth my while to go into work late so as I could come and get you.'

'You have had a most extraordinary morning,' said Holmes.

'You can say that again, Mr Holmes,' he sighed.

Henry Holland was a thin, rather sickly-looking young man, perhaps in his early twenties. His pale features had an agitated aspect about them, no doubt as a result of the sight he had discovered in Hanbury Street. Yet I was more intrigued by the man who had sent him to inform us of the murder. How was it that Benjamin Bates was at the site of the murder so soon after its discovery? In truth, I felt as anxious to meet Holmes' new contact, who evidently kept himself extremely well-informed, as I was to examine where the poor woman had met her demise.

Hanbury Street was a long road which ran off the northern end of Commercial Street. Its tall buildings fought against the burgeoning morning sunlight to keep the road ahead of us in a gloomy haze. We passed two public houses, after the second of which Holland ordered our driver to stop.

'That's it, Mr Holmes. Number twenty-nine,' said Holland, pointing out a three-storey house whose front was filthy with grime, its façade long ago eroded by time and neglect. Outside was a knot of people of both sexes talking in low voices, who gave scant regard to our arrival. Above the wide-open street door was a vestige of pride in the form of a white sign written in a straggling hand which announced: 'Mrs A. Richardson, rough packing-case maker.'

We passed two constables, both of whom merely nodded as we followed Holland through the doorway. We then proceeded along a narrow passage which went straight out into the back yard.

'It was just out there I found her,' said Holland, gesturing towards the yard.

'Thank you, Mr Holland,' said Holmes, sensing Holland's trepidation. 'I think we shall be alright from here.'

The back door was swung right back and as we approached, I saw the head of a man who was bent over as though inspecting something on the ground beneath him. Upon hearing our steps, the figure stopped and stood up, viewing us through squinting eyes in the pale dawn light. He was of middle age, with prominent whiskers and dressed in such old-fashioned yet immaculate style, that he might have just stepped out of a century-old painting.

'Apologies for our intrusion,' said Holmes airily. 'I take it the poor woman lies just beneath you?'

'That is correct, Sir. And whom do I address?'

'Forgive me. My name is Sherlock Holmes and this is my colleague, Dr Watson.'

'I have heard much about you, Mr Holmes. I am Dr Phillips, the Police surgeon.'

Dr Phillips stepped aside that we might pass him, and I followed Holmes as he descended the three steps that took us into the yard. It was perhaps four or five yards square, the bare earth pockmarked in places by flat stones.

My attention was drawn immediately to a prostrate figure to the left of the door and covered by sacking.

'Good morning, Mr Holmes,' said a man standing further inside the yard. 'What a stroke of luck to see you here. This is the worse one yet.'

'Good morning, Inspector. Watson, this is Inspector Chandler, currently one of the force's more able detectives.

'You flatter me, Mr Holmes. Good morning, Doctor Watson,' said Inspector Chandler, offering his hand. He was a tall man of about forty, possessed of dark features and a strong, expressive face.

'Good morning, Inspector,' said I. 'Do you think this poor woman murdered by the same hand as the others?'

'I do, Doctor. Dr Phillips was just about to examine her when you arrived. I cleared the passageway of people and covered the body as soon as I got here. An elderly fellow named John Davis discovered the body. He lives on the third floor. No-one else has been in the yard since I arrived.'

'You have done commendably well, Inspector,' said Holmes. 'Now, let us not detain Dr Phillips from his task any longer.'

35

Dr Phillips nodded in gratitude and stooped down to carefully peel back the filthy sacking which covered the dead woman. It was a terrible sight that confronted us. She was laid with her head facing the back door, her body parallel with the wooden palings that fenced the yard off from its neighbour. A jagged incision ran across her throat. So fierce was the cut that it appeared almost an attempt at severing the head completely. A large quantity of blood had oozed from this terrible wound and formed in a large pool underneath her head. Part of the poor woman's intestines had been pulled over her right shoulder, while over the left was draped what appeared to be part of her stomach.

'Dear God,' said Holmes.

'As I said gentlemen, this is the worst of the lot,' said Chandler.

'I have never seen anything like it,' I said, gazing at the stricken figure before me.

'Can you tell us anything, Dr Phillips?' asked Chandler, reaching for his notebook. The aging Doctor rose unsteadily to his feet and turned towards us slowly.

'The cause of death was massive blood loss caused by the wound to the throat. She was strangled first, as indicated by the swelling to the face. The abdomen has been entirely laid open and the intestines have been severed from their mesenteric attachments and, as you have no doubt observed, placed on the poor woman's shoulder. If you can have her removed to the mortuary, Inspector, I shall make a more detailed examination there.'

Chandler ordered the two constables to have her conveyed to the police ambulance. After they had performed this grisly task, the four of us began an examination of the yard. While I of course focused my utmost on this duty, I suspected my efforts would be quite superfluous in the presence of Sherlock Holmes. Yet the first thing that came to our attention scarcely required my friend's powers of deduction. Near the fence, just where the woman's feet had laid, I made a macabre discovery. There, quite neatly arranged, were a scrap of coarse muslin, a small toothcomb and a pocket comb in a paper case.

'Holmes!' I gasped, as the others gathered around. 'Why would someone arrange these things in such a fashion?'

'He's playing with us, Watson,' said Holmes, inspecting my discovery.

'You think they belong to this woman?' asked Inspector Chandler.

'Undoubtedly. You may have noticed the large pocket tied with string around the woman's waist. It had evidently been torn with a sharp instrument. No doubt the murderer plundered it before commencing his frightful incisions. The splashes of blood you can see upon the wooden panels make it clear that her throat was cut after she was laid on the ground. You will also notice a torn portion of envelope placed quite incongruously where her head would have rested.'

'There's part of an address written on it,' said the Inspector as he stooped down to pick up the scrap of envelope. 'A letter "M" and beneath it "Sp". There's also a red postmark: "London, Aug.23, 1888". The Inspector turned the envelope over in his hands. 'And on the back there's a seal and the words "Sussex Regiment".'
Chandler passed the envelope to Holmes, who studied it intently.

'It's written in a man's hand. "Sp" no doubt refers to "Spitalfields"'.

'Is it a clue, Mr Holmes?' asked Chandler. Holmes shook his head.

'I do not think so. If our man has the time to arrange the poor woman's belongings, then he had time to leave a clue if he wished to do so. From the chalk marks on the inside of the envelope, I would suggest this was used by the victim to store her pills. You may have also noticed the fresh abrasions on the third finger of her left hand where two rings had been removed, almost certainly by her killer. This really is a most extraordinary murder, gentlemen.'

Dr Phillips, who had never been witness to my friend's gifts, shot him a disbelieving glance.

'Thank you, Mr Holmes,' said Inspector Chandler. 'You never fail to astonish me. But we still have no clue as to this madman's identity.'

'On the contrary, Inspector. If you inspect the water tap in the corner, I believe you will find something of great interest.'

At Holmes' words, I swung around and looked in the opposite corner nearest the kitchen window. There, soaking wet and not two feet from the tap, was a leather apron.

5.

Leather Apron

'Dear God!' I exclaimed, as Chandler inspected the apron. 'Holmes, can it be possible?'

'That the murderer is Jack Pizer and that he has left his eponymous leather apron at the murder site? I do not believe so, Watson. The apron has clearly not been unfolded in some time and is visibly absent of bloodstains. Forgive me, Chandler, if I momentarily gave you false hope.'

'So, it is nothing?' said the clearly dejected Inspector, replacing the apron where he found it.

'Do not look so forlorn,' said Holmes. 'With each murder, our man is revealing himself. I know more about him now than I did before I arrived. I can tell you, for example, that he takes a size eight shoe. Do not look astonished, gentlemen, for the evidence is in the earth where the body lay. The marks are fresh and quite distinct.

'My word, Holmes!' I exclaimed. 'The man's shoe print must surely provide a clue to his identity?'

'I am not without hope. Watson, I think we have seen all we can here. Gentlemen, I will bid you both good morning.'

We emerged through the passage amongst a rabble of sightseers, whose numbers had swelled considerably since our arrival. We were barely noticed as we made our way past them, each speculating on the events that had occurred just yards from where they were standing.

'Sherlock Holmes!' exclaimed a shrill voice that caused us both to stop and turn around.

'Ah! I suspected that London's most intrepid reporter must be about here somewhere.'

'So, you made it then, Holmes?' said the man cheerfully, seemingly quite oblivious to the sombre scene around him. He appeared to be in his late twenties, of above average height and lean build. His angular features gave him an arrogant, almost haughty air, while his dress of a Newmarket coat and shiny billycock hat made the young man before me cut a rather dashing figure.

'Good morning,' said Holmes. 'I must convey my thanks on behalf of both myself and Dr Watson here for the kind transportation. Watson, this is Mr Benjamin Bates.'

'Think nothing of it, Holmes. A pleasure to meet you, Dr Watson,' said Bates, shaking me firmly by the hand. I must admit that the awful spectacle we had witnessed in the back yard had caused me to entirely forget that we owed both our visit to Hanbury Street and our means of arriving there to a man who had until now proved absent from the scene himself.

'And how was it, Bates, that you were informed of events here with such astonishing alacrity?' asked Holmes.

Benjamin Bates appeared to take much delight at my friend's evident bewilderment, greeting the question with a wide and self-satisfied grin.

'As I explained to you in the Blue Coat Boy, Holmes, I am perhaps the best-connected reporter in all of London. Little happens in this great city of which I do not hear about before my rivals.'

Holmes narrowed his eyes and fixed them sternly upon the young man, evidently unimpressed with Bates' response. The reporter's jocular expression faltered momentarily before he collected himself under Holmes' unwavering gaze.

'When the old man who found the body went into the street for help, one of the men who helped him was James Green. He works just up the road there as a packing-case maker. He's been of use to me before in return for the occasional shilling. He knew it was worth his while to send me the tip on his way to find a policeman.'

'I see. Well you certainly live up to your self-anointed reputation, Bates. I must confess to marvelling at both your capacity for acquiring informants, as well as your generosity at providing them with shillings.'

'All reimbursed to me by The Star, Holmes. I assure you that my pocket is never lighter for the information I receive.'

'A most enviable condition of employment, Bates. Now, might I be privy to such information that you have discovered this morning of which I may be unaware?'

'A deal is a deal, Mr Holmes. Benjamin Bates never reneges on his word,' said Bates good-naturedly, as though eager to impress Holmes. 'I didn't manage to get into the back yard, no matter what I offered Inspector Chandler. But while he was surveying the dreadful site himself, I managed to interview several of the residents, including the old man, Davis, who found the body. Neither he nor anyone else I spoke to heard the slightest sound. But my man, Henry Holland, ventured into the yard and tells me that there was a leather apron to be seen in the corner near the kitchen window.'

'Mr Holland was quite correct,' said Holmes laconically. Bates seemed to be most surprised that my friend did not offer a more animated response to his intelligence.

'But Holmes, surely it indicates that Jack Pizer is the murderer?'

'I do not think so,' replied my friend tersely.

'Well its presence in the yard is certainly newsworthy at any rate,' said Bates defiantly. 'Might I ask if your observations of the yard can offer me anything of interest, as my own information is apparently without merit?'

'I can tell you that the man who was in this yard is local and of similar class to his victim,' said Holmes. 'That is to say, someone who can traverse such streets without attracting attention.'

Benjamin Bates' sulky expression evaporated as he eagerly jotted down Holmes' observations. Rather than any clues which might provide a means of catching the murderer, Bates seemed preoccupied with whatever details Holmes could offer which might provide his newspaper columns with the most lurid of headlines.

'And you are perfectly happy for me to report that the great Sherlock Holmes believes the man to be of the lower class?'

'I am satisfied that this is the case. You may of course prefix my name to any such comment to that effect with my blessing, Bates.'

Bates appeared gratified at this information, his eyes widening as Holmes described the discovery of the poor woman's belongings arranged alongside her body. He recorded Holmes' narrative with some vigour, although his lack of questions of the more salient points suggested he intended to use them in only the most arbitrary manner. The single omission I noted in the account which Holmes gave of the murder was any mention of the footprint, which at present appeared the most tangible clue he had yet discovered. I had no doubt, of course, that the exclusion was an intentional one.

'You're a Godsend, Holmes. An absolute Godsend!' said Bates, pocketing his notebook before shaking first Holmes and then myself enthusiastically by the hand. 'O'Connor's going to love this stuff.'

'I am glad to see that you are pleased,' said Holmes, smiling at Bates' barely contained excitement. 'But please remember your side of the bargain. I expect to be kept informed of your own enquires whenever they might turn up something of interest.'

'Take it for granted, Mr Holmes.' said the young journalist. 'Now, let me call you a cab.'

'I imagine you are intrigued as to why I did not mention the footprint to young Mr Bates?' said Holmes, as we were sitting at the table later that morning, devouring a much-needed breakfast.

'I am, Holmes,' I said. 'I cannot see what has been gained by withholding the intelligence.'

Holmes studied me with a broad smile.

'Ha! I knew that would puzzle you,' he exclaimed, leaning back in his chair and crossing his arms in good-natured defiance. 'But I shall cease playing games and enlighten you.' He stood up theatrically, his aspect assuming a sudden seriousness. 'You recall the footprints which we observed in the yard?'

'Of course, Holmes. They were quite clear.'

'Exactly, Watson!' he cried, thrusting out his long arms to punctuate his exclamation. 'The print was perfect. There were no marks where the sole had been scuffed or worn. They were clearly brand-new shoes. Immediately, I question how many men walk about Whitechapel clad in brand new footwear. A typical man of the area would have his shoes re-soled. Now, a cheap re-soling invariably leaves some imperfection, yet I could detect none on the prints in the yard. Of course, a local man who happens to have purchased a new pair of shoes is unlikely, if not impossible. But the sole of the shoe print was quite distinctive, Watson. The layered, riveted heel and that distinctive pattern could only have come from a John Lobb.'

'John Lobb!' I exclaimed. 'But they must be fifty pounds a pair!'

'Perhaps more, Watson. I cannot be sure, but I would guess that the shoe in question was a Saddle Oxford or Half Brogue. Now, how many men walk the streets of Whitechapel in shoes which cost more than six months' salary?'

'But, Holmes,' I protested. 'You have told Bates that the man we are looking for is local.'

'That is correct. But you must remember what I told you following your visit to The Blue Coat Boy. I have played him, Watson. I want Benjamin Bates to publish the entirely erroneous statement that I believe the murderer to be a local man. It must seem obvious to you now that the man we are seeking isn't to be found in a common lodging house. If we are to catch this man, then we must look up and not down.'

'But this is incredible, Holmes!' I blustered. 'You are saying that a gentleman has descended thrice upon Whitechapel to murder a woman of the lowest class in the most unspeakable way?'

'In the absence of a better theory, Watson, I consider it the only possibility. And I do not think that this morning's outrage is to be his last such venture.'

'Then we must catch this man before he can strike again.'

'It is imperative, Watson,' said Holmes. 'And I believe that our most pressing enquiry regards our friend, the young Mr Bates.'

'Bates!' I cried. 'You mean you suspect him?'

'Of murder, Watson, I do not. But perhaps you failed to observe that the toe of his left shoe was slightly caked with earth. Then consider his statement that Holland informed him of the leather apron to be found in the yard. Holland would have been in the yard for a mere second or two, his gaze surely fixed on the awful sight at the bottom of the stairs, not looking about earnestly for clues. Remember that even Inspector Chandler failed to observe its existence until I remarked upon it. No, Watson, it is a certainty that Benjamin Bates was in that yard before our arrival and that of Inspector Chandler. I would dearly love to know how he came to be there at such an hour, and why he saw fit to lie about it.'

Despite the imponderables which Hanbury Street presented, events moved more quickly than Holmes or I imagined. At seven o'clock that

43

evening, shortly after Mrs Hudson had cleared the remains of an excellent fish dinner, she returned to our sitting room to announce that Inspector Lestrade and another gentleman were at the door and wished to see Sherlock Holmes. Holmes implored her to fetch the men up immediately and moments later, for their footsteps devoured the stairs to our sitting room with some ferocity, stood Lestrade and his companion.

In contrast to the thin Inspector, the man standing next to him cut a rather portly figure. He was perhaps in his mid-forties and something above the middle height, with dark brown hair and hazel eyes. He possessed a thick moustache and side-whiskers, and I thought his appearance to be more that of a bank manager than the police officer I took him to be.

'Good evening, gentlemen,' said Lestrade. 'I understand you were at Hanbury Street this morning, although devil knows how you learned of the murder so quickly. This is my colleague, Inspector Abberline. He was drafted in after the Nichols murder.' He indicated his companion, who was standing almost shyly near the door, as if awaiting permission to join us.

'Ah, Inspector Frederick Abberline of Scotland Yard. Recently promoted to Detective Inspector first class, I believe?' said Holmes matter-of-factly. Our visitor appeared astonished at this address, a light crimson flushing across his cheeks as his glance darted between Lestrade and I.

'Why, that is certainly correct, Mr Holmes,' he said. 'Although I confess that I have no idea how you come to know who I am.'

'Really, Inspector, you are too modest. I am, of course, only too aware of your exemplary record, not to mention the esteem with which you are held by your colleagues. It is indeed an honour to have so distinguished a practitioner of your profession here in our humble rooms.'

'Thank you very kindly, Mr Holmes,' replied Inspector Abberline. 'Your name is of course known to all of us at Scotland Yard, and talked of in the highest regard, I might add.'

Holmes merely smiled in response and signalled for the two Inspectors to make use of the sofa, while he himself drew up an armchair.

44

'I take it, Inspector Abberline, that you have no objection to my friend, Dr Watson here, sitting with us while we discuss the delicate matter of this morning's outrage?'

Inspector Abberline assured Holmes that I was a welcome addition to proceedings. We completed the required pleasantries, with Holmes requesting some tea from Mrs Hudson, before Lestrade began to avail us of his investigations.

'It has been an awful day, Holmes,' said the Inspector. 'I understand that you departed Hanbury Street just before I arrived. By late morning, there were hundreds of sightseers clogging the streets, all trying to get a glimpse of the murder scene. And that was besides the dozens of reporters who began to swarm around the place as soon as word spread about the murder. There was even a man selling what he called "Leather Apron" toffee.'

'Quite the circus, it would appear, Lestrade.' said Holmes impatiently.

'In any case,' said Lestrade, consulting his pocketbook. 'We at least know who the poor woman was. Her name's Annie Chapman, known to some as Dark Annie on account of a quick temper. Both her brother and the dosshouse keeper who turned her out last night have identified her. She became estranged from her husband in about 1882 and since his death the year before last, lived by whatever means presented themselves. For the last few months, she'd lived at a lodging house on Dorset Street called Crossingham's.'

'Most enlightening, Lestrade,' said Holmes in a faintly sardonic voice. 'And as to her murder?'

'I have here a copy of Dr Phillips' post-mortem report,' said Lestrade testily, passing Holmes a slim folder. 'I know that you have viewed the body yourselves and, I believe, were privy to Dr Phillips' initial examination before it was removed to the mortuary. What you may like to know is that certain portions of the body were missing.'

'Missing?' I asked incredulously, leaning forward in my chair with such force that it threatened to empty me onto the carpet. 'There must be some mistake.'

'There was no mistake,' said Inspector Abberline softly. 'I spoke to Dr Phillips, who assured me that parts of the womb and a portion of

45

the bladder were absent. That is to say, they were taken by the murderer.'

As Holmes sat there in dumbstruck silence, I took the report from between his long fingers and availed myself of the facts. The posterior two-thirds of the bladder had been entirely removed, along with the belly wall, womb and part of her lower organs. It was unfathomable to me that Annie Chapman's killer had left the yard with these grotesque trophies, before slipping into the early morning streets without notice.

'But this is quite unbelievable,' I said, returning the report into Holmes' tremulous hands. 'He has removed part of the viscera and taken it with him.'

'It is appalling, Watson,' remarked Holmes. 'Gentlemen, we are dealing with that greatest of enemies: the unknown. I believe the annals of crime to be entirely absent of anything comparable to such macabre purloining of bodily parts.'

'But what is the point of it, Holmes?' asked Lestrade. 'I can see no purpose to such an act.'

'The worrying aspect is that neither can I, in point of fact.' confessed Holmes. 'If one can understand the motive, then one can understand the crime and hence the criminal. But the reasoning of this man escapes me.'

'Does he hope to sell the organs?' I asked. Holmes shook his head.

'Too risky.'

'There must be some reason,' said Lestrade. 'A man did not remove those organs with such care for the sheer devilment of it.'

'Care?' asked Holmes.

'I'm sorry?'

'You said that he removed the organs with care.'

'And he most certainly did, Holmes. Dr Watson has just read the report and Inspector Abberline here spoke at length to Dr Phillips this afternoon.'

'It is true, Mr Holmes, that Dr Phillips thought the killer to have shown professional skill in some of the incisions which he inflicted upon his victim,' explained Inspector Abberline in a measured tone. 'The cuts were clean and done so as to avoid injury to the adjoining organs. He felt that the ability to secure the pelvic organs with one sweep of the knife showed clear signs of anatomical knowledge. The Doctor's opinion was that only the precarious conditions in performing such mutilations inhibited further evidence of surgical skill.'

'Thank you, Inspector Abberline. I could not have wished for a more concise appraisal of the matter. Might I trouble you further with regards to any information you feel is wanting in my knowledge of events?'

'We spoke to a young carpenter earlier this evening,' he replied. 'Name of Albert Cadosch. He lives at number 27 Hanbury Street, next door to the murder site. He said that he was in his backyard at about half past five this morning and heard voices coming from next door. The only word he could catch was 'No'. He went indoors but returned three or four minutes later. He then heard what sounded like something falling against the fence that separated the two yards.'

'Undoubtedly he heard the poor woman conversing with her killer,' said Holmes. 'And minutes later her descent to the ground already, I imagine, insensible to the world.'

'That is what we believe,' said Abberline in a low voice.

There was little else that either Inspector could add to our understanding of events, and they must have departed Baker Street in a rather dejected state if they had expected any illumination upon the matter from Sherlock Holmes. The removal of Annie Chapman's organs had clearly astonished Holmes. I could scarcely recall a crime whose solution proved so resistant to his powers of logic. His early retirement to bed that evening appeared to me almost a resignation to failure.

6.

The Whitechapel Vigilance Committee

The week following the murder of Annie Chapman was to prove notable only for the lack of success on the part of Sherlock Holmes in deciphering the slightest clue as to her killer's identity. Jack Pizer was discovered, arrested and questioned, only to be exonerated of any compliance in the murders. While there seemed little doubt that Pizer was the ubiquitous phantom known as Leather Apron, it become equally apparent that he was an entirely separate villain to the man whose butchered victims were to be found with increasing regularity across Whitechapel.

Holmes' spirits were briefly lifted by a telegram from Lestrade, advising that a witness might have seen Dark Annie and her killer moments before the murder took place. A Mrs Long claimed to have passed along Hanbury Street en route to Spitalfields Market at about five-thirty. She observed the deceased conversing with a man outside number twenty-nine. Yet she could describe him in only the vaguest of terms as 'shabby genteel' and confessed that she would not recognise him again.

Benjamin Bates continued to produce the most bombastic of prose within the pages of The Star, while making much of his supposed relationship with Sherlock Holmes. On the 12th September, in the wake of Jack Pizer's innocence, he informed his readers that the police were still in search of a local culprit:

While the Police have proclaimed the innocence of Jack Pizer, thought to be the man known as Leather Apron, it is known that they are still certain that the culprit is a local man. Mr Sherlock Holmes, the consulting detective who was amongst the first at the scene of Annie Chapman's murder, gave an exclusive interview to The Star. He remains convinced that the murderer is of a similar class to his victim and can thus traverse the streets of Whitechapel without attracting undue attention. It is this ability to come and go quite unnoticed which makes him only the more sinister. Mr Holmes, who's gifts in the detection of crime are widely acknowledged as unparalleled, is conducting enquires in the lowest establishments of Whitechapel with a view to capturing the assassin before he strikes again. This he has promised to do, courtesy of information supplied to him by The Star.

'Ineffable twaddle!' I exclaimed, throwing the offending paper to the floor.

'Fear not, Watson,' said Holmes, with perfect equanimity. 'Such twaddle, as you rightly call it, assists our cause rather than harms it.'

'I appreciate your thinking, Holmes,' I said, still simpering with rage. 'But really, the man has taken an enormous liberty.'

'Please calm yourself, Watson. I confess that when your features turn that particular shade of red, I invariably have concerns for your well-being. Now, to turn matters towards a more productive avenue, I received this intriguing missive by the morning post.'

Holmes produced a cream-coloured envelope from his jacket pocket and thrust it into my hand. Inside was a letter, written in a man's hand on foolscap paper of common quality which read as follows:

Alderney Road
Mile End

Dear Mr Sherlock Holmes

I write in connection to the most outrageous murders presently being committed in Whitechapel. I beg an audience with your good self with regards to the capture of the foul miscreant responsible for these crimes. As you will no doubt be aware, a vigilance committee has been formed by a number of concerned denizens, of which I am president. We feel it would be most advantageous were I to consult with you regarding such knowledge upon the matter that we have gathered, and which might assist your endeavours in apprehending the culprit.
If it is at all convenient, I shall call upon you at seven o'clock this Wednesday evening.

Mr George A. Lusk

'What do you make of him, Watson?' asked Holmes, once I had finished reading.

'Mr Lusk? His intentions certainly appear to be entirely honourable,' I replied. 'I believe I have seen his committee mentioned in several newspapers.'

'Quite. Their notices are also to be found in several shop windows about Whitechapel and for some distance beyond. This group intrigues me, Watson.'

'You suspect them of something more sinister?'

'Not yet.' he replied. 'But it has been my experience, Watson, that when such a group forms itself in consequence of a crime, it is a curious fact that at least one of its number will eventually prove guilty of some degree of compliance in its execution. You may recall the infamous Smithfield scandal of some years back. A night watchman is easily corrupted. But what can you tell of this Lusk chap from his letter?'

I examined both the letter and envelope in my hands for some seconds.

'I confess, Holmes, that I can see nothing which tells me anything about George Lusk's habits or disposition.'

'Ha! I knew you would fail to see what was in front of you,' cried Holmes triumphantly as I passed the letter back to him.

'And I suppose that it is all perfectly obvious to you?' I answered indignantly.

'Apologies, Watson. If it affords you any consolation, I could hand this letter to Lestrade, or half of Scotland Yard for that matter, and find them in total ignorance of any clues it presents.'

'Which are?'

'George Lusk is a man whose usual routine has been severely disrupted in recent months in consequence of his wife's passing. He remains an outward veneer of self-order, but I fear that his habits have fallen into some disarray. He also has at least one child.'

'You joke, surely, Holmes?' I said incredulously. 'How on earth can you make such grand deductions on the mere basis of this letter?'

51

'The letter and envelope do not match, Watson. They are from different sets which have evidently become mixed with one another. The first two lines are evidently written using ink which has dried due to ill-usage. There is also, you will observe, some fading on one side of the envelope where it has been allowed to absorb the sun. These facts would usually suggest a person of less than particular habits with regards to his stationery. However, the rigid, uniform hand suggest an altogether more ordered nature. Clearly this is a man who has experienced some great upheaval which has caused his usually impeccable conduct to slip so dramatically. The use of wax to seal the envelope speaks of a man determined to maintain appearances.'

'I see. But how can you tell that he has lost his wife?' I asked. 'Surely that is mere speculation?'

'I never speculate, Watson. I balance probabilities on occasion, but I never speculate. You will observe on both the letter and envelope a total of six small indents to the paper which have been caused by the pressing of a fingernail. The angular appearance of these marks suggests the writer has neglected his nail clippers of late. What wife, Watson, would allow her husband to grow his nails in such a fashion?'

'But he might be a bachelor, or his wife may merely be staying with relatives,' I countered, certain that I had found a flaw in Holmes' reasoning. Yet Holmes merely shook his head dismissively.

'If you hold the letter to the light as I have done, you will observe the outline of a tiny handprint at the bottom, evidently that of a very young child. No doubt this young fellow was sat on Lusk's knee as he composed his missive. A man who has suffered a recent upheaval, has a child and yet no wife allows for but one conclusion. No woman would depart her household without so young an infant. It is a matter of probabilities, Watson.'

'Most ingenious, Holmes,' I said. 'If your conclusions prove to be correct, that is.'

An assessment of Holmes' deductions was not long in arriving. Later that evening, at precisely the appointed hour, the bell rang and Mrs Hudson introduced George Lusk into our sitting room. Holmes invited our visitor to take a seat. Mr Lusk was a middle-sized man, aged perhaps fifty and whose round face and pale features where accentuated by a heavy, brown moustache. He had a retiring aspect about him, yet possessed also something of an agitated manner as he sat fidgeting absently in his seat.

'I hope I do not trouble you too greatly,' he said softly.

'Not at all, Mr Lusk. Both myself and Dr Watson are delighted to make your acquaintance. Let me also offer our condolences on the recent loss of your wife.'

'Thank you, Mr Holmes. It is the children who have taken it hardest. You have read of Susannah's passing then?'

'Only in your letter and the solemn manners I see before me, Mr Lusk. The bereaved have a haunted aspect which is quite distinctive to the trained observer.'

'I have heard of your abilities in deduction, Mr Holmes. Yet I had no idea that they were so extraordinary. I do not wish to take any more of your time than is absolutely necessary, so I will not trouble you for a denouement of your methods and get straight to the point.'

'The vigilance committee?'

'Precisely. We mean to assist you, Mr Holmes.'

'In what way, might I ask?'

'I- that is, the committee- feel that we may be able to gather information which may help you identify the killer.'

'Your letter in fact hinted that you have already acquired such intelligence?'

'That is quite correct, Mr Holmes. Am I to take it that this conversation is entirely confidential?'

'You may rest assured, Mr Lusk, that whatever you care to tell us within this room shall remain the solemnest secret between the three of us.'

'Thank you, Mr Holmes. We have become aware on our nightly rounds of a mysterious figure who is often seen around Spitalfields. Several locals observed a man with bloodstained clothing on the night of Annie Chapman's death.'

'I see,' said Holmes flatly. 'This is quite the occurrence.'

'Has it been reported to the police?' I asked.

'We informed Scotland Yard.'

'Good. Any description?' asked Holmes.

'Not very much, I'm afraid. Tall, aged about forty and dressed in a long, dark coat.'

'Well that is something, at least.'

'Mr Holmes, I hope I do not compromise your own enquires by asking, but is there anything which you have discovered that might assist the vigilance committee in its duties? Anything which you feel may narrow down our searches would be of enormous help.'

'Of course, Mr Lusk. I believe our man to be local and of the same class as his victim. I also believe that he will strike again if we do not apprehend him. My advice would be to continue your excellent work. I would suggest paying particular attention to the darker thoroughfares of Whitechapel, for it is in these foul alleyways that you have most likelihood of capturing the miscreant.'

Mr Lusk thanked Holmes and drew the interview to a rapid close, vowing to inform Holmes of any information that the committee discovered.

'A most earnest fellow,' said Holmes upon our visitor's departure. 'Whether the Whitechapel Vigilance Committee proves to be a help or hindrance to our cause, I am not yet prepared to wager, Watson.'

'His commitment is certainly beyond question,' I said. 'But surely if he is working under false information, any help he provides is certain to be of negligible value.'

'Ah! You wonder why I gave him the entirely erroneous direction towards the lower strata?'

'I do, Holmes. I fail to see what can be gained by such subterfuge.'

In truth, I felt not a little anger towards my friend. A respectable gentleman such as Lusk, despite his recent loss, had taken it upon himself to mobilise a unit in response to the murders, only to have his efforts thwarted by Holmes' deliberate misdirection.

'You are perhaps quite right to admonish me, Watson. But I confess that we appear to be dealing with something that I do not yet fully understand. I feel it is therefore wise to keep our own findings a secret to outside agencies, no matter how altruistic their efforts may be. In the meantime, if Mr Lusk and his associates are patrolling the less salubrious byways of Whitechapel and thus keeping its lower inhabitants in check, I fail to see that his efforts may be considered wasted.

'Consider too, Watson, that our man's wearing of John Lobbs may have been a rare blunder. He might adopt a disguise which will bring him to Lusk's and, therefore, our own attention. Meanwhile, we shall follow his lead of the blood-stained man. I believe our combined approaches should cover all eventualities, for nothing in this case would surprise me.'

As ever, Holmes' irresistible reasoning left me floundering for a response.

'I understand your motive, Holmes.' said I. 'But is this business really as dark as you say?'

'I believe so,' said Holmes. 'Which is why I propose to engage an agent to infiltrate Lusk's rabble and report back to me.'

'Do you wish my assistance, Holmes?'

'My dear fellow, I have no doubt you would do a commendable job,' said Holmes. 'But I am afraid I require a charge possessed of a rather less refined aspect than yourself: one who can appear above suspicion of any counter-dealings. And of course, Mr Lusk has already met your good self.'

'Then who, Holmes?'

'Watson,' he replied with a wide grin. 'I think it is time that you met Squibby.'

7.

Dear Boss

I was constantly astonished at the apparently endless connections which Sherlock Holmes had cultivated with the less desirable inhabitants of our great city. The ease with which he could avail himself of such persons at the shortest of notice was little short of extraordinary. It seemed incredible to me that a man whose name was so illustrious in Whitehall- and known to half the heads of states of Europe- had associates in the most unwelcoming establishments of what the halfpenny press called 'The East End'. On more than one occasion we had encountered some vile ruffian, who seemed about to waylay us for some nefarious purpose, only for him to desist upon recognising Holmes and greeting him as if an old friend.

Thus, it was little of surprise to discover that 'Squibby' was of the worst possible antecedents, and that he himself had forged an infamous career as a noted exponent of petty crime. Holmes arranged to meet him in the Princess Alice Public House a few days following George Lusk's visit. The Princess Alice was a large, three-storey building on the corner of Wentworth Street, just off the southern end of Commercial Street. To judge from the ornate brickwork and mullioned windows on its upper floor, the establishment had evidently known better days.

In common with so many buildings in the area, however, it had fallen into a gradual decay since the decline of the silk weavers. Its grim façade and filthy windows gave it an altogether unwelcoming aspect as we entered. Holmes ordered us two pints of ale while I studied our surroundings. Rabbles of women gossiped noisily in the corners while merrily sipping their gin. Men were standing at the bar in conversation, or else playing cards at a table. A lone man was sitting across from them smoking a pipe, his hat tucked over his eyes. The air was filled with smoke, while the smell of tobacco mingled with the odour of sweat and stale ale. Holmes directed us to a roughly hewn table in the corner, purposely chosen to afford us a perfect view of the door. Holmes gave a shrill laugh as he observed my disgust at the filthy condition of my tankard.

'My apologies, Watson,' said he. 'I fear I have placed you at the mercy of some of London's less salubrious hostelries in the course of this investigation. You will accept it, I hope, as an entirely necessary evil.'

'It is nothing, Holmes,' I said, with a faint air of embarrassment. 'Just a little smeared.'

'Ha! We shall soon have you a regular of the gin palace, Watson! Although I do not expect our visit to last too long once Squibby has arrived.'

Holmes had arranged the meeting for six o' clock, yet it was half past the hour before his visitor arrived. Squibby was a short fellow, perhaps in his late thirties, whose stature merely added to the menace of his immense build. He was possessed of the broadest shoulders I had ever seen, while his shaved head and tattoos adorned every visible aspect of his torso, endowing him with the most fearsome of appearances. He saw Holmes and lumbered towards us.

'Mr Holmes, Sir,' said our guest in a guttural growl. 'Is it past six?'

'By some minutes, I am afraid,' said Holmes. 'But no matter, Squibby. This is my associate, Dr John Watson.'

Squibby surveyed me with his weak, narrow eyes and offered both a scarcely intelligible salutation and fleshy hand by way of greeting.

'Here,' said Holmes, handing our guest a penny. Squibby looked gratefully at the coin before departing to procure an ale.

'He is certainly a most formidable figure, Holmes,' said I, as we watched Squibby shouldering his way to the bar.

'Ha! He is quite the pocket Hercules, is he not, Watson? In truth, even I have struggled to contain him in the past. Yet he has been somewhat mellowed by a recent brush with death.'

'What on earth happened?'

'Some weeks ago, Squibby, for quite his own reasons, was engaged in throwing bricks at a policeman. When one of his errant missiles struck a child he went into hiding, only to be coaxed out by news of the Chapman murder. Mingling with the crowds at Hanbury Street, he was spotted by an officer and made good his escape. The ensuing pursuit caused a most ghastly hue and cry, during which the crowd unfortunately assumed poor Squibby to be suspected of murder. He found refuge in a house, which was promptly surrounded by an angry mob perhaps a hundred strong, each of them baying for Squibby's blood. Only a most determined effort by the police saved Squibby's life. Since that day, he has proved to be as docile as a kitten.'

'Good Heavens!' I exclaimed.

Squibby returned with his ale and squeezed into a seat next to me.

'Ah, Squibby,' said Holmes. 'Now, I will not detain you for very long. I wish to engage your services.'

'Usual terms?'

'Better, Squibby. For this is a most special commission. Your wages are to be thirty shillings per week.'

'Thirty shillings!' said he, spluttering over his ale. 'Why, whatever do you want me to do? I warn you that I'll not do anything criminal. I'm a changed man, Mr Holmes.'

'Fear not, Squibby. I wish you, in fact, to act on behalf of the authorities. You have been requested especially.' Squibby eyed Holmes quizzically. 'There is a group known as the Whitechapel Vigilance Committee who patrol Whitechapel at night. Have you heard of them?' Squibby nodded. 'Good. I wish you to join them. The fellow in charge is named George Lusk. I wish you to pay special attention to his activities. You will volunteer your services tomorrow. You will report to me every Friday with any information you have gathered, whereupon you shall receive your wages. Are you agreeable to these terms?'

'I certainly am, Mr Holmes.' he replied, his immense chest visibly swelling with pride.

'Excellent. Here is fifteen shillings in advance. I expect results, Squibby.'

'Of course, Mr Holmes.' replied Squibby, finishing his drink in one gulp and standing up to leave.

'Can he be trusted, Holmes?' I asked, as our companion made his way to the door.

'Entirely, Watson. A mind such as Squibby's runs along unfailingly straight lines. Provided that the task is within his intellectual remit, he will carry it out with quite blinkered single-mindedness. It also never hurts to give the exercise a certain illusion of grandeur. Convince a being such as Squibby that his actions carry some weighty purpose and he will prove as faithful a servant as you could wish to find. I have no doubt that we shall find him to be a most excellent set of eyes and ears.'

Holmes was proved correct on his assumption, for the following Friday, much to the alarm of Mrs Hudson, Squibby duly presented himself at Baker Street armed with the most enthusiastic reports of his exploits. The Whitechapel Vigilance Committee, it appeared, were a well-organised and determined gathering who seemed above any kind of suspicion. It was noted by our singular correspondent, however, that Mr Lusk had on occasion absented himself from the night-time proceedings, with no-one able to account for his whereabouts. Holmes instructed Squibby to trail the Committee President more closely over the following week, which our friend faithfully promised to do.

Holmes' own enquires again took him away from Baker Street for days at a time, with the occasional telegram bemoaning a lack of progress remaining my only contact with him. I was still curious about our friend Benjamin Bates, who continued to fill the pages of The Star with idle gossip and tittle-tattle upon the murders. We had heard nothing from the intrepid reporter for some days when early one afternoon, not long after Holmes had returned from one of his sojourns, Bates raced into our sitting room, his face flushed with crimson and creased into a look of wild excitement.

'Mr Holmes! My word, Mr Holmes!' he gasped breathlessly.

'Good Heavens!' cried Holmes, rising from his seat in surprise at our visitor. 'Why, whatever is the matter, my dear boy?'

'He's written to us, Mr Holmes!' cried Bates, gripping an astonished Holmes by his lapels.

'Who? Who has written to you?' asked Holmes.

'The murderer, Holmes! Jack the Ripper!'

With these words, he thrust an envelope into my friend's hands. Holmes unfolded the letter and read in silence for what seemed an eternity.

'Watson,' he said eventually. 'I think you should read this.' He passed me the missive, which I took in my tremulous hand. Written in red ink, it was dated 25th September 1888 and read as follows:

Dear Boss

I keep on hearing the police have caught me but they wont fix me just yet. I have laughed when they look so clever and talk about being on the right track. That joke about Leather Apron gave me real fits. I am down on whores and I shant quit ripping them till I do get buckled. Grand work the last job was. I gave the lady no time to squeal. How can they catch me now. I love my work and want to start again. You will soon hear of me with my funny little games. I saved some of the proper red stuff in a ginger beer bottle over the last job to write with but it went thick like glue and I cant use it. Red ink is fit enough I hope ha.ha. The next job I do I shall clip the lady's ears off and send them to the police officers just for jolly wouldnt you. Keep this letter back till I do a bit more work then give it out straight. My knife's so nice and sharp I want to get to work right away if I get a chance.
Good luck.
            Yours truly

            Jack the Ripper
Dont mind me giving the trade name

Wasn't good enough to post this before I got all the red ink off my hands curse it. No luck yet. They say I'm a doctor now ha ha

'I've never read anything like it, Holmes,' I said, handing him back the letter.

'Where did you get this, Bates?' asked Holmes.

'My editor, Mr O'Connor, received it from an associate at the Central news agency.'

'Ah, yes. I see from the envelope that it is to that same organisation to whom the letter is addressed.'

'That is correct. The owner of the agency, Mr Saunders, is a personal friend of Mr O'Connor and thought it may interest him. He loaned it under strict terms that we wouldn't publish it without his say so. It only arrived this morning.'

'That much is evident from the post mark. I observe also that it was posted in the East Central district. How very interesting.'

'It is?' asked Bates, leaning forward in his seat. 'In what way?'

'I am not yet sure,' said Holmes tersely. 'Do you require this letter back immediately?' Bates nodded.

'I must have it back within the hour,' he replied. 'Mr O'Connor thought it would be of interest to you.'

'And it certainly has, Mr Bates. Please extend my gratitude to your employer.'

'I certainly will, Mr Holmes.'

'And I should be intrigued to meet him if it would prove at all convenient.'

'I am sure that can be arranged,' said Bates. He took the letter back from Holmes.

'Excellent. I shall hope to hear from you soon.'

Benjamin Bates bade us farewell before disappearing out of the room, clutching his prized missive in his hands.

'An extraordinary development, Holmes,' I remarked. 'Jack the Ripper? Have you ever seen anything like it?'

'Nothing, Watson,' said Holmes. 'It is quite the most macabre correspondence I have ever laid eyes upon.'

'Was it written by the murderer?' I asked.

'I am certain that it wasn't. But I am equally certain that someone is playing a very nasty game with us, Watson.'

'You mean Bates?' Holmes shook his head.

'Unless his acting matches that of Irving, I would wager that his excitement upon his arrival was entirely genuine. He also failed to ask me whether I felt the document to be genuine, something he would have undoubtedly done had he been complicit in its manufacture.'

'In order to be certain that the subterfuge had been successful?'

'Precisely, Watson. No, I am afraid I am not the only one who is deliberately leading young Bates along an entirely false path.'

'But who, Holmes?'

'I cannot be certain, Watson. But I would most certainly wish to meet Mr T.P O'Connor, or Tay Pay, as I believe he is known in some circles.

'The editor of The Star? Do you know him?'

'Only by reputation. Watson. And he is as wily a fellow as exists in the newspaper industry.'

8.

Squibby

The last Saturday of September found me idling about Baker Street of a late afternoon. I had returned from my practice quite unable to lend myself to the simplest of pursuits. It therefore came as something of a relief to hear the familiar sharp tread of Holmes' footsteps clipping their way up our staircase at shortly after four o 'clock.

'Watson, my dear fellow,' he greeted cheerfully, as he entered the sitting room. 'Why, what the devil have you been doing?'

'I have been sorting through my correspondence, Holmes,' I replied, observing the sea of letters and documents scattered across the floor in untidy heaps. 'I confess I have been quite beside myself with boredom this afternoon.'

'Well, I have the cure for that, my dear boy,' said Holmes rubbing his hands together. 'An adventure! The streets of Whitechapel await us, Watson!'

'But what has happened, Holmes?'

'Squibby has been in contact, Watson. And a more intriguing story than the one with which he regaled me in The Queen's Head this afternoon, I have not heard in many years.'

'Then I should be glad to hear it.'

Holmes sat down, slowly positioning his long frame on the edge of the chair as though to heighten the anticipation.

'Contacting Squibby, let me tell you, Watson, is not an endeavour to be undertaken lightly. No postal service or telegram wire can penetrate his elusiveness; no enquires can yield an address beyond the vaguest of geographical terms. He is at once amongst the most visible yet evasive figures of London's lower strata, while his methods of communication may be charitably described as arbitrary. I was astonished, therefore, to receive a message from him this morning in the form of as wretched a looking child as I have ever laid eyes upon. This straggling young emissary mumbled something about Squibby wanting to meet me here this evening.

'Of course, such an unprecedented dispatch aroused my curiosities to the extent that I was compelled to venture in search of the fellow that instant. Only by the sheerest luck was I able to find him in so quick a fashion. I had given up hope of finding him for today when Mrs Ringer of the Britannia informed me that she had served him a half pint of ale not ten minutes before my arrival. I was informed by the landlady that after finishing his drink, he declared his intention of visiting the cookshop across the street. I eventually found him meandering along Commercial Street, eating out of a brown paper bag the most unappetising offal that I have ever seen consumed by a human being.

'After devouring his unedifying victuals, I had little trouble tempting him to another half of ale at The Queen's Head.

'"I was making my way to come and see you later, Mr Holmes," he barked, as he gulped down the contents of his glass in one thirsty mouthful. "Did you get my message?"'

'I most certainly did, Squibby,' I replied. 'I see that your recent upturn in shillings has afforded you a more efficient means of communication.'

'"You mean the lad?"' he asked. '"My sister's boy. A good lad is our Eddie, Mr Holmes. A sharp mind on the young man, too. Could be an apprentice if we can find someone that'll take him on."'

'Let us hope so, Squibby,' I replied. 'Now, I confess that I can wait no longer in discovering what it is that you felt so worthy of my attention.'

'"Of course, Mr Holmes,"' he said, adjusting his seat with a great roll of his gigantic shoulders. '"It's like this: last night, I went out with the Vigilance lot, same as ever. I got talking to Mr Harris. He's the secretary, I think. Well, I'm as regular as clockwork, aren't I? The best of the patrollers, if I say so myself."'

'For thirty shillings a week, I should expect no less an accolade, Squibby,' I said drily.

'"Exactly, Mr Holmes. And I think they like having me about, too. They always get me to do the roughest parts. Of course, it don't scare me none. Last night I got talking to Mr Harris before setting off on my rounds. Now, remembering what you said about that Mr Lusk who, I have to tell you, Mr Holmes, I don't like one bit, I starts bringing him into the conversation, don't I? But it was all just casual questions and he didn't think nothing of it. Not as if I'm a reporter now, is it? Anyway, Harris said this Lusk is a fair sort; pillar of the community and all that. It's just he can be a bit pompous now and again. And he's always wandering off on his own during the patrols, saying he's got such and such a business to sort out.

"'Now, my ears pricked up good and proper, 'cause I'd noticed that very same thing myself and told you about it, as you'll remember. Now how am I supposed to find out what the old devil is up to, I thinks to myself. Then a stroke of luck comes my way, Mr Holmes. My rounds took me up Dorset Street way. I don't know the time, but the pubs were shut and I'd been roaming for a couple of hours, so best I can guess is that it was about one o'clock. I'd just come past the Horn of Plenty and onto Dorset Street when I spot a couple about fifty yards away.

"'Now, we're told to look out for men and women what's together in the street after dark, so I keep an eye on them, don't I? And I'm sure I recognise the man. I cross to the other side of the road and I've got this new coat I bought for four shillings in Brick Lane and I pulls it right up to cover my face, so even though the road's narrow, they can't see who I am. They're stood outside an alleyway, the man and woman, and as I gets closer, I can see that it's Mr Lusk. The girl he's talking with was a fine sort, Mr Holmes. Half his age and a right buxom thing she was. She's got her arms around him and they're talking in low voices. So, he kisses her and she goes into the alleyway and he heads off towards the Commercial. I followed him down Commercial Street, all the way to the High Street and saw him get a cab.'"

'Was there anyone else in this cab?' I asked.

"'Not as far as I could tell.'"

'And he did not see or recognise you at anytime during this observation?'

"'I'm sure of it, Mr Holmes.'"

'Remarkable!' I exclaimed when Holmes has finished his story. 'What do you reason Lusk is up to?'

'We can but guess, Watson. Beyond the obvious vulgarity of such actions so soon after the sad departure of his wife, I'm afraid I cannot yet say what George Lusk's game is.'

'It throws into question his motives for forming a vigilance committee, I suppose?'

'Perhaps, Watson. Although if he proves to be involved in some tawdry love affair, what is to be gained by having several members of his own committee, all of whom should know him in an instant, trawling the streets each night? Surely he could absent himself from his own household on occasion without the need for such a charade.'

'Well, he certainly seems to be using the committee to mask his own affairs,' I countered.

'I agree, Watson. And his letter troubles me.'

'His letter?'

'Yes. I suspected it at the time, but now I am almost certain that the entire purpose of Lusk's letter, as well as the subsequent visit it proposed, was merely to create an impression which might allow him to conduct his affairs, whatever they may be, without suspicion.'

'Now that I think of it, his main objective when he came to Baker Street seemed to be determining what you could tell him of your own findings, rather than any information which he could impart.'

'Exactly, Watson! And the man he claims was observed in Dorset Street intrigues me.'

'Why, of course!' I said, having quite forgotten the blood-stained man of whom Lusk had spoken. 'And now he has been observed in the very same street!'

'Which is precisely what intrigues me, Watson. Tonight, we must endeavour to find out the truth.'

'Tonight?'

'Yes, Watson. We shall discover the identity of Lusk's mysterious paramour with the assistance of our friend Squibby. He thought he would recognise the girl again and it never hurts, in any case, to have a man of his dimensions as company on a midnight stroll through the lowest portions of Whitechapel.'

After fortifying ourselves with dinner courtesy of Mrs Hudson, we steeled ourselves for the long night ahead and departed Baker Street at just past eleven o'clock. By the time we arrived at The Commercial its patrons were already spilling out onto the street as closing time

68

beckoned. We shouldered our way past soldiers and their sweethearts, vagabonds, ladies of obvious ill-repute and their inevitable associates, all of whom ignored us in their drunken stupor.

At a table in the furthest corner sat an oddly subdued looking Squibby. He was dressed in a thick black coat which fitted his enormous bulk perfectly, but whose length was evidently intended for a man of much greater stature than our friend. Thus, it appeared as if Squibby were some enormous infant wrapped in a swaddling blanket. Along with his hat, which was something approaching that of a sailor's, he cut a surprisingly innocuous figure as he hunched over his tankard of ale.

'Good evening, Squibby,' said Holmes as we approached the table. 'A fine night, is it not?'

'Not for me, Mr Holmes,' he said sulkily.

'And why ever not, Squibby?'

'I'm not sure about tonight, to tell the truth. I don't want to get mixed up in anything that will get me in trouble again. And I like my patrolling. My Ma's proud of me for once. If Mr Lusk finds out I've been spying on him, he's not going to keep me on, is he?'

Holmes took the seat next to Squibby.

'My dear Squibby,' said Holmes in a most soothing voice. 'You have my unreserved assurance that tonight's escapade, whatever its eventual outcome, will not prove in any way detrimental to your current position. You may even find it enhances it. I did not tell you this previously for fear of alarming you, but my investigations have been commissioned by Royal appointment, Squibby.'

'The Queen?' he asked.

'One of her subordinates, certainly. And I need not remind you that it is I who am paying you a generous salary, not Mr Lusk. Of course, if you wish to resign your post, then I shall have no alternative but to reluctantly disengage you from your duties.'

'No, no!' he implored, gripping Holmes by the shoulder in earnest. 'I'll do it, Mr Holmes!'

Squibby released Holmes from his well-meaning, but no doubt painful grip, and was assured that he would not regret his decision.

We departed the Britannia shortly before midnight, by which time Squibby was already supposed to be patrolling the High Street and its foul tributaries. When we reached the corner of Dorset Street, Holmes and I stayed back while Squibby slowly walked along the street, glancing either side of him. He appeared to observe nothing which excited his interest, reaching the end of the narrow street before promptly turning on his heel and making his way back to Holmes and I.

'I couldn't see her,' said Squibby dejectedly.

'No matter, Squibby,' said Holmes. 'We at least know where she lives.'

'In the alley where Squibby saw her with Lusk?' I asked.

'I believe so, Watson,' said Holmes, his pale features reddened by the cold. 'If Squibby has described events accurately, then I believe he observed Lusk accompanying her home and bidding her goodnight.'

'Could we not return in the morning and look for her then?' I asked, uncertain what might be gained by searching for the woman at such an hour.

'We may very well do that, Watson,' said Holmes. 'But I wish in the first instance to discover whether last night's meeting was an isolated dalliance on the part of Lusk, or whether Squibby was privy to a regular meeting between him and his young beauty. There is nothing as satisfying as pre-empting a fellow and then catching him red-handed.'

Yet, if Squibby had observed George Lusk in the course of what was a uniform arrangement between himself and the young girl, he had absented himself from such an appointment on this occasion. We stood loosely at either end of Dorset Street for the next hour, during which time we observed little save for the commotion of its many lodging houses. Amongst the steady throng of people who came in and out of these establishments, Squibby was certain that he could not spy Lusk's companion.

It was past one o'clock before I ventured the suggestion to Holmes that we might do best to admit defeat and retire home to our warm beds. Observing both the weather, which had turned wet and dismal, as well as the futility of our remaining in Dorset Street, Holmes acquiesced. We made our way towards Commercial Street in the vague hope of acquiring a cab at such an hour.

We passed the alleyway outside which Squibby had seen Lusk and his companion. It was a narrow, stone-flagged passage, above which a sign, much rusted with age, proclaimed it to be Miller's Court. Our attention was drawn to a man on the opposite side of the streets, whom was standing outside one of the lodging houses.

'Good evening, Sir,' said Holmes cheerfully as he crossed the narrow street, beckoning us to follow.

'Evening,' replied the man gruffly, eyeing the three of us suspiciously. He was a stout fellow in his fifties and possessed of great side whiskers which gave him a rather stern aspect.

'Are you the keeper of this lodging house?' asked Holmes.

'That I am, Sir. Can I help you?'

'I believe that you can. I am looking for a young lady who lives in the court just across the road there.'

'Are you now? You know what sort live in there, don't you?'

'I am afraid I do not.'

'A likely story. Be away with you,' he snarled, dismissing Holmes with a shake of his fist. In an instant, Squibby had dashed past me and grabbed the man by his coat, trapping him in his iron grip. The poor fellow writhed and turned in a futile attempt to release himself from Squibby's unyielding grasp, a mixture of fear and astonishment across his features.

'I believe my friend told you that he was looking for a girl,' said Squibby menacingly, fixing a hard stare on the man.

'What girl?' he stammered.

'Last night I saw a girl standing outside that alleyway. She had long dark hair and had on a white apron. She was tall and pretty and perhaps five and twenty. I want you to tell me if you know her.'

'It's alright, Squibby. You may let him go,' said Holmes. 'I believe our friend will answer your question, will you not?'

The man nodded as Squibby released him, straightening his back and rubbing his chest in pain.

'I think I know who your friend saw,' he said to Holmes, still appearing rather shaken. 'Her name's Mary Kelly and she's well known around here. Often drinks in The Ten Bells. She's from Ireland and she lives in the court with her man; a fellow called Joe. That's all I know about her.'

'And you have never observed her with a well-dressed man? One considerably older than herself?'

'With the greatest of respect, a sort like her is often seen in the company of various men. But no, I haven't seen her with such a man of late.'

Holmes thanked the man, who eyed Squibby narrowly as we departed the grim shadows of Dorset Street. Our companion gave us a muttered farewell before turning northwards up Commercial Street while we headed south in search of a means home. Commercial Street, stripped of its traffic and trade, had a rather foreboding air. The hazy, rain-flecked light cast by the gas lamps were but shallow pools in the darkness. Aside from pockets of vagrants and idlers who inhabited its foulest corners, we appeared quite alone in the eerie silence. I confess that as our footsteps echoed off the smog-stained facades of the shop fronts, I was rather glad to have the company of Holmes.

We reached the junction onto Whitechapel High Street without sight of a single vehicle. As I was preparing myself for an ungodly walk back to Baker Street, we heard the clattering of wheels and moments later, a cab streaking past us in the direction of Commercial Road.

'That fellow has certainly had more luck than us in procuring a hansom,' I lamented.

'Regrettably so, Watson. Halloa, he has stopped in the middle of the road,' said Holmes, as the cab came to an abrupt halt. A man stepped down onto the street, peering earnestly into the darkness.

'Holmes?' shouted the man. 'Dr Watson. Is that you?'

'My goodness!' exclaimed Holmes, as the man dashed towards us. 'It is Benjamin Bates!'

'Bates? Whatever can he be doing in Whitechapel at this hour?'

'I rather think he may ask the same question of us, Watson. But whatever has brought him here, it seems to have done so in some hurry, to judge by his attire.'

I observed that Benjamin Bates was in rather a bedraggled state of dress. His shirt hung out of his trousers in loose flaps and his hair stuck out wildly from beneath a hat which sat at an ungainly angle upon his head.

'You have heard then?' he cried breathlessly.

'What on earth do you mean, Bates?' asked Holmes, shooting the reporter a worried glance.

'You mean you don't know?'

'What has happened?' I asked earnestly.

'Another murder, Doctor,' he replied. 'Jack the Ripper has struck again.'

9.

Dutfield's Yard

'Another murder?' I gasped. 'But where?'

'Berner Street. A place called Dutfield's Yard. I can take you both with me. Come on!'

'And how was it that you came to hear of this murder, Bates?' asked Holmes as we ran to the awaiting vehicle.

'I'll explain on the way. Please, hurry!' cried Bates anxiously, no doubt keen to arrive at the scene before his rival pressmen. We crammed into the cab three abreast and were soon galloping off towards Berner Street.

Dutfield's Yard, according to Holmes' encyclopaedic knowledge of London, was so-named due to its former occupancy by one Arthur Dutfield's cart building business. It proved to be but a few minutes from where we had met Benjamin Bates. Berner Street was a mean thoroughfare of small two-storey slums. As we came to its southern point, a great crowd indicated the spot where the poor woman had evidently met her fate. A policeman was standing just outside the yard.

'Holmes! Dr Watson!' called the familiar voice of Lestrade, whom neither of us had noticed in the grim blackness.

'Lestrade,' said Holmes, as the Inspector advanced towards us. 'This is becoming something of a habit.'

'Do you know who she is yet?' asked Bates.

'And who might you be?' asked Lestrade sharply.

'Benjamin Bates of The Star,' he said, offering Lestrade a hand which the Inspector ignored.

'We don't talk to the press,' said Lestrade curtly.

'Then I shall make my own enquires,' replied Bates in an equally brusque tone, setting forth amongst the rabble of sightseers.

'Tell me what you can, Lestrade,' said Holmes, as soon as the reporter was out of earshot. The Inspector signalled for us to follow him past the policeman on sentry duty and through the wicker gates into Dutfield's Yard.

'This is Chief Inspector West and Inspector Pinhorn,' said Lestrade, gesturing towards the two detectives stood just inside the gates. 'Gentlemen, this is Sherlock Holmes and his colleague, Dr Watson.'

The two men greeted us and obligingly moved aside to reveal the prostate form of a woman. Over the body was knelt a man clearly in the midst of examining her. He stood up when he saw Holmes and I approach.

'I'm Dr Blackwell,' said a tall, amiable-looking fellow in his late-thirties. 'Good evening to you both.'

'Good evening, Dr Blackwell. Lestrade, might we have a little light?'

Lestrade beckoned a constable into the yard and instructed him to flash his bull's-eye upon the grim figure laid across the ground. In the flickering light, I saw it was a woman of about forty with curly black hair. Her throat had been fearfully cut, a stream of blood flowing from the wound and clotting near her feet. Her eyes were open, eerily reflecting the glow of the lantern.

'What can you tell us, Dr Blackwell?' asked Holmes.

'She has been dead about thirty minutes,' he said.

'It is one thirty-three now,' said Holmes, consulting his pocket-watch. 'So, this poor woman was murdered at about one o'clock, you say?'

'I believe it could not have been much later than that, Mr Holmes. I arrived at just after the quarter hour and she had been dead no more than twenty minutes.'

'Thank you, Doctor. Please continue.'

'The cause of death was haemorrhage due to blood loss from the wound to the throat, although there are no further cuts or abrasions. I believe that she was pulled to the ground by her scarf and then had her throat cut.'

'There are no signs of strangulation?' I asked in surprise.

'None, Dr Watson,' replied Blackwell. 'Nor are there any mutilations of the type found upon the previous victims.'

76

'Surely he was disturbed before he could commence such a task?' ventured Lestrade. 'The man who found the body evidently interrupted her murder before he could plunder her further.'

'That would be the most likely explanation, Lestrade,' said Holmes. 'But perhaps if you were to furnish me with the details of this poor lady's discovery, I may be able to give you a more qualified assessment.'

Whatever deficiencies in the arts of observation and detection of which Holmes considered Lestrade guilty, even he had never questioned the thoroughness of his enquiries. Thus, while consulting his notebook, the Inspector provided us with a comprehensive summary of events at Berner Street. The building next to Dutfield's Yard was the International Working men's club, patronised by socialist Jews of mainly Russian or Polish extraction. After their evening's discussions had ended at around midnight, a few dozen had remained behind, chatting or singing in the upstairs meeting rooms. Several of them had entered the yard in the hour before the body was found, yet none observed anything suspicious. At 12.40, a member of the club named Morris Eagle passed through the yard and all was quiet.

Yet at one o'clock, Louis Diemschutz, the club secretary, entered the yard with his pony and barrow. When the animal shied to the left, Diemshutz inspected the entrance. He saw a form on the ground which, by the meagre light of a match, he observed to be that of a woman. No-one from the club or the surrounding houses heard the slightest noise, nor was there anything that could be found in the yard that might afford a clue.

'You may find it helpful in the identification of this poor woman, Lestrade, if I tell you that she has worked recently as a charlady and has also done a considerable amount of sewing. She is no stranger to violence and has been married.

'How the devil do you deduce that?' asked Lestrade.

'Her hands have the tell-tale signs of the charlady. You may notice the slight discoloration to the fingertips caused by prolonged contact with the cleaning agents employed by that profession. The fingers are pock-marked, clearly evidence of much sewing. There is also the slight indent of a wedding ring just visible on the left hand. Her missing front teeth and the scar of a torn ear-lobe convince me that she has not been immune to the violence to which her position in life has exposed her.'

'Yes, well I suppose that is a sensible enough conclusion,' blustered Lestrade. 'And what of the murderer?'

'That is rather less evident, Lestrade,' confessed Holmes.

We emerged from the yard to find Bates interviewing the ashen-faced club members, eagerly taking down their comments with barely suppressed glee.

'Well, there is at least someone who is making the best of tonight's horror,' I said, gesturing towards the reporter.

'As you no doubt expected him to, Watson. As for ourselves, I am afraid that all we can do for this evening is to retire to Baker Street and hope that Lestrade can acquire us some clues. At present, I confess that events here quite confound me.'

Benjamin Bates requested some words from Holmes on his observations in the yard, something my friend acquiesced to only begrudgingly and with the most truculent manner. Never had I seen him so despondent as in the blackness of Berner Street. Unable to avail himself of any clues, it must have seemed to Holmes that Jack the Ripper was a yet more elusive figure than before our arrival at Dutfield's Yard. The singular saving grace of Benjamin Bates' presence, it seemed, was the cab which he had ordered to wait for him, no doubt at the expense of The Star. Given the turn of events, it was of some comfort when he offered to transport us home immediately upon the completion of his interviews.

At something after two o' clock, he informed a weary Holmes that he was at last ready to depart. As I sat myself heavily into the cab, and Holmes was in the act of joining me, I was jolted from my fatigue by the shrill cry of Inspector Lestrade. I leaned forward to see his thin frame racing towards us.

'Holmes! Dr Watson! Wait!' he cried.

'What in Heaven's name is wrong, Lestrade?' asked Holmes as he stepped back onto the pavement, his features almost as startled as those of the Inspector. 'What have you found?'

'I have had an urgent message from Leman Street station,' he gasped. 'Another murder has been committed!'

'Where?' demanded Holmes.

'Mitre Square,' said Lestrade. 'This one is terrible.'

Barely had he said these words than Bates alighted the hansom, fervently repeating the destination to the driver as Holmes jumped aboard the half-moving vehicle. In seconds, we were driving into the blackness of the night towards Mitre Square and Jack the Ripper's second victim inside the space of an hour.

10.

Murder in Mitre Square

We hurtled through the barren streets, the wheels of our cab rattling wildly against the ancient cobbles as we galloped towards Mitre Square. Holmes' eyes were fixed straight ahead, his features unflinching in the icy wind which swept across us. Hemmed in firmly by the angular figure of my friend, Benjamin Bates hung on grimly to the side of the hansom, his shirt flapping loosely about him. His countenance was quite aghast; swept with a mixture of anxiety and excitement as he no doubt considered the story that lay ahead of him at our journey's end. For my part, I was merely content to fight the fatigue with which my body ached, although my imagination ran wild as I peered through the swirling blackness.

We arrived at Mitre Street a mere five minutes or so after our alighting at Berner Street. There were several policemen just inside the wide entrance to Mitre Square, their faces partly illuminated in the faint glow of the lamp by which they were standing. They nodded upon the sight of Sherlock Holmes and we proceeded silently past them. Mitre Square was perhaps twenty-five yards across and flanked on every side by tall warehouses which cast long, oblique shadows that stretched its entire length. There were but a few houses crouched in these grim silhouettes, most of which were unoccupied and possessed of crumbling brick and broken panes. Save for the low mutterings of the police officers, the faint echo of our footsteps was the only sound audible in what seemed to be the loneliest spot in all of London. Our way ahead was cloaked in impenetrable darkness, save only for the solitary lamp in the square's furthest corner which gave the faintest glimmer of our surroundings.

Holmes' remarkable senses proved our saviour, for he heard the indistinct murmuring of voices and took us around the right corner to where, in the very darkest spot of the square, laid the poor woman. As we approached the handful of police officers gathered around the prostrate figure, one of them turned and evidently recognised Holmes.

'Mr Holmes?' asked the man, his eyes straining in the darkness.

'That is correct,' my friend replied, as the man drew towards us and shook Holmes by the hand. 'I'm afraid that your name is not so familiar to me.'

'Apologies, Mr Holmes. I am Inspector Collard of the City Police.'

'A pleasure,' said Holmes, as the Inspector surveyed Bates and I with a polite smile.

'You will want to view the body, no doubt,' said Inspector Collard. 'Dr Sequeria is already here, but no-one is to touch it until Dr Brown has arrived.'

We followed the Inspector, a tall, well-built fellow of about forty, and joined those officers partly encircling the poor woman, who had appeared a mere bundle in the gloom of the square. Bates was notable only for his silence, skulking about just to my side where he might cause the least attention. I surveyed the body before us which, by the light of the two obliging constables' bull's-eyes, became the most grotesque spectacle that I had ever seen.

Before us was a woman of about forty-five, her head turned across her left shoulder and her face fearfully bloodied and mutilated. The throat had been cut across savagely, the thick wound still trickling blood which had pooled upon the cobbles beneath her. Her skirts had been pulled up to expose her abdomen, which had been slashed in the most fearful manner. Part of the poor woman's intestines had been drawn out and placed on her right shoulder. Another piece was lodged between the body and the left arm, around which was a pool of clotted blood that had flowed from her throat.

'Dear God, Watson,' said Holmes, his eyes fixed upon the horror before him. 'What has he done?'

'It is horrific, Holmes,' I said, observing my friend's despair. 'The man is out of control.'

'That he is, Watson. Inspector Collard, who found this poor woman?'

'Constable Watkins here,' he replied, indicating a clean-shaven young man of about thirty-five who was standing just across from us.

'I found her at just before a quarter to two,' explained Watkins shakily. 'I'd come here just a quarter of an hour earlier and all was well.

The next time I entered the square, I saw this poor woman in the beam of my lantern. It's the worst thing I ever saw.'

'And what did you do upon making so terrifying a discovery?' asked Holmes, eyeing the Constable intently.

'I went to the warehouse across the square, for I know Mr Morris, the watchman. The door was ajar, so I shouted that another woman had been done in and I needed assistance. He came with me and I kept watch while he went in search of help.

'You have acted commendably,' said Holmes. 'Is there no-one else who lives in this square?'

'It's mostly businesses here, Mr Holmes. Warehouses and the like,' replied Watkins. 'But PC Pearce and his wife live just across the square. I don't think they have been knocked up yet.'

'I see. They evidently heard nothing to arouse them from there beds at any rate,' observed Holmes.

'It is extraordinary, Mr Holmes. It is as though the man appeared by magic and then vanished into the night.'

Holmes mumbled his concurrence with this remark and made his way to the centre of the square.

'Are we without hope, Holmes?' I asked, as I drew alongside him.

'I am never without hope, Watson. Although I admit that this fellow is proving a most worthy adversary.'

'But how did he make his escape without being observed?' I asked in wonderment. 'It appears impossible.'

'It is far from that, Watson. Consider that our man has three possible means of egress: the carriageway by which both ourselves and Constable Watkins entered, as well as two passages at the opposite end of the square, each lit by but a single lamp. He must have used one of these, for if he had exited via the carriageway, Watkins could not have failed to observe him as he made his own way into the square. Its lack of residents was of course to the killer's advantage, as no-one was close enough to hear him carry out his foul deed. No, the most worrying thing is that he has again left no clue as to his identity.'

'You could tell nothing?'

'Again, I can tell you more of the poor woman than of the man who slayed her. She has recently returned from hop-picking with a male friend who has purchased new boots within the last month.'

'How on earth can you tell that, Holmes?

'Some deductions, Watson, rely on a series of tiny inferences which, when taken together, form a chain of logic from which the truth becomes an irresistible certainty. Consider that her apparel includes a waistcoat which is clearly that of a man's, and that she is also wearing a pair of men's laced boots. Immediately, I could not fail to be struck by the presence of a man in her life with whom she evidently shares an intimate relationship. The boots troubled me, Watson. They were far from new, but equally some way from being considered battered enough to warrant casting them off to an acquaintance. Evidently, the man who possessed them had purchased a new pair recently and hence could afford to present these to his lady in such a serviceable condition.

'Even in the gaudy light of a policeman's lantern, I observed that her face was lightly tanned, as were her hands. These facts told me that the woman had been hop-picking with her man. He had bought new boots upon his return to London, whereupon he passed his old ones to her. It is quite the tradition, I believe, for hop-pickers to acquire new boots upon leaving Kent and often leave their old ones strewn along the roads back to London.'

'Of course! That is quite ingenious, Holmes!' I exclaimed in admiration.

'Yet I am afraid I can offer no such assurances as to her killer,' said Holmes, his vexed features betraying his frustration. He turned and re-joined the rabble of officers, who were still muttering amongst themselves. Dr Brown had evidently arrived, for I could make out the form of a man hunched over the body. After he had completed his examination, he ordered that the body be removed to the mortuary.

'I rather thought that Lestrade would have arrived by now,' I said, my pocket watch informing me that the hour was approaching half-past two.

'Your geography of this great city has always been notable only for its remarkable ambiguity to detail. We are in the great square mile, Watson, of which the City of London Force have charge.'

84

As I replied in defence of my ignorance, the attention of the officers surrounding us was taken by the arrival upon the scene of a middle-aged man flanked by several detectives. He was tall and possessed of strong, if rather gaunt features, his eyes and aspect suggesting a formidable bearing and intellect. He was availed of events by Inspector Collard, and I gathered from their hushed conversation that the man was Major Henry Smith, whom Holmes informed me was the Acting Commissioner of the City force. He spent some considerable time amongst his officers, talking to each in turn and nodding as they spoke.

'They tell me that you are Mr Sherlock Holmes?' said Major Smith, turning his attention to my friend.

'That is correct,' replied Holmes. 'I believe I address Major Henry Smith of The City Police force?'

'You do, indeed,' said he, appearing surprised that Holmes should recognise him.

The two men conversed cordially upon the night's events, with the Major voicing his distress that a murder had occurred on his territory. I was able to interject my own minor observations, principally on medical matters, as the dialogue turned to embrace the previous murders. Major Smith assured us of the elaborate precautions he had taken since the spate of murders began, explaining how he had placed extra men in plain clothes onto the streets in the hope of catching the man red-handed. His officers had been instructed to challenge any man seen in the company of a woman and yet the killer, much to Major Smith's obvious embarrassment, had entered Mitre Square with his victim to the complete ignorance of The City Police.

It was past three o' clock when it became apparent that there was little more to be gained by our remaining at the murder scene. The body had long since been conveyed to the mortuary, while most of the officers had dispersed in order to perform house-to-house enquires amongst the nearby streets. Even the intrepid Benjamin Bates appeared to have tired of events, having exhausted every means of acquiring the details with which to furnish his report of this extraordinary night.

Yet just as I was successfully persuading Holmes of the attractions of our beds at Baker Street, a young Constable ran breathlessly into the square and raced towards the first officer of sufficient rank he could find.

'I've been sent from Commercial Street Station,' he stammered to Inspector Collard. 'They've found part of the dead woman's apron in Goulston Street.'

'They are certain it is hers?' asked Collard. The Constable nodded.

'It is blood-stained, Sir. Inspector Halse is certain it belonged to the dead woman.'

'Then we shall proceed to Goulston Street immediately,' said Collard.

'There is something else, Inspector,' said the Constable earnestly. 'Above the apron was a message written by the murderer.'

11.

Goulston Street

We stood in astonished silence at this remarkable intelligence, until at last Holmes implored us to depart for Goulston Street without delay. Inspector Collard joined Holmes and I in the cab by which the Constable had arrived, while Bates held on gingerly to the back of the vehicle, his legs dangling alarmingly at the side as we clattered our way north.

Goulston Street was a long thoroughfare just off the western edge of Whitechapel High Street. The Constable ordered our driver to stop as we reached its northern end. We followed him to a Model Dwellings, the entrance of which was already choked with officers.

'I'm Inspector Halse, Mr Holmes,' said a middle-aged man with a sandy moustache and whiskers. 'I was told you were on your way. One of our men found a piece of apron that was taken from the woman at Mitre Square. Above it was some writing.'

He moved to his side so that we could see the graffito for ourselves. Just inside the doorway, on the black-bricked facia, was written in chalk the following cryptic message:

> The Juwes are
> The men That
> Will not
> be Blamed
> for nothing

'Extraordinary!' I exclaimed, as I read the words. They were in a cursive, if rather sloping hand. 'Do you think it was written by our man, Holmes?'

'Undoubtedly, Watson,' said he, his eyes fixed upon the message. 'He has left the piece of apron here to prove that the writing was his work.'

'But what does it mean?' I asked, re-reading the bizarre message.

'That is not immediately clear,' said Holmes. 'If I am right and the word 'Juwes' is a misspelling of 'Jews', then it is either a subterfuge

87

to cast blame upon those people, or else an admission of the man's faith. Either way, I do not see that it tells us much about his motives.'

'Is there some other layer to it, do you think, Holmes?' asked Bates from over my shoulder. 'Perhaps a code of some sort?'

'That is of course possible, Bates. Although if the killer wished to leave a message, I fail to see what is to be gained by encrypting it and thus obscuring its meaning.'

'Is it to photographed?' I asked.

'Inspector McWilliam has sent for a photographer,' said Halse. 'Although we shall have to wait until it is light, of course.'

Despite his enigmatic communication, the killer had again left us floundering for clues as to his identity. Holmes employed our wait for the photographer in making as accurate a facsimile of the message as he could in his notebook.

It was just getting light, my pocket-watch informing me that it was five o'clock, when the tall, robust figure of Sir Charles Warren, the Commissioner of the Metropolitan Police, arrived at Goulston Street. He was instantly recognisable from the thick moustache that punctuated his stern features which, together with his military stance and piercing gaze, gave him a most formidable air.

There was much muttering between Sir Charles and Superintendent Arnold, who had arrived shortly before him, to the effect that they wished the writing to be washed away.

'But Sir, surely it is unwise to remove such an important clue?' protested Inspector Halse.

'It is getting light, man!' barked the commissioner, his features flushing with anger at this unexpected dissent. 'Superintendent Arnold informs me that this area will soon be teeming with people for the Sunday market. I cannot be responsible for an anti-Semitic riot.'

'Could we not merely remove the top line, Sir? That would remove any association with the Jews.' replied Halse.

'You are aware that this tenement building predominantly houses Jewish people?' blustered Sir Charles. 'It matters little whether the message refers to Jews or not. If the public observe the Police guarding this building in the wake of two murders, I fear that they will rapidly draw their own conclusions. And that, Inspector, can only result in trouble.'

The Commissioner spat out these words with such an air of finality that I believe even the intervention of Sherlock Holmes would have proved futile. Sir Charles observed as a Constable applied a wet sponge to the message, while I looked on in horror as a direct clue to the murderer was erased forever.

'A confounded idiot!' I ejaculated, when Sir Charles had brushed past us and hurried out of Goulston Street.

'Calm yourself, Watson,' said Holmes, placing his hand on my shoulder. 'Commissioner Warren has made quite an unpardonable blunder. I cannot claim to have anticipated his actions, although I felt it wise to record the exact wording and script of the message in case of such an event.'

'But Holmes!' I protested. 'The man has destroyed a valuable clue.'

'You heard his reasoning, Watson. We may question his decision, but not the fact that it was his alone to make. In any case, I am certain that the solution to this mystery lies beyond the enigmatic riddle which we have just observed being so graciously effaced from existence.'

'Then where?'

'That, I am sure, will soon become apparent, Watson. There is little else we can do here tonight. I suggest we engage Bates' talent for procuring hansoms and return to Baker Street. I for one require much rest and a little sustenance before I am able to give this problem the full benefit of my attention.'

Benjamin Bates, himself rather weary of visage and sagging of limb, agreed with Holmes that the extraordinary events had run their course. He took mere minutes to procure us a vehicle and were soon headed west towards the comforting prospect of our rooms at Baker Street. By the burgeoning dawn light, I soon observed the gleaming spires of Westminster ahead of us.

'I feel utterly defeated,' I said, as we wearily reached the top of our staircase. 'The man must surely be a phantom.'

'I assure you that he is as real as you or I, Watson,' replied Holmes.

'But he has left no trace, Holmes. How can a man murder two women in such a manner without being seen?'

'I do not believe he can, Watson. He has quite miraculously avoided detection. But someone will have observed him. Someone who is yet to realise the importance of what they have seen. I expect no less than a flurry of witnesses once tonight's events are detailed in the papers and become the talk of London. We shall have him eventually, Watson.'

With these words, Holmes retired to his room, as I went in search of my own bed and much needed sleep, quite exhausted by the extraordinary deeds of Jack the Ripper.

Sherlock Holmes was proved correct in his belief that there would be a deluge of information once the particulars of the murders had been laid before the public. The following day's papers were replete with the fullest of accounts of the murders, providing in the most lurid prose whatever details the reporter had cobbled together. Benjamin Bates exceeded himself in his wonderfully vivid report, combining the facts he had gained from his presence at both murders with the questionable details acquired from his numerous interviews.

It was well past midday when I was fully dressed, while Holmes stirred later still as we both struggled to recover from the effects of the previous night. Finally, as evening approached and we had fortified ourselves with an early dinner from Mrs Hudson, I believe we had regained something of our zeal for the task at hand. Our return to strength proved rather fortuitous, as minutes later Mrs Hudson returned with a telegram from Lestrade, which Holmes duly passed to me:

Please come at once to Leman Street Station. We have a witness who saw attack upon Berner Street victim. I think you should meet him. Lestrade.

Scarcely had I read the message than I was once again donning my hat and coat and following Holmes onto Baker Street in search of a cab. We quickly procured a rather rickety example of the vehicle and made our way to Leman Street in jolting fashion. Upon our arrival, the duty Inspector recognised Holmes and quickly ushered us past the rabble of drunks and vagabonds who were loitering at the main desk. We were shown into a small, wood-panelled interview room, where sat a tired-looking Lestrade, his unkempt hair and dishevelled shirt evidence of the long hours he had worked since the previous night. Across the table from him were two men, both of whom appeared of continental extraction.

'Good gracious, Lestrade,' exclaimed Holmes upon eyeing the weary Inspector. 'Why, you look positively exhausted.'

'You don't know the half of it, Holmes,' he said wearily. 'These murders will be the end of me, I tell you.'

'You mentioned something of a witness, did you not?' said Holmes, his attentions turning rapidly to the matter at hand.

'This is Mr Schwartz,' he replied, gesturing to the smaller of the two men, who had a rather theatrical air about his neat costume and swarthy features. 'He is Hungarian and speaks no English. Mr Lechner here is a friend of his and has agreed to act as an interpreter.'

Mr Lechner, a stout, well-proportioned man with a ruddy countenance, greeted us warmly. At Holmes' request, he availed us in halted English of his friend's extraordinary story. It appeared that at quarter to one on the morning of the murders, Mr Schwartz had turned onto Berner Street on his way to his new lodgings in Backchurch Lane. Upon passing Dutfield's Yard, he observed an attack on the very spot where the body was discovered just fifteen minutes later. He saw a man stop and talk to a woman, who was standing just outside the yard. The man then attempted to pull the woman into the street. When she resisted, he threw her to the ground, whereupon she screamed three times, although not very loudly.

Being of a rather nervous disposition, Schwartz crossed to the opposite side of the street, where he observed a second standing, casually lighting his pipe. The man who had thrown the woman to the ground cried 'Lipski!' across the street, apparently to the man with the pipe. Schwartz continuing walking, but on finding that he was being followed by the second man, ran as far as the railway arch, although the man did not follow so far. Schwartz could not be sure whether the two

91

men were acting together. On being shown the body found in Dutfield's Yard, he positively identified her as the woman he had seen.

'My goodness, Holmes!' I said, when my friend had exhausted all possible questions to Mr Schwartz. 'He has seen the killer in the midst of his murderous assault!'

'I believe he has, Watson,' said Holmes, with rather less ardour than I might have expected.

'And what of the cry 'Lipski!'? Did the man mistake Mr Schwartz for someone else?'

'No, Watson. I believe it was meant as a derogatory term in consequence of Mr Schwartz's semantic appearance. You may remember the case last year of a certain Polish poisoner by the name of Israel Lipski, who was hanged for the murder of a young woman. His name has become something of an unfortunate insult to his fellow Jews.'

'Of course! I recall there was a great fuss about the verdict,' said Lestrade. 'And what do you make of this second man?'

'He was unquestionably a look-out for the murderer,' said Holmes.

'So, Jack the Ripper is in fact two men?' said the Inspector, visibly sagging at the possibility.

'Perhaps. But I am convinced that we would be wrong to attribute this killing to the same hand that slayed the other women.'

'What?' gasped Lestrade. 'You are saying there are two maniacs roaming Whitechapel plundering women?'

'Only one maniac, I am happy to say, Lestrade. And one murderer of the far more mundane variety.'

'You are sure?'

'Mr Schwartz has furnished you with excellent descriptions of the men he saw in Berner Street. But I am afraid neither of them is the man who struck an hour later in Mitre Square.'

Lestrade appeared confounded at this intelligence. I confess that I was taken aback by Holmes' dismissal of the Dutfield's Yard victim.

'You are quite certain, Holmes?' asked Lestrade, 'Her throat was dreadfully cut.'

'But nothing else besides. There were no mutilations, you remember. I thought perhaps the killer had been interrupted by the

92

fellow and his pony. But Mr Schwartz was clear that he saw the attack take place some fifteen minutes before the woman was discovered, proving that the murderer had ample time to indulge himself should he have wished. It is also impossible for me to reconcile the cunning and dare exhibited by the stealthy figure of Mitre Square with the rather haphazard assault witnessed at Berner Street.'

'Because the two murders were entirely separate,' groaned Lestrade. 'Well at least the Mitre Square phantom is the City lot's problem and not ours.'

'Exactly, Lestrade. Please let me know of any developments you think demand my attention. Watson, I believe there is nothing more to be gained here.'

'You feel that this evening's excursion has been without merit then, Holmes?' I said, as we exited the station onto a chilly Leman street.

'On the contrary, Mr Schwartz's account has filled me with intrigue. Did nothing strike you as odd about it?'

'How do you mean, Holmes?'

'Firstly, let us consider the man he observed to be casually lighting his pipe during the assault upon the poor woman. We must assume that he was there in the role of a lookout, for surely he would have otherwise intervened, or at the very least raised the alarm. And yet something about his presence at the scene troubles me, Watson.'

'And why is that?'

'As Schwartz described it, the murder resulted from the dead woman engaging in conversation with her attacker. When this quickly became an argument, he attempted to drag her into the yard. It was clearly, therefore, not a premeditated attack. Rather, it seems to have been typical of the sort of squalid encounter you might observe in Whitechapel on any given night, save for its fatal conclusion. So from where did this apparent lookout appear so conveniently?'

'I see what you mean, Holmes,' I said. 'There could have been no possible warning that an assault was about to take place.'

'Precisely! When considering an account such as Mr Schwartz's, we must always look for that which does not ring true. It is this man with the pipe which elevates the matter above the commonplace. A frightened man is never a good witness and Schwartz may have misinterpreted the scene entirely, of course. But I fear there is something sinister about this business that we are yet to fully comprehend.'

'Yet it has nothing to do with the other murders?'

'The more I consider the matter, Watson, the less certain I am that that is indeed the case.'

12.

Lawende and the Letter

The day following the murders found me in bed at an uncommonly late hour, quite exhausted by our recent pursuits through the grim streets of Whitechapel. Thus, when it was approaching midday and the shrill tones of Mrs Hudson announced that we had a visitor, I remained undressed and half-asleep in my room. Holmes, whose inestimable fortitude during an investigation knew no bounds, was evidently awake and dressed, for I heard his alert voice assuring our landlady that he would greet them at the street door. Moments later, I heard him return to our sitting room accompanied by someone who I took to be Benjamin Bates, to judge by the boisterous tones audible above those of Holmes.

As I emerged from my room, Holmes spun around and greeted me with a keen smile that hardly spoke of the strains of the last few days.

'Ah, Watson, I see that you are awake at last,' said he. 'I do hope we did not wake you from some badly needed rest?'

'I'm afraid I was quite exhausted, Holmes,' I replied with a faint air of embarrassment. 'But I feel much better now.'

'Excellent. Bates has brought Mr Lawende here with him, whom he thinks may be of great assistance to our investigation.'

Both men nodded their heads at Holmes' introduction.

'I shall look forward to hearing Mr Lawende's account just as soon as I am dressed.'

'Nonsense, my dear fellow. Your dressing gown is perfectly reasonable attire for your own sitting room. Bates promises a revelation which I for one wish to hear without delay.'

Placing myself upon the sofa, I observed as Bates pulled out a postcard from his jacket pocket in a rather theatrical manner for Holmes and I to view.

'He's written in again, Holmes,' he said dramatically, handing the missive to my friend. 'It came by the first post this morning.'

Holmes took it with a studied expression and held it to the light, reading it only briefly and muttering the words as he did so.

'It is written by the same hand that authored the previous correspondence,' he announced flatly. 'Take a look, Watson.'

I took the postcard, across the length of which appeared to be a bloodstain. The message read as follows:

I wasn't codding
dear Old Boss when
I gave the tip.
youll hear about
saucy Jackys work
tomorrow double
event this time
number one squealed
a bit couldnt
finish straight
off. had not time
to get ears for
police thanks for
keeping last letter
back till I got
to work again.
Jack the Ripper

'Extraordinary, Holmes,' I said, handing the postcard back to Bates. 'It has the same mocking tone as the last letter.'

'Precisely, Watson,' said Holmes. 'I notice, Bates, that it was sent to the Central News Agency, as was the previous correspondence. Did you acquire it by the same route?'

'That I did, Holmes,' said Bates. 'Mr O'Connor has loaned it on the same conditions as last time and thought it would interest you.'

'And it most certainly has, Bates. Please extend my gratitude to Mr O'Connor for his consideration.'

'And you believe it is genuine?' asked Bates expectantly.

'I do not yet know what to think,' said Holmes. 'I am intrigued as to how your friend, Mr Lawende here, is connected to this letter.'

'He is not connected at all, Mr Holmes,' said Bates, evincing a look of great curiosity from Sherlock Holmes. 'Mr Lawende was discovered during the house-to-house investigations yesterday afternoon. I tracked him down and brought him to The Star's offices this morning for an interview, only to find upon my arrival that Jack the Ripper had sent us another letter. I thought you would be equally interested in the man as in the missive, so to speak, so I brought both along to see you.'

'The courtesies you afford me continue to astound, Bates,' said Holmes drily. 'And you do not object, Mr Lawende, to being brought here in this manner?'

'Absolutely not, Mr Holmes,' assured Lawende. 'I have read much of Dr Watson's accounts of your exploits and am only too pleased to meet you both.'

'I assure you that the pleasure is entirely reciprocated, Mr Lawende. Now, Mr Bates leads us to believe you have information that will be of some interest to us?'

'I believe that I do, Mr Holmes,' said our visitor. He was aged about forty and neatly dressed in a grey morning suit. He had a lean, intelligent face whose sharp lineaments benefitted from whiskers which gave him the appearance of a clerk. I had thought him of Germanic extraction, but the cultured consonants and soft vowels of his speech marked him as of Polish origin.

'On the night of the murder, I and two friends were at the Imperial Club on Duke Street. We stayed there until one-thirty in the morning in consequence of the rain. We left the building at about 1.35. Crossing Church Passage, we saw a man and woman standing at the corner. One of my friends commented on them due to their unsavoury appearance. I walked a little apart from my friends and noticed the woman to be short and wearing a black jacket and bonnet. She was facing the man and had her hand on his chest. They were talking in very low voices and I could not hear what was being said. I was shown the body at the mortuary this morning and am sure that it was the same woman whom I saw.'

'And the man?' asked Holmes, his eyes fixed upon Lawende. 'Did you see him?'

'I did, Mr Holmes. He was a little taller than the woman, perhaps five-feet-seven, and aged about thirty, I should say. He was of medium build and had a fair complexion and moustache. He was dressed in a loose jacket, which was pepper-and-salt in colour, a grey cloth cap with a peak and a reddish neckerchief which gave him the appearance of a sailor.'

'Would you recognise him again?' asked Holmes.

'Alas, I do not believe I would. The spot on which they stood was poorly lit, and I had little reason to observe them in any particular detail. I am sorry I cannot be of more help.'

'On the contrary, you have been of wonderful assistance, Mr Lawende. I am indebted to your faculty of observation, however casually it has been employed.'

'Do you believe that he has seen the murderer, Holmes?' I asked.

'Undoubtedly, Watson,' said he. 'The woman was found less than ten minutes after Mr Lawende observed her with this man. It is absurd to suggest that the killer left this woman, procured another almost immediately and then proceeded to murder her in time for her corpse to be found by P.C Watkins at 1.44. No, he has seen our man, Watson.'

'Excellent,' said Bates, clearly pleased by this endorsement of his witness. 'And I can print that, can I?'

'You may print anything I have said verbatim and with my blessing, Bates,' replied Holmes cheerfully. 'And when shall I have the pleasure of meeting Mr O'Connor, to whose generosity of information I am so indebted?'

'Soon, Holmes,' said Bates, standing up to leave. 'I guarantee it!'

'A most extraordinary development,' said Holmes, once our visitors had left. 'I can scarcely recall a case with so many twists.'

'I'm afraid I don't know quite what to make of it all,' I confessed.

'Let us start with the postcard, Watson.'

'You think it a fake?'

'Undoubtedly it is a fake. But let us consider matters for a moment. Although it is stamped with today's date, I would venture that the postcard was sent yesterday. It said, you will recall, that we would hear more about Saucy Jacky's work tomorrow, referring, of course, to today's papers. That it was also received with the first post this morning would seem to confirm this. It was posted, as was the letter that preceded it, in the East Central district, which encompasses Fleet Street and the offices of almost all the major newspapers, including The Star. Moreover, if you or I wished to send a hoax letter purporting to be from the murderer, we would, I imagine send it to a newspaper.'

'I should think that would be the instinct of most people.'

'Quite. Now, this man has written to the Central News Agency, suggestive to me of someone who knew where to send a letter in order that it would receive maximum exposure.'

'That would also prevent the suspicion of it having been penned by someone at a particular newspaper.'

'Bravo, Watson,' said Holmes. 'You understand my thinking entirely. Then there is the composition of both the postcard and the letter which preceded it. There are clues abounding in both missives which suggest an educated man attempting to appear less so. The layout and handwriting are neat and careful. While he dispenses with apostrophes and question marks, capital letters and full stops are perfectly employed. And despite containing words which might be expected to test a semi-literate man, both letter and postcard are absent of a single spelling mistake.'

'I take it that you believe them to be the work of a journalist?'

'I do. I was immediately struck by the comment that the first victim-that found at Berner Street- squealed a bit. Now, that is a detail which any journalist might have invented with little fear of anyone proving him wrong. But you remember that Mr Schwartz told us that he heard the lady cry out three times; information which was not included in The Star interview. When we consider this, it appears as though the author of the postcard is suggesting knowledge of the crime which he could not have gathered from the newspapers.'

'Goodness! I believe you may be right, Holmes!' I exclaimed.

'The postcard writer is playing a game with us, Watson. He is careful to include a detail of the Berner Street killing which he could not have learned from the newspapers.'

'You think the Dutfield's Yard murderer and the letter writer are one and the same person?'

'I do. Or he is at least the man Schwartz saw with a pipe. The postcard is implicit in admitting that both killings were part of a 'double event' and committed by the same hand. I believe that the letter which gave us the name of Jack the Ripper was a hoax, designed purely as a means of boosting newspaper sales and perpetuating interest in the murders. It's author, or at the very least someone who was involved in its manufacture, plan to commit their own murder. This is executed in a similar style to that of Jack the Ripper. That same night, a second communication is sent, claiming responsibility for both murders. The sender knows that a second murder will take place later that night and will thus provide the perfect cover for his own.'

'But wait, Holmes,' I said, quite baffled. 'You are saying that whoever wrote the letters knows who Jack the ripper is and when he will strike?'

'As extraordinary as it may sound, that is the only conclusion at which I can arrive. Murder, Watson, is surprisingly rare on the streets of Whitechapel and Spitalfields. There were none last year, and but one the year before that. You may encounter a violent brawl or the occasional bludgeoning on any night of the week. If you are particularly unfortunate, you might even prove witness to a stabbing. But murder, even in an area where a handgun might be bought for 4 shillings, is uncommon. Murder by means of a cut throat is, to my knowledge, virtually unheard of. Two such attacks on the very same night, yet apparently by different hands, place events beyond the realm of mere coincidence.'

'And do you know who the author of the letters is?' I asked.

'I do not, Watson,' said Holmes, shaking his head. 'But I think it is time that we finally made the acquaintance of Mr T.P O'Connor.'

13.

The Star and The Strangers' Room

The day following our latest visit by Benjamin Bates found Holmes and I taking the short walk from Baker Street to Pall Mall. The cause of our visit was a most unusual summons by Holmes' brother Mycroft, requesting our presence at the Diogenes Club that same day at twelve o'clock.

'It is most irregular, Watson,' said Holmes, re-reading the message in his hand with a look of great anxiety. 'I cannot imagine what has caused my brother to telegram me in such a manner.'

'Could it be his health?' I asked, mindful of Mycroft' Holmes' corpulent physique and advancing years.

'I fancy not, Watson. My brother possesses the most robust of constitutions and scarcely have I ever known him to be unwell, save for a bout of influenza many years ago. In any case, he is possessed of the most peculiar sensibilities, and I fear that he would not consider something as trivial as a life-threatening malady cause enough to warrant such a communication.'

We entered the hall of the Diogenes Club, passing along its course with a necessary silence until we had arrived at the Strangers' Room. In this small chamber, the only room in the club where members might converse with each other, we found Mycroft Holmes in the company of a portly gentleman of somewhat aristocratic bearing.

'My dear Sherlock and Dr Watson,' he greeted warmly, as he saw us approach. 'Please come in.'

'I presume this to be an important matter, Mycroft?' said Holmes coldly.

'Sherlock, please. A little cordiality for the sake of my guest if not for myself,' he said with a smile.

'Good afternoon to you both,' said the man in brusque, heavy tones. He was of rather short stature and possessed of a thick, dark beard which framed a rather wistful countenance. He was immaculately attired in a grey morning suit and top hat, which rather gave him the appearance of a statesman. We returned his greeting before Mycroft interjected.

'This is The Duke of Buckingham,' he said, indicating the man with a sweeping gesture of his enormous hand.

'I believed that was whom I addressed,' said Holmes. 'The Chairman of Committees in the House of Lords, no less.'

'That is correct' said The Duke, exhibiting only mild surprise that Holmes should recognise him.

'I struggle to imagine what might cause the presence of so illustrious a personage,' said Holmes in a faintly mocking tone.

'It is a matter which demands the utmost discretion, Sherlock,' said Mycroft, his great frame rising as though to emphasise this statement. 'Concerning Jack the Ripper.'

In an instant, the sneering expression Holmes' features vanished. I confess that I shuddered at the use of the chilling sobriquet, coming as it did from the lips of Mycroft Holmes.

'Jack the Ripper? And what concern is he of yours, Mycroft?' asked Holmes sullenly.

'When his name is spoken by every citizen of the realm; when the whole of London is in a state of abject panic, it becomes of great interest to Whitehall. They fear a panic, Sherlock. These murders are an embarrassment to the government. The French claim the British police to be bunglers. They openly state that the murderer would be caught within a few days were he to attempt to replicate his vile acts upon the streets of Paris. Lord Salisbury is under great pressure from the Queen to apprehend this killer. This burden has passed to his cabinet and, by extension, myself. The Duke and his fellow peers received word that my younger brother was engaged in the hunt for Jack the Ripper and were most anxious to know how near you were to success. I have assured The Duke that your powers should effect an arrest in the very near future.'

'I wish I could share your great optimism, Mycroft. The truth is that Jack the Ripper is proving a most elusive adversary. I cannot proclaim when I might capture him or if, indeed, I shall at all.'

'This is not good news, Sherlock,' said Mycroft, with a shake of his head. 'Do you see any hope at all?'

'I do not discount the possibility of success, but I cannot provide you with any information that might be considered a clue as to his identity.'

'What exactly do you know, Mr Holmes?' asked The Duke earnestly.

'I believe he is a local man who lives alone, is of the same class as his victims and may have the appearance of a sailor,' said Holmes. 'Beyond that I cannot tell you little about him.'

'Well, it certainly appears as though this fellow is as elusive as you say. You are quite certain he is of the lower order?'

'I have discovered nothing which dissuades me otherwise, your Grace. How else could he traverse the streets of Whitechapel and attract so little attention?'

'Quite. And what did you make of the chalked message?' asked The Duke. 'Was that not a clue from the murderer?'

'In all probability I believe it was,' said Holmes. 'Although I cannot see that it tells us anything about the man beyond the extremity of his nerve.'

'I see. Well, I wish you every success with your investigation,' he replied stuffily. 'It appears as though you shall need it.'

Holmes did not respond, although Mycroft, no doubt observing his brother's anger, hastened the meeting to its conclusion.

'I am relying on you to bring this unfortunate matter to a satisfactory conclusion, brother,' he said, as we were leaving. 'I need results, Sherlock.'

We reached Baker Street without a word, Sherlock Holmes not venturing any comment upon our visit to The Diogenes Club until he was settled in his armchair and smoking absent-mindedly on his pipe.

'I simply refuse to allay the fears of the government, Watson,' he growled suddenly. 'I am not answerable to Whitehall.'

'I noticed that you told them very little of what you have discovered.'

'Until I know what we are dealing with, Watson, I consider it wise to keep our suspicions to ourselves.'

'You still believe Jack the Ripper to be of the higher classes?' I asked. Holmes held down his pipe and eyed me thoughtfully.

103

'I was certain, Watson. I cannot forget the John Lobbs. Someone with considerable influence is at work here. Yet, I cannot reconcile this belief with Mr Lawende's description of an apparently sea-faring man.'

'Could it have been a disguise?' I asked

'I have certainly considered that possibility. But there is more than one man involved here, of that I am certain.'

'We have still to discover what George Lusk is up to.'

'Yes, we have rather neglected the Whitechapel Vigilance Committee Chairman in the wake of the double murder,' agreed Holmes. 'But rest assured we shall rectify that in the very immediate future. For now, however, I feel a visit to the offices of The Star is in order. After a suitable luncheon, of course.'

At three o'clock that afternoon, having taken a hansom as far as The Strand, I found myself following Holmes through a series of impossibly narrow alleyways upon our way to The Star's offices. Innumerable such lanes flowed off Fleet Street like arteries suggestive of some great organ, from whose crouched darkness was audible the dim roar of that vibrant heart of the British Press. We emerged onto Fleet Street from its western end, the dome of St Paul's emerging above the shops, offices and hostelries in the crisp autumnal air.

'This is a perfect time to find Mr O'Connor at the helm,' whispered Holmes as we entered the lobby of The Star's offices. 'He will have returned from lunch and be overseeing production of this evening's edition.'

Holmes asked the young clerk at the desk for Mr O'Connor, a request which he was told was unlikely to be met. The mention of my friend's name, however, sent the clerk scurrying up the stairs to report our visit. He returned some minutes later with the news that the editor's office was on the first floor, and that O'Connor would be pleased to see us.

O'Connor's office was at the end of an enormous room divided by glass panels and containing several dozen journalists clattering away on typewriters or scribbling furiously in longhand. Such was the noise of this activity that we arrived at the large door marked with the name of the editor with scarcely a glance in our direction.

Holmes' knock upon the door was greeted with an immediate cry of assent from within. We entered to the sight of T.P O'Connor smiling at us from behind his desk.

'Mr Sherlock Holmes!' he exclaimed, rising from his seat and shaking my friend warmly by the hand. 'And Dr Watson. A pleasure to finally meet you both.'

'The sentiment is mutual, Mr O'Connor,' said Holmes flatly. 'I hope that we do not intrude too greatly upon your work.'

'Nonsense, Mr Holmes. Please take a seat,' he said, gesturing at the two chairs opposite him. He took his seat, apparently quite unperturbed by our presence. 'Now, to what do I owe this great pleasure?'

'In the first instance, I wish to thank you for your great kindness in forwarding the letters received by the Central news Agency to ourselves so swiftly after they were received,' said Holmes.

'Think nothing of it,' said O'Connor, with a broad smile. He was aged about forty, with broad shoulders and an expressive, if somewhat weather-beaten face. A sandy moustache gave his features something of a cultured aspect. 'I am only too glad to help the great Sherlock Holmes.'

'Secondly, I wish to know what you hoped to gain by providing this intelligence and whether you are in anyway connected with these murders.'

O'Connor's smile faltered only slightly at this extraordinary demand, while I was quite incredulous at Holmes' forthright manner.

'I had heard something of your tenacity, Mr Holmes,' said he, with a false, bellowing laugh. 'But I scarcely imagined you to be so pugnacious.'

Holmes' stare remained fixed upon O'Connor, and I observed that the editor's grin rapidly dissolved as he retuned Holmes' gaze.

'I can see, Mr Holmes, that you are a man with whom it is ill-advisable to trifle,' he said thoughtfully.

'I assure you that I am not, Mr O'Connor,' said Holmes. O'Connor drew himself closer to his desk and eyed both of us carefully.

'Firstly, my reasons for passing the documents purporting to be from the murderer to you were not entirely altruistic. This is a

105

newspaper, Mr Holmes. We have financial backers who expect a return for their investment. Consequently, each day is a battle to gain new readers while satisfying existing ones. Tomorrow, we shall have been in print five months, and I will not deny that the murders which began this summer have been, with the utmost respect to those unfortunate women, a fantastic stroke of luck. Our coverage of these regrettable events has been far more extensive then any other paper, I'll grant you. But you must understand our market. These are changing times, Mr Holmes. On the streets today we have a great number of literate working men to whose sensibilities we are squarely aimed.

'In having Benjamin Bates contact you at every turn of this awful affair, I have sought merely to add the weight of your considerable merits to his reports and thus give a fledging newspaper some credibility. If the information you receive is of help to your investigations, then so much the better. All I seek is to bring news that the man in the street wishes to read. Bates is impetuous, but he is also the most tireless worker I have known in over thirty years in this business.'

'And what of my more serious charge?' asked Holmes unrelentingly.

'As I have explained, Mr Holmes, I am in the business of selling papers. Like my competitors, I am not above the occasional underhand tactic to keep us ahead of our rivals. Publishing is not a profession conducive of scruples. But, like any man, I have my morals and I state now and quite categorically that I am no way connected with these murders, nor have I any idea whom Jack the Ripper is. I sell news, Mr Holmes, I do not create it.'

'And you have no idea who wrote the letters to the Central News Agency?'

'The murderer, I imagine,' he said, with a faint sneer. 'I passed them to you as I thought they may be of interest.'

'I assure you that they were,' said Holmes. 'And I have already thanked you for your consideration.'

'And you wish to continue with this arrangement?'

'As you have assured me that your intentions are genuine, I see no reason to do otherwise.'

'Excellent!' said O'Connor, his features brightening in an instant. 'It is nice to know that The Star has friends like yourselves. Now, if you'll excuse me, gentlemen, I am afraid this paper does not run itself.'

'Do you believe him, Holmes?' I asked, the moment we were back on the pavements of Fleet Street.

'I cannot be sure, Watson,' said Holmes thoughtfully. 'I am certain that someone is influencing young Bates for their own purpose. I am equally certain that that man was O'Connor.'

'If it is him, he is certainly an accomplished liar.'

'I can introduce you to a thousand of those, Watson,' said Holmes, with a withering look. 'I do not trust the man.'

'I confess that your endorsement of Bates' articles appears insufficient reason for the assistance he has given us.'

'Those were my thoughts exactly, Watson. No, there is some greater purpose to this arrangement, although I am certain that Bates is not aware of its existence.'

'Then who is behind it all?'

'I still believe O'Connor is our man, Watson. But it seems as though proving that fact will require a little more ingenuity on our part.'

14.

Lusk at Dusk

The day following our visit to Fleet Street, Holmes announced that we would be transferring our efforts towards the redoubtable Chairman of the Whitechapel Vigilance Committee, Mr George Lusk. That morning's papers announced that the Mitre Square victim had at last been named. She was Catherine Eddowes, a forty-six-year-old from Wolverhampton and had been identified by her lover, John Kelly. Holmes was proved correct upon her hop-picking exploits. Kelly confirmed to the police that he had purchased new boots shortly upon their return, a pawn ticket for which was found upon the dead woman. The Berner Street Victim was proving rather more difficult to identify. Lestrade reported to Holmes a quite farcical series of setbacks at the inquest. A Mrs Malcolm assured the coroner that the deceased was her sister, Elizabeth Watts, only for that same woman to present herself before the inquest alive and well!

We took a hansom as far as Whitechapel High Street and, on account of the mild weather, completed our journey to Dorset Street on foot. Since the so-called 'Double Event', Whitechapel had become a subdued and forlorn place. Following the early murders, the initial wave of shock and despair was quickly replaced by something of a carnival atmosphere. The huge crowds that had gathered at the murder sites attracted tradesmen offering all manner of victuals and souvenirs. While both Mitre Square and Berner Street were still attracting crowds of morbid sightseers, a mood of fear now pervaded the streets of Whitechapel. The usual bustle of the High Street was replaced by a most unnerving silence, the shrill cries of the vendors eerily absent as people hurried past us, as though anxious to return to the safety of indoors.

We turned up Commercial Street and at last reached Dorset Street at approaching eleven o'clock. I noticed that The Britannia already boasted several patrons visible through its windows. Millers Court, with its grim façade and crumbling brick, appeared only marginally less foreboding in the narrow bands of daylight which streaked overhead. It was with some trepidation, therefore, that I followed Holmes through its narrow, stone-flagged entrance. We emerged into a paved yard which contained about half a dozen ramshackle houses that were in obvious want of repair. To the left was what appeared to be a chandler's shop, from which emerged a respectable looking man in his mid-thirties dressed in a loose brown jacket and sporting a light-coloured moustache.

'Can I help you, gentlemen?' he asked quizzically, a light Irish lilt evident in his tones. 'Perhaps you are lost?'

'Not at all,' Holmes assured him. 'We are looking for a young lady by the name of Mary Kelly. We were informed that we might find her here.'

'Mary?' asked the man, glancing between us suspiciously. 'Yes, she lives just there in number thirteen. Are you friends of hers?'

'I confess that we are yet to meet the young lady. We have a mutual friend who believes she may be of some help to us.'

'I see. Do you mind if I ask your names, Sir?'

'Not at all. I am Mr Sherlock Holmes and this is my friend, Dr Watson.'

'Mr Sherlock Holmes!' he exclaimed. 'I have of course heard the name, although I cannot imagine what you might want of young Mary.'

'Merely to ask her a few questions regarding a suspicious character seen in the area, as reported to me by Mr George Lusk of the Whitechapel Vigilance Committee.'

'Mr Lusk, you say?' he stammered. 'You are friends of his?'

'We are acquainted with the gentleman professionally. I take it that you are the proprietor of this court?'

'That is correct,' he said nervously. 'My name is Jack McCarthy.'

'Forgive us, Mr McCarthy, if we intrude upon your business,' said Holmes. 'Do you know of Mr Lusk yourself?'

'Mr Lusk? Well, certainly I believe I have heard the name, Mr Holmes.'

'But you have never met him?' asked Holmes.

'Not to my recollection.'

'And you were unaware that he is acquainted with Miss Kelly?'

'Mary's a girl as keep's herself to herself, Mr Holmes,' said McCarthy. 'And I don't pry into the affairs of my tenants.'

'Quite commendable, Mr McCarthy,' said Holmes brightly.

'Is Mary in at present?' I asked, not wishing to stand in the dank confines of the passageway longer than was necessary.

'I believe I saw her go out earlier this morning,' he replied quickly.

'Well, it is of no matter,' said Holmes. 'We shall try again another time. Good day, Mr McCarthy.'

McCarthy watched us make our way through the passage and out onto Dorset Street.

'Now there is a man who is not a good liar, Watson,' said Holmes, once we were out of ear shot. 'His every word betrayed a darker intelligence he could barely suppress.'

'You think he knows something of the murders?' I asked, as we turned onto Commercial Street. Holmes shook his head.

'I do not think so. But you noticed how he hesitated when I asked if he knew Lusk? My guess is that he is assisting Lusk to carry out his sordid affair with the Kelly woman.'

'That was my thought on the matter,' said I. 'So, it has nothing at all to do with Jack the Ripper?'

'I am always loath to embrace a simple explanation when my instincts tell me that something far more intriguing lurks just beyond it. There are still questions to be answered, Watson.'

'If McCarthy knows nothing of the murders, I fail to see what remains of interest.'

'You disappoint me, Watson. How does McCarthy know Lusk? Why is he helping him? How did Lusk meet Mary Kelly? What was his reason for forming the vigilance committee? Or, for that matter, his decidedly odd visit to us at Baker Street? No, Watson, I am certain that we are justified in questioning the motives of at least one of these men.'

Once the curiosity of Sherlock Holmes had been aroused, it was quite impossible to dissuade him from his task. He followed the criminal scent with the unwavering tenacity of a bloodhound, desisting only once he had run his unfortunate quarry to ground. On observing his alarming capacity for exertion and his infinite faculty for reason and deduction, I was on more than one occasion thankful that I was not a criminal whom he had in his unyielding sights. I was quite sure that the mind of Sherlock Holmes was something utterly unique in the cerebral physiology of humankind, and I had long since desisted my efforts in fathoming his unworldly gifts.

Thus, that same evening, and despite my misgivings on the matter, we made the now rather familiar trip to the desolate streets of Whitechapel. Holmes was largely silent during our journey east, although there was an alertness to his aspect which told me that his senses were primed for the task ahead. We alighted at the western end of Dorset Street, where Holmes directed us to the Horn of Plenty Beer shop. It was a rough little establishment that was thankfully rather empty on this cold, dreary evening. We soon found ourselves tucked into a corner seat, where our words were inaudible to others above the crackle of the open fire.

'There is something I do not like about George Lusk, Watson,' said Holmes thoughtfully, as he leaned forward in his chair.

'I do not question your professional instincts, Holmes. But could it be that your dislike for the man is clouding your opinion of him? His efforts are directed at capturing the murderer, after all.'

'You do me a great disservice, Watson, if you believe I would in any way allow my personal feelings to impact upon my actions on so important a matter. In any case, I did not state that I did not like him. I merely said there is *something* about him which I did not like. Not withstanding the obvious vulgarity of so recently a widowed man seeking comfort with another woman, which itself speaks of a reprehensible nature, I am certain that his actions cover a far darker secret that is yet to reveal itself.'

'You are referring to the vigilance committee, I take it?' I said.

'Yes, I am talking of the ubiquitous Whitechapel Vigilance Committee, Watson. Its very existence shall vex me until I know its true purpose.'

'But surely if you suspect Lusk of using it as a cover for some other purpose, then that purpose is perfectly clear?'

'You refer to his apparent romance with Mary Kelly, I take it?'

'I do, Holmes. What else could it possibly be?'

112

'Watson, a man who finds himself embroiled with a woman and wishes to keep his relations with her clandestine, might be expected to take certain measures in order to preserve his secret. But I fail to be convinced that these measures would extend to the forming of a vigilance group, which necessitates the mobilisation of dozens of men upon the streets of Whitechapel night after night. Surely it is far too elaborate a deception to mask a mere dalliance on the part of its chairman? What is there to be gained? Not only is his own profile raised, thus increasing the likelihood of his being observed in the act, but in addition he gains a role from which he must absent himself each night. You remember that our suspicions were first aroused by Squibby's intelligence that Lusk had a penchant for disappearing during his nightly patrols?'

'I can see your reasoning,' I conceded. 'And so you hope to observe him with Kelly and confront him?'

'I do, Watson. Now, let us finish our drinks, for we have work to do.'

We walked the length of Dorset Street, crossing over Commercial Street to the Ten Bells Public House. It was situated on the corner of Church Street and offered a far more raucous environment than the Horn of Plenty. We were forced to endure the swaying groups of drunken market porters who stumbled about the place, seemingly quite oblivious to our presence. I ordered us two ales and Holmes acquired us as quiet a spot as he could find, although I could barely discern him through the choking wisps of smoke that spiralled from innumerable cigarettes and pipes.

'It is unfathomable to me how anyone would wish to drink here,' I said, with a spluttering cough. 'The smoke is insufferable. It is quite the worst hostelry I have ever encountered.'

'Ha! Come now, Watson. At least this unedifying mist gives us a certain invisibly to our game, does it not? You are entirely correct, of course. The Ten Bells is quite amongst the most notorious Public Houses in the whole of London.'

We sipped our ales as I cast furtive glances about me, although I found we were completely ignored by any of the less desirable patrons, all of whom were too busy wallowing in their drunken stupors to cause us any inconvenience. It was eight o'clock when a nudge from Holmes alerted me to the presence of a young woman who was just approaching the counter. The air had cleared somewhat since our arrival, allowing me to observe that she was rather tall, with waist-long dark hair and of shapely, if somewhat stout, build. As she turned to procure a seat in the corner diagonally opposite our own, I saw that she was of some considerable beauty and clad in a white apron.

'Do you think that is her, Holmes?' I asked in a whisper.

'From the descriptions of both Squibby and the lodging house keeper, I am sure of it, Watson.'

'Is she here to meet Lusk?'

'Undoubtedly.'

We observed her for some minutes, her personal attractions affording her the attentions of several men, one of whom was attempting something akin to a drunken courtship. She smilingly bade them away, seeming not the least nonplussed by their intrusions, and I judged her to be of formidable nature. Presently, I observed Lusk enter the hostelry, his hurried manner and glancing at his pocket-watch suggesting that he was late for whatever appointment he had arranged. I turned to Holmes, whose smile told me that he too had observed the man's arrival. Lusk greeted the woman with a kiss and sat down opposite her. We drew our chairs back towards the wall so that our figures were slunk into the shadows and beyond Lusk's view. Yet so engrossed was he in his conversation with the woman that such measures were entirely superfluous.

'We have been very fortunate, Holmes,' I said. 'I quite feared we would be here all night in vain'

'Not at all, Watson. I suspected that they would meet here and at this exact time.'

'And how could you possibly know that?' I asked incredulously.

'The location is a simple matter, Watson. As we know Kelly woman shares a room with a man called Joe, we are hardly likely to find Lusk meet her there. We are informed that she is a regular at this establishment, while I can think of no other place which would provide a more convenient place to meet. As for the more troubling matter of the time, I confess I neglected to inform you of another visit by Squibby's ragamuffin messenger this morning while you were at your practice. He informed me that in the last few days, Lusk has redoubled his efforts at the helm of his committee, having taken to accompanying several of his volunteers on their nightly patrols. Apparently, he no longer absents himself from duties during those late hours when the killer is most likely to be caught. I considered it probable, therefore, that any meeting between himself and his paramour must naturally take place before he commences his nightly search for the killer.'

'You have certainly been proved correct, Holmes,' said I. 'And what shall we do now that he is here?'

'I have pondered that question, Watson. We do not yet know if Lusk has any involvement with these murders. I have hesitated, therefore, in my decision of whether to reveal ourselves or not. We are, after all, still attempting to unravel this mystery. But I have decided on a course of action. I see nothing to be gained by approaching Lusk in here, save for the unedifying spectacle of his mortification at being discovered. We shall therefore wait until they have departed before following them as Lusk walks Miss Kelly back to Millers Court. We will await until he has bade her goodnight, whereupon we shall accost him as he makes his way back on to Commercial Street in search of a cab.'

We waited patiently for the better part of an hour as Lusk and his companion completed their meeting. From where we were sitting, their words were inaudible above the dim roar of hoarse laughter and drunken oaths. Yet the intimacy of their gestures and unwavering gaze upon each other marked them undoubtedly as lovers. At last, a little after nine o' clock, we observed them preparing to leave. Holmes signalled for us to remain seated as they weaved their way through the swelling crowd of drunkards and disappeared beyond our sight. We waited for perhaps a minute before making our way out of The Ten Bells. We caught a fleeting view of Lusk and Kelly as they ambled along in the darkness of Commercial Street. Their hazy figures merged with the dark shadows around them, and we next saw them as we arrived at the corner of Dorset Street, their outlines clearly visible standing outside Millers Court.

The narrow confines of Dorset Street, coupled with its tall buildings, gave it a curious acoustic quality. Thus, we were afforded snatches of Lusk and Kelly's conversation as we stood on the street corner, just beyond the hazy glow of the Brittania. They appeared to be arranging their next meeting, and the name of McCarthy was clearly audible from Lusk, to which Kelly replied with a low muttering. They embraced and parted, Lusk turning on his heels and heading back towards us, quite unaware of our presence as we darted swiftly back onto Commercial Street and beyond his sight. In the still quiet, we heard his measured tread approaching us, whereupon Holmes nudged me to follow his lead as he began walking casually towards Lusk, who was just turning off Dorset Street in front of us.

'My word, Mr Lusk!' cried Holmes. George Lusk stopped in his tracks and turned so quickly that it appeared as though some invisible hand had spun him around.

'My goodness!' he blustered, his face quite aghast before he managed to smooth it into a troubled smile. 'It is Sherlock Holmes and Dr Watson. I hardly expected to see you both here.'

'Nor us you, Mr Lusk. It is rather early for the commencement of your patrols, is it not?'

'Ordinarily, Mr Holmes,' he sputtered. 'You remember, though, that I told you of the man who had been seen in Dorset Street with bloodstains? I decided to pass along this way in order to see if I could observe any suspicious characters.'

'Forgive me for questioning your logic, Mr Lusk, but one might expect to find any number of suspicious characters in such a street.'

'Well, I of course thought it an unlikely enterprise.' he replied awkwardly. 'But since these latest murders, I have taken it upon myself to try anything in order to bring their perpetrator to justice.'

'Most commendable,' said Holmes sardonically. 'Allow me to ask you, Mr Lusk, if you know of a young lady by the name of Mary Kelly?'

Lusk eyed Holmes in astonishment as he stammered for a response.

'I, I- why do you ask that?' he cried eventually.

'Because I have just observed you with her in The Ten Bells,' said Holmes coldly.

'I never met her before this evening,' he said. 'She merely accosted me while I was sitting there.'

'We also observed you walking the young lady home to Millers Court and arranging to meet her again.'

'You followed me?' gasped Lusk in astonishment.

'I confess that we did, Mr Lusk. We are aware of your relations with Miss Kelly and wish to ask you some questions.'

'But I do not know this woman, I swear. I can tell you nothing,' he said pleadingly.

'Do not imagine that you can play games with me, Mr Lusk. I will give you one chance to tell me the truth. After that, I cannot promise that matters will remain between us gentlemen here. I can acquire my facts elsewhere but that, I fear, shall entail matters entering a more public domain.'

'Please, Mr Holmes,' he implored. 'I will tell you everything. But I beg of you not to reveal anything of what I have done. I should be a ruined man if people knew the truth.'

Holmes smiled grimly, although I myself viewed the pathetic figure before me with a degree of pity.

'Excellent. Now, I fear that the air is growing chill. I take it that you would not object to continuing this conversation indoors?'

Such was Holmes' mastery of men at these moments that he had turned on his heel before Lusk could fumble a response. Minutes later, we found ourselves sat around a table in The Brittania, to whose confines I found myself becoming increasingly accustomed.

'Now, Mr Lusk,' said Holmes, leaning back in the chair and studying the man contemptuously. 'Please tell us about your relationship with Miss Mary Kelly. I implore you to be frank with me and omit no detail concerning the circumstances under which you met her.'

'You must understand, Mr Holmes, that it is difficult for me to articulate the nature of my gross indiscretions,' said Lusk, his head lowering as he spoke. 'I feel a great shame that I can scarcely put into words. I fail to see how availing you of the circumstances would serve any purpose.'

117

'Rest assured that I do not wish to judge you, Mr Lusk. My concerns run far deeper than your domestic arrangements. Please tell me everything from the beginning and I promise that events will benefit you for it.'

'Very well, Mr Holmes. As you know, my wife died earlier this year. She was a fine woman, my Susannah, and I always did right by her. With God as my witness, I loved her as much as any man could love a woman. We were happy until last year when she grew ill. It was a terrible strain on me. We have seven children and I had our painting and decorating business to run. I hired a nanny, but still I spent every evening attending to the children or nursing Susannah through her confinement. I am not ashamed to say that I struggled, Mr Holmes. I have not lived a life of temperance, but rarely have I sought consolation in drink. Yet I found myself turning to it more and more as my despair grew. I fear this caused me on occasion to exhibit a foul temper upon the children. The nanny I employed departed in disgust, at which point I sank further into a decline from which there appeared no prospect of recovery.

'Then I met Mary Kelly. My business specialises in music hall restorations, Mr Holmes. Through this work, I met some years ago a fellow named Jack McCarthy. He owns Millers Court, but that is merely a fraction of his true estate. He has several properties about Whitechapel and runs prize fights with the infamous Smith family of Brick Lane. He mixes in some high circles, and I have even heard him mention nobility amongst his business acquaintances, however true that might be. He also owns several music halls. It was during renovation work for one such establishment that I first met him several years ago. In recent years, he has employed my services on several occasions and we have always got on very well.

'At the beginning of this year, after the stress of providing a Christmas for the children, I chanced upon McCarthy. He took me to some of the drinking dens around Dorset Street. Well, I was rather apprehensive at first, but soon got into the spirit of things and confess that I had quite a fine time of it. It was, as McCarthy had promised, just what I needed. At the end of the evening, we went back to his shop in Millers Court, where he said there was someone whom he would like me to meet. In my drunken state, I of course obliged, and he took me to the Ten Bells and introduced me to Mary Kelly. She seemed to be quite as beautiful a woman as I had ever seen. You have seen her yourselves, of course.'

'She is quite the buxom beauty,' agreed Holmes.

'She was a lady of the night, he told me, which seemed only to add to her lustre. She lived with a fellow by name of Barnett, but the union had ceased to be a happy one. McCarthy suggested we spend the night together, and so I took her to Crossingham's and paid eightpence for a double room. I awoke the following morning in absolute horror at what I had done, solemnly vowing never to see her again. And yet in the weeks which followed, I could not help but think of her. I resisted, of course, and as Susannah grew sadly weaker, my only thoughts were to provide her with what comforts I could. She passed away this April and in the lonely days that followed, I eventually found solace in Mary's arms.

'I could not forgive myself, yet I had prepared myself long ago for Susannah's passing. I knew I could not hope to continue with the business and care for the children alone. I fell in love with Mary Kelly, Mr Holmes. I am not ashamed to admit that. I employed another nanny and, with the affections of Mary, I believe I may yet put the awful loss of Susannah behind me. But I fear that I would be ostracised by my family and friends were the truth to emerge.'

George Lusk sat back in his chair and sighed as if he had just been relieved of some great burden. I stared at him in wonder at this remarkable account. Holmes, who was usually entirely detached in such matters of emotion, was not himself unaffected, surveying the man before us with studied humanity.

'Thank you, Mr Lusk,' said Holmes softly. 'I do not believe I could have asked for a more comprehensive summary of events. I do, however, wish you to expand on one principal aspect. I am rather curious as to the events which lead to the formation of the Whitechapel Vigilance Committee.'

'Certainly, Mr Holmes,' said Lusk. 'When these terrible murders began, I was quite appalled, as were my fellow businessmen and associates. After the murder of the Chapman woman, I discussed with some friends the possibility of assisting the police in their efforts to catch this man before he could strike again. I believe I needed something on which to focus my energies, rather than dwelling on the loss of Susannah. I confess that perhaps I wished to atone for my relations with Mary by doing something of which my wife would have been proud.'

'And I certainly do not doubt she would have been, Mr Lusk,' said I. 'You have nothing of which to feel ashamed.'

'Thank you, Dr Watson. Mr Holmes, if I may, can I ask as to why my relationship with Mary caused you such interest in the first instance?'

'Certainly, Mr Lusk. Such honesty as you have exhibited deserves reciprocation. I confess that your letter and subsequent visit to Baker Street intrigued me. I instructed a friend of mine to join the ranks of your committee and ascertain your character. When he observed that you absented yourself from duties and were seen with a woman in Millers Court, I was naturally keen to discover more upon the matter.'

'I see,' said Lusk with an air of embarrassment. 'It is true that I often visited Mary at night while supervising the patrols.'

'I have nothing further to ask you, Mr Lusk. If you are quite ready, I think we shall bid each other goodnight.'

We waited until George Lusk had departed before making our way along Commercial Street and hailing a hansom.

'What do you make of it, Watson?' asked Holmes, as we rattled west. 'A most curious development, is it not?'

'You surely do not still suspect Lusk?' said I. 'His motives appear entirely genuine.'

'I believe they are, Watson,' he replied. 'Although it begs some very searching questions of our friend, Jack McCarthy.'

'He claimed to have never met Lusk.'

'Exactly. That is why I harbour suspicions. Why should McCarthy lie about knowing him? He might have easily admitted as such without fear on his part.'

'And if he and Lusk are as well acquainted as we are led to believe, surely it was inevitable that we would discover they were known to each other?'

'Exactly, Watson. No, McCarthy panicked because he is hiding something. And I fear it goes far beyond the wandering affections of George Lusk.'

15.

Three men

Sherlock Holmes cut rather a detached figure in the days following our meeting with George Lusk. He skulked about Baker Street like a caged animal and constantly I observed his expression to be creased in one of the utmost vexation. Although as near to an automaton as any man who had ever lived, there were times when I observed in Holmes a fallibility which hinted that his gifts, however ungodly they may be, were possessed by a man every bit as human as myself. Although loath to admit it, I felt that Holmes had long harboured a quite inappropriate suspicion of George Lusk, who had struck me as nothing less than a gentleman of unquestionable morals.

The confession of his relationship with Mary Kelly was as impassioned and heartfelt as any I had ever heard. Yet I sensed that the apparent exoneration of Lusk irked the guarded sensibilities of my friend, whose affirmations of the man's questionable motives had proved to be entirely erroneous. Thus, although Holmes would not entirely discount the possibility that the Chairman of the Whitechapel Vigilance Committee was involved in matters, it appeared that suspicion must be passed to the sinister figure of Jack McCarthy.

I was far from convinced, however, that his deliberate falsehood of not knowing Lusk was borne from any involvement in the murders. Holmes, for his part, remained steadfast in his belief that Jack McCarthy knew something of events. From his low mutterings as he made his haphazard circuits of our sitting room, it was evident that it was he who occupied my friend's thoughts. Yet, while such ruminations from Holmes might be expected to portend a solution, just as black clouds might precede a rain shower, it appeared as though Jack the Ripper was proving impervious to his powers of deduction.

Precious few details had emerged since the night of what had become known as 'the double event' which might afford the slightest clue as to the identity of the murderer. The Berner Street victim had finally been identified as Elizabeth Stride, a forty-five-year-old Swedish woman who had apparently resided in England for the last two decades.

It transpired that she had been observed by several witnesses in the few hours before her murder. Two witnesses claimed to have seen her leaving the Bricklayer's Arms at 11 p.m. in the company of a man, while a third saw her with possibly the same man in Berner Street at 11.45 p.m.

A notable aside to the affair of Stride's murder was the unfathomable conduct of one Matthew Packer. He was an elderly fruiterer who sold his wares from his front window, mere yards from the murder site. Having advised the police on the night of the murder that he had observed nothing of note, he then proceeded to claim that he had sold grapes to a man in the company of Stride shortly before she was discovered in Dutfield's yard. There followed a farcical series of events, in which two private detectives of dubious repute accompanied Packer to view Stride's body, which he positively identified as the woman he had seen. He was then frogmarched by these same men to Scotland Yard in order to relay this information first-hand, only for his story to unravel and Packer discredited entirely as a witness.

Yet the inquest into Elizabeth Stride's death, while producing the desultory ignorance which might have been expected, was not entirely void of interest. A colourful account of Stride's past was provided by Michael Kidney, who had been her lover for the last three years of her life. She had earned a living by the precarious pursuits which befall women of her circumstances, latterly being employed as a charlady in several Jewish households. While the fanciful narrative of her past, which encompassed the notorious Princess Alice disaster of some years ago, gave the newspaper reports a certain lustre, it was the man who recounted them for whom Holmes held chief interest. Kidney admitted to a stormy relationship with Stride, during which she frequently absented herself without explanation.

On one occasion, he had had cause to padlock her indoors. It also emerged that he had been briefly imprisoned for three days, just two months prior to Stride's murder, for being drunk and disorderly. Dr Phillips asserted that the weapon used upon the victim's throat was quite unlike that used in the other murders. It seemed to me entirely plausible that Kidney himself had killed Stride, with Holmes himself keen to make the man's acquaintance.

Yet the prospect that Michael Kidney was responsible for Stride's murder presented Holmes with a problem. It forced him to question his belief that the perpetrator of this outrage had some foreknowledge of the Mitre Square killing, and thus some connection with Jack the Ripper. That Elizabeth Stride's death was perhaps merely the result of a squalid domestic argument threatened to expose yet another of Holmes' pronouncements upon the murders.

A week following the murder, Sherlock Holmes was absent from our rooms for two consecutive nights, with neither prior warning, nor hint as to when he might return. Although I feared for his welfare upon such disappearances, I confess that on this occasion I found myself welcoming his absence from Baker Street. Despite the extreme vagaries of his personal habits, Holmes was most often an entirely tolerable man with whom to share quarters. Yet the respite afforded me by his latest excursion into the ether of London's underworld brought with it a joyous calm, one which our rooms had so sorely lacked recently during his insufferable maladies of the mind.

Upon the third morning of his absence, I returned from a visit to my practice to find the figure of Lestrade sitting in one of our armchairs. An empty teacup upon the table and an agitated aspect to his lean figure told me that his wait had not been a short one.

'Good morning, Inspector,' said I. 'I am afraid that Sherlock Holmes is not at home.'

'Good morning, Dr Watson. I had hoped it was Holmes whom I heard upon the staircase. Do you know what has kept him?'

'I am afraid I have not seen sight of Holmes for these last two days. Am I to take it that he has arranged to meet you?'

'At ten o'clock, here in Baker Street,' said Lestrade angrily. 'The telegram said it was important. Yet here I am at nearing eleven o'clock and there is no sign of him.'

'I am sure Holmes would not make an appointment if he was not certain that he could keep it. Something must have waylaid him.'

'Very probably it has, Doctor,' said Lestrade. 'But I am afraid I can wait no longer.'

As Lestrade was rising out of his chair, I heard the slam of the street door and the rapid strides upon the staircase that could only be those of my friend.

'Ah, Lestrade!' greeted Sherlock Holmes, as he entered our sitting room. 'Please accept my sincerest apologies for my lateness.'

'I have been here almost an hour, Holmes,' said the Inspector reproachfully. 'I have better things to do than wait around for you all morning.'

'Of course you do, Lestrade. But I am afraid my poor time keeping was unavoidable. I trust that you have been well-attended to?'

'Mrs Hudson was very courteous, thank you. Now, Holmes, I have three murders to investigate, so I would be grateful if you could tell me what it is that you considered so important.'

'My dear Inspector, I would not wish to keep you any longer than is absolutely necessary,' said Holmes, making himself comfortable in the chair next to my own. Holmes often returned from his self-imposed exiles dishevelled of clothes and filthy of skin. Yet I observed at close quarters that not only was he freshly shaven, but as clean as though he had just emerged from a hot bath. Most noticeable, however, was the keenness of eye and quickness of manner which he invariably possessed when on the scent of a solution.

'Is this concerning the murders, Holmes? Because I have little time for anything else at present.'

'It is indeed about the murders, Lestrade. And rest assured that I have used my own energies upon little else since they were first brought to my attention.'

'I am glad to hear it, Holmes. I confess that this Jack the Ripper fellow is running rings around us. The City lot are faring no better with the Mitre Square murder.'

'It may please you to know that I myself have been left baffled by events, Lestrade.'

'But you are on the track of a solution?' asked the Inspector eagerly.

'I am never without hope. But capturing Jack the Ripper is proving not unlike catching a fish with one's bare hands. As soon as you

126

imagine it is within your grasp, it darts away and proves as elusive as ever.'

'You have suspicions of someone?' asked Lestrade.

'I do. But I admit that I am still yet to decipher events to my satisfaction. Before I avail you of my own findings, might I ask for any information you have discovered of which I may not be aware?'

'I am afraid that will not take very long, Holmes,' sighed Lestrade. 'Our investigations have turned up nought. We have investigated the history of each of the victims, yet can find no-one who bore them ill-will, nor any reason why someone may have wished them murdered. They appear on the whole to have been rather well-liked and popular with those who knew them. Nor do we believe that any of them were known to each other. Other than the fact that they all lived in the lodging houses around Flower and Dean Street at one time or another, we can find no link between any of them.

'As to the murders themselves, we have turned up nothing new. I had hoped Israel Schwartz might have been the breakthrough we were looking for, but you were quick to scotch that possibility. I confess that every light we shine upon these murders merely makes the darkness surrounding it only blacker.'

'What of the medical reports?' I asked. 'Do they provide any clue?

'The doctors have confirmed that our man is right-handed. They seem unanimous upon the fact that he is well-used to a knife, but most of them do not feel he possesses much in the way of actual skill above some rough anatomical knowledge. They have offered nothing which narrows down our search, Dr Watson.'

'So you can offer me nothing whatever on the matter?' said Holmes, with a mischievous smile. 'Perhaps it is time I informed you of what I know.'

Holmes proceeded to give Lestrade a somewhat truncated account of events, omitting only his belief that the killer was of considerably higher class than his victims. He concluded his narrative with a summary of our meetings with Lusk and McCarthy. Lestrade listened to the story with growing astonishment.

'My goodness,' exclaimed the Inspector, once Holmes had finished. 'I can scarcely believe it. But you no longer suspect George Lusk of any wrong-doing?'

'I do not. Now, Watson, I believe I have enlightened the Inspector of events up to my departure of a few days ago. I imagine you wish to know what I have been doing since then?'

'But of course, Holmes,' I enthused.

'I must warn you, Watson, that the waters have grown only murkier since I left Baker Street. Before my departure, I expressed my interest in meeting Michael Kidney, Elizabeth Stride's lover. This I did at his house in Devonshire Street, a narrow thoroughfare off Commercial Road which is little more than five minutes' brisk walk east of Dutfield's Yard. I found him to be a taciturn, somewhat abrasive man, who was extremely guarded upon matters and refused to answer any question I asked of him.

'Yet the offer of a beer at The Star Public House proved harder to resist. I soon found that beneath the harsh countenance and rough manners, Kidney was possessed of a surprisingly quick mind, allowing him on several occasions to pre-empt me. He deduced immediately that I had him under suspicion, providing me with a most comprehensive, if uncorroborated, account of his movements on the night of Stride's murder and challenging me to prove otherwise. Yet he appeared genuinely troubled by her death, the consumption of several ales producing a torrent of melancholy sentiment which left me in little doubt as to the veracity of his emotions. Shortly after these inebriated professions of love, he descended into an unsightly spectacle of weeping histrionics and I quietly departed.'

'You do not suspect him of murder?' I asked.

'I do not, Watson. Stride's death has shaken him. And yet-'

'And yet what, Holmes?' interjected Lestrade, as my friend's voice drew silent and his features furrowed in deep thought.

'And yet I could not escape the feeling that he was hiding something from me. When I asked if he knew any reason as to why someone may have wished to murder Stride, he shot me a contemptuous glance and burst into a bellowing laugh. "You would not dare believe what that woman knew," he said bitterly. "It will take more than you have to fathom it out." When I asked what he meant by this enigmatic comment, he sneered and refused to say anything further.'

'What do you think he could have meant?' I asked.

'I hadn't the least idea, Watson. But during his drunken stupor, he alluded to someone called 'Aaron' and said that this gentleman, whoever he may be, was to blame.'

'Intriguing. I wonder what connection this fellow had with Liz Stride.'

'This is all well and good,' interrupted Lestrade. 'But does any of this help our case, Holmes?'

'That is what I endeavoured to establish. Kidney was not a difficult man to follow. He is a labourer of simple habits whose daily routine might be observed many times over with little in the way of variation. Yesterday, however, he did not return straight home from work, but took a considerable detour to Mile End. There he knocked upon a door of a house whose location was evidently unfamiliar to him, for he walked up and down the street before satisfying himself that he had the correct address. A maid answered, who eyed him suspiciously before disappearing, presumably to inform her master of this uncouth visitor. A man duly appeared at the door. That man was George Lusk.'

'Lusk!' I gasped. 'Are you sure?'

'I confess that I could scarcely believe it myself, Watson. And yet as soon as I had noted we were entering Alderney Road, I recalled that this was Lusk's address, as printed in the newspapers. I waited for over half an hour before Kidney emerged from the house and made his way back along the same road by which he had come. Not long after him, I observed Lusk open his front door in the company of a second man. They were in conversation and shook hands before Lusk bade the man farewell. The man departed in the opposite direction to Kidney and I followed him at a distance. Neither the felt hat he wore, nor the creeping darkness of the evening assisted my recognising him, but as I drew closer, I saw that it was none other than Jack McCarthy.'

'But this is remarkable, Holmes!' I cried.

'What's their game, then?' asked Lestrade, appearing quite bewildered by events.

'I do not yet know, Lestrade. But it would seem apparent that somewhere in what I have observed lies the answer to the murder of Elizabeth Stride.'

'Evidently one of these men is responsible,' said Lestrade, rising to his feet and gesticulating at Holmes. 'And the other two played some part in it.'

'I fear that the solution may prove somewhat more taxing, Lestrade,' said Holmes. 'If Israel Schwartz is to be believed, we are looking for two men, so whence comes the third? Lusk strikes me as an unlikely killer and Kidney suggested that a man called Aaron knew what had happened. That leaves us with McCarthy, whom currently invites the most suspicion.'

'But what is it linking them together?' I asked.

'That is what most puzzles me,' said Holmes. 'We know that Lusk and McCarthy are associated. But how does Kidney know either of them? McCarthy was already present in the house when Kidney arrived. His presence may therefore have been merely a coincidence. Yet Lusk and Kidney are evidently acquainted, although not well, for Kidney was unsure of Lusk's address.'

'And just who is this Aaron fellow?' asked a bemused Lestrade. 'I confess, Holmes, that I cannot see where this leads us.'

'Kidney was implicit in stating that he knew something of the events which led to Stride's murder,' said Holmes impatiently. 'When I subsequently find him in the company of two men who have already fallen under my suspicion, surely it is suggestive that something extremely interesting is going on, Lestrade?'

'Admittedly, Holmes,' sighed the Inspector. 'Although I am still sceptical that this enquiry holds any merit.'

'I feel you would be unwise to ignore what I have told you,' implored Holmes.

'So, what would you have me do, Holmes?'

'I cannot follow the movements of three men simultaneously, Lestrade. I have Squibby who can shadow Lusk, while I myself can investigate McCarthy. If you can deploy someone to follow Kidney, I should be extremely grateful.'

'Follow Kidney, indeed! The Metropolitan Police do not exist to prove your own wild theories, Holmes!' cried Lestrade. 'I have heard nothing which warrants such a use of resources.'

'Then I fear you shall never catch this man, Lestrade,' said Holmes, as the Inspector made to leave. 'I implore you to do as I have asked.'

'You have been of assistance before. I will not deny that,' sighed Lestrade. 'Very well. I shall have a man keep an eye on Kidney for the next week. But I warn you, Holmes, that I need a breakthrough on this case. I am placing my trust in this exercise to yield results.'

'I believe you shall have them, Lestrade. Thank you.'

'One week, Holmes,' said Lestrade, as he stood up and made towards the door. 'I shall keep you informed.'

'The man is an insufferable fool!' cried Holmes, once Lestrade had departed. 'He fails to grasp the enormity of the web in which he finds himself entangled.'

'I struggle to comprehend the incessant twists of the case myself.'

'It is a most unseemly business, Watson. But if we can only solve the murder of Elizabeth Stride, then I suspect we shall unravel the thread which leads us to Jack the Ripper.'

16.

From Hell

A week following his visit to Baker Street, Inspector Lestrade gained
what he must have considered a rare victory over Sherlock Holmes
when announcing the desultory results of the investigation into Michael
Kidney. The man, Lestrade gladly announced, appeared completely
innocent of any wrongdoing. He certainly presented no evidence of his
complicity in the murder of Elizabeth Stride. The officers assigned to
follow him had found evidence only that Kidney was possessed of a
proclivity for drink, no doubt brought on by his recent loss. He had not
been observed in the company of Lusk, McCarthy or anyone else whom
aroused the least interest. Holmes was forced to concede that Michael
Kidney may have been a false lead, although he steadfastly refused to
dismiss him entirely, to the great scorn of Lestrade.

Holmes stayed true to his instincts that Kidney knew something
of what had happened to Elizabeth Stride. His presence at Lusk's house
appeared to confirm that there was an intrigue afoot which had yet to be
fully understood. Lestrade's reasoning was that Kidney had been
summoned to Lusk's house with the offer of labouring work. Lusk, he
argued, may have felt compelled to offer him a position as an act of
kindness on account of his being so personally affected by Stride's
murder. Then again, the Inspector argued, perhaps Kidney, being
inspired by his loss, had arrived there unannounced to offer his services
to the Whitechapel Vigilance Committee. In the absence of any
subsequent cause for suspicion, Lestrade's arguments appeared justified.
I confess that I found myself agreeing with the Inspector on this
occasion.

Holmes took the suggestion that his triumvirate of suspects had
been a waste of both his and Lestrade's efforts with great disdain. His
response was motivated not, it appeared, by vanity or a consideration of
his own fallibility, but rather frustration at Lestrade's failure to observe
the obvious.

Yet Holmes conceded that he could provide no further evidence
against Kidney, agreeing with Lestrade that it was impractical to

continue such observations when they had yielded no results. For several days following this disappointment, Holmes spent long hours away from Baker Street. He would arrive home late each evening and immediately slump languidly in his chair, a look of exhaustion swept across his crumpled countenance. He said nothing of where he had been and, given his irascible mood, I declined to enquire.

The afternoon of Thursday, 18th October found Holmes and I in Baker Street, engaged in reading our respective newspapers in studious silence. At just past one o' clock, Mrs Hudson interrupted our reverie to announce that we had two visitors, one of whom was Mr George Lusk. I gasped in astonishment at this intelligence and Holmes sprang to his feet, immediately questioning our landlady as to whether he had heard her correctly.

'My goodness, Holmes!' I exclaimed, when Mrs Hudson, having repeated Lusk's name, left to send that same man and his companion up to our rooms. 'What can this mean?'

'I haven't the least clue, Watson,' said Holmes, as he eagerly awaited our visitors' arrival.

There was a faint knock upon the sitting room door and George Lusk appeared before us, ashen-faced and clearly in a state of great agitation. Whereas I had expected either Jack McCarthy or Michael Kidney to be his unannounced companion, the man who followed him shyly into the room was one whom I had never seen before. From Holmes' description, he could not possibly have been Kidney. He was a small, neatly dressed man with a rather pale complexion.

'Good morning to you both,' said Lusk, in a most troubled voice. 'I trust I do not inconvenience you too greatly? I confess that I am at my wits' end.'

'It is an unexpected pleasure to see you once again in our humble rooms, Mr Lusk,' said Holmes graciously. 'Although I cannot help but observe that you appear to be in a state of some anxiety.'

'I am afraid that I do not know quite what to do, Mr Holmes,' said Lusk. 'This is my friend, Mr Joseph Aarons. He is the treasurer of the vigilance committee.'

Holmes and I stared at each other in astonishment at the name of Lusk's companion. My friend gave Mr Aarons a distracted greeting and bid both of our visitors to sit down.

'Now, what appears to be the matter?' said Holmes, still eyeing Aarons suspiciously.

'It is like this, Mr Holmes. Two evenings ago, I received through the post a most grotesque communication in connection to the recent murders, the contents of which left me quite aghast.'

'I see. I should perhaps advise you, Mr Lusk, that the police themselves are receiving hundred of letters a week purporting to be from Jack the Ripper, no doubt penned by idle fantasists. As the Chairman of the vigilance committee, I imagine you have attracted the attention of a similar hoaxer.'

'It is far worse than that, Mr Holmes,' said Lusk, shaking his head. 'For you see, I received what you may describe as a parcel.'

Reaching inside his coat pocket, he retrieved a paper bag from which he produced a small cardboard box wrapped in brown paper. It was stained with what appeared to be blood. He passed it gingerly to Holmes, who scanned it dubiously as he took it in his hands. He slowly opened the lid of the box and peered at its contents. His face suddenly convulsed in disgust, and I momentarily feared that he was about to throw the offending object across the room.

'My God,' said Holmes, closing the lid and averting his eyes in horror. 'Take a look, Watson.'

He handed me the parcel, which I accepted with the utmost trepidation. Steeling myself, I opened the box and peeled back the blood-stained paper wrapping. Before me was half a kidney, divided longitudinally and apparently of human origin. It smelled foul and I quickly closed the box and handed to back to Lusk, who took it in his rather tremulous hand.

'You say that you received this two evenings ago?' asked Holmes. Lusk nodded.

'I thought it was someone trying to scare me, for I have received several hoax letters in the past few weeks. I should have gone to the police, but I considered it was just a macabre joke. I mentioned the parcel last night to Mr Aarons, who agreed to come to my house this morning to inspect it. He felt certain that he was not looking at a sheep's kidney, so I was confronted by the possibility that Jack the Ripper had sent me a grizzly trophy of his foul deeds.

'I took it to my local surgery where my doctor's assistant, Mr Reed, examined it and opined that the kidney was certainly human. He is a rather thorough man and decided to take it across to the London Hospital, where it was looked at under a microscope. It was confirmed as being a left human kidney which had been preserved in spirits, rather than formaline, which I am told is the usual practice with such organs. They could not say, however, when it had been removed from the body. But I am certain that it must have come from the poor woman in Mitre Square.'

'A most singular sequence of events,' said Holmes. 'You have had quite the morning of it, Mr Lusk. But there is one point on which I remain unclear. In your capacity as the chairman of the Whitechapel Vigilance, it is entirely possible that you have unwittingly raised the ire of the murderer. However, I fail to see how you can be quite so certain that this singular enclosure was sent to you by Jack the Ripper.'

'Because of the letter, Mr Holmes.'

'Letter, Mr Lusk?' asked Holmes, his eyes widening.

'This came with the parcel,' said he, passing a small sheet of paper to Holmes, who scanned it in silence for several seconds.

'Quite extraordinary,' said Holmes, before passing me the letter.

It was written in black ink in a most unsightly, ragged scrawl. The bizarre message ran as follows:

From hell

Mr Lusk,
Sor
I send you half the
Kidne I took from one woman
prasarved it for you tother piece
I fried and ate it was very nise I
may send you the bloody knif that

136

took it out if you only wate a while
longer
      signed   Catch me when
                       you can

            Mishter Lusk

'It is indeed macabre,' I said, returning the letter to Holmes. 'But do you think it came from the killer?'

'I do, Watson,' he replied.

'So, it is from Jack the Ripper?' said Lusk, his voice quivering with fright. 'I felt certain of the fact myself. Yet I had hoped that you would find some objection to it having been sent by that foul miscreant. I feel quite distressed at the prospect that this beast of a man knows where I live. I have seven children, Mr Holmes.'

'Calm yourself, Mr Lusk, please.' said Holmes gently. 'He is certainly a beast, but one who preys upon lone women at night in deserted alleyways. I am certain that neither your safety, nor that of your family, will be compromised by the author of this grotesque missive.'

'That is all very well for you to say, Mr Holmes. But it is not you to whom he has sent a kidney.'

'Can you tell anything from the letter which affords us a clue to the murderer's identity, Mr Holmes?' asked Aarons.

'Assuming that I am correct, and this communication was indeed sent by Jack the Ripper, it tells us a great deal, Mr Aarons.'

'Anything which will assist us in catching this man would be greatly appreciated, Mr Holmes,' said Lusk anxiously.

'The man who wrote this letter is semi-literate and has benefitted from only the most rudimentary of learning. The writing is cramped, with crowded letters and retraced vertical strokes. This is caused by moving merely the fingers when one writes, rather than the forearm. It allows only the slightest of lateral freedom to one's script and is thus the hallmark of one who has not the ease of command with a nib of the more practiced penman. I am something of a student, as Watson will attest, to the burgeoning discipline of graphology. I have read several books by Crèpieux-Jamin, the man whose work in the field threatens to turn an art into a science.

'It seems clear that the letter is not that of an educated man who has merely adopted a crude script in order to disguise his own hand. The consistency of the author's minute idiosyncrasies upon his stokes, as well as the speed with which he has written his words, dismisses the possibility that he composed the letter slowly in an attempt to appear less educated than he actually is. The numerous ink blots in so short a missive is another tell-tale sign of a man who is quite at odds with the tool with which he is working, while possessing scant regard for the clarity of his script. You will also have noticed both the absence of punctuation and the atrocious spelling. Yet our correspondent has knowledge of both the silent 'k' and 'h', and neither could he have arrived at the correct spelling of the word 'piece' phonetically. The setting out of the letter likewise conforms to that taught in copybooks, so our man has had at least a little formal schooling.'

'You are saying that Jack the Ripper is of the lower classes, Holmes?' I asked.

'If he and the letter writer are one and the same, then that is the only conclusion at which I can arrive, Watson.'

'A quite remarkable analysis, Mr Holmes,' said Aarons appreciatively. 'I wonder how any man could discover so much upon so little evidence.'

'You flatter me, Mr Aarons,' said Holmes dismissively. 'To the trained eye, the letter presents a wealth of clues. I can tell, for instance, that the letter-writer is almost certainly of British origin.'

'How on earth can you deduce that, Holmes?' I asked. 'I have read the same letter as you. Yet I fail to see in it any clue to the writer's nationality.'

'The abbreviation of 'Mr', with the r raised above the line is a peculiarity unique to the English hand, Watson. Equally, and with the exception of Wales, the contraction of 'tother' in place of 'the other' is common throughout the British Isles. Perhaps more specifically, the words 'prasarved' and 'Mishter' suggest a man who is local to the eastern portions of this great city. 'Er' you will find is often pronounced as 'ar' east of the City of London, and 'sh' widely substituted for 's'. I feel our writer has unwittingly tightened the net upon himself.

'Extraordinary!' I exclaimed.

'It is nothing of the sort, Watson. Perhaps you have failed to read my monograph on London dialects. To my ear, a fellow from Shoreditch sounds as distinct to a man from Bow as a Swallow does a Robin.'

'You are a most remarkable man, Mr Holmes,' said Aarons. 'We must surely catch the fellow now.'

'I am afraid it will not be quite that straightforward, Mr Aarons,' warned Holmes. 'We know something of the letter writer's background, but nothing with which we might single him out from a hundred others of his kind. The attributes you have heard me ascribe to the author might equally apply to half the men in the East End.'

'But we have his handwriting, Holmes,' said I. 'Surely that will be enough to find him?'

'I fear not, Watson,' said Holmes, shaking his head. 'The evidence suggests that this letter is a rare instance of its author being compelled to commit pen to paper. If that is so, what other examples of his handwriting may exist? Besides his signature, perhaps none. He has certainly made no attempt to disguise his hand, which suggests that he feels he has nothing to fear from the prospect of it being made public.'

'So, we have nothing whatever to go on?' said Lusk, appearing quite beside himself.

'We shall catch him, Mr Lusk. Have no fear of that.'

'Before he strikes again?'

'Of that,' said Holmes softly. 'I cannot be so sure.'

17.

Kidney and The Star

'You are certain the package came from Jack the Ripper?' I asked, once our visitors had gone to take their grisly parcel to the police.

'The more I think upon the matter, the more I am convinced that it was sent by the murderer.'

'But can we be sure?' I asked. 'Could it not have been a cruel hoax?'

'In the first instance, Watson,' said Holmes. 'Let us consider the kidney which you, as a medical man, have yourself just observed. It has been confirmed as a left human kidney which has been preserved in spirits. Now, Lusk was informed that such organs are usually kept in formaline. Is that correct?'

'It certainly is, Holmes. Formaline is a preserving fluid which any body delivered to a hospital for dissection is charged with.'

'Thank you, Watson. So, you agree, no doubt, that there is an immediate objection to the most obvious theory of it being a crude hoax, perhaps perpetrated by a medical student possessed of a singular sense of humour?'

'That would appear to be the case,' I conceded.

'So whence came the kidney? And why, if it were a prank, did our joker procure a left kidney and then send only part of it? We know that Catherine Eddowes had part of her left kidney removed. I question how many hoaxers would go to the trouble of recreating as exact a replica of that organ as possible for the cause of a mere prank. If they meant to frighten Lusk or cause a panic, would they not have merely sent a whole kidney, or for that matter a sheep's kidney? By the time its provenance was established and the hoax identified, the required effect of placing Lusk at his wits' end would have been achieved.'

'I see your reasoning,' said I. 'Perhaps the thought of Jack the Ripper taunting Lusk with the plundered remains of his victim is simply too obscene a notion. But I must confess, Holmes, that I have doubts as to its origin.'

'Your pragmatism is surely one of your most prized assets, Watson,' replied Holmes. 'And it may be that your doubts will be proved entirely correct. But let us turn our attention to the letter with which the kidney arrived. There was something missing from it, Watson.'

'Missing? Do you refer to the absent letters of the misspelt words?'

'I do not, Watson. We have referred to the letter as being from Jack the Ripper. But were I to give it to a man who had no knowledge of this case, it is extremely unlikely he would use that name, is it not?'

'Because it is not signed by Jack the Ripper!' I cried.

'Bravo, Watson!' said Holmes, clapping his hands in delight. 'The murderer concludes with the enigmatic challenge to Lusk of catching him, yet purposely omits the sobriquet by which he is known throughout the country. The police are beleaguered by hundreds of letters each week, with Lusk himself having received several, all purporting to be the work of the murderer and signed Jack the Ripper. The man who posted the kidney did not. Why?'

'Because he is the real killer.'

'Precisely. Jack the Ripper is a name bestowed upon him by the letters which Bates showed us in this very room, most probably composed by someone at The Star. It is not what our man calls himself. He therefore proceeds to distinguish his letter from the veritable sea of derivative nonsense, of which Lestrade's men are in receipt of by the sack load. How? He sends his victim's kidney as a way of proving it is genuine.'

'I believe you are right, Holmes,' I said with a shudder. 'Then surely the piece of Eddowes' apron found by the graffito in Goulston Street had the same purpose?'

'You have outdone yourself, my dear Watson. That is precisely why I made what proved to be a most fortuitous copy of the message before it could be erased. I was certain that the words had been chalked by the murderer.'

'And you consider that the parcel sent to Lusk confirms this?'

'Precisely, Watson. Consider that the murderer takes from Catherine Eddowes two things: he removes a portion of her kidney and a part of her apron. The piece of apron is later found next to a scrawled message. Two weeks later, George Lusk receives a letter claiming to be from the murderer. Enclosed with this missive is a portion of a human kidney. The indisputable fact is that Jack the Ripper departed Mitre Square that night with two items as trophies of his grisly work. We now find that both, should we accept the kidney as being genuine, are found accompanying a message.'

'I am sure that you are correct, Holmes. But Lestrade still believes that the murderer took the apron simply as a means of wiping his knife, and that its discovery next to the graffito was coincidental.'

'Lestrade is a fool!' cried Holmes. 'Why should a killer take the time to cut away part of the lady's dress for such a purpose when he could have cleaned his knife upon the spot in half the time? All he need do is wipe it upon any part of her clothing before making good his escape. No, he set out that night with the intention of obtaining from his victim items by which he might prove his communications to be authentic. The calculating mind of this man quite unnerves me.'

'He is certainly a bold fellow,' I agreed. 'And still as elusive as ever.'

'That he is, Watson. And every turn of this extraordinary affair leaves me baffled as to who he is. I am certain, for instance, that he is well-connected and affluent. Yet how on earth do I reconcile that notion with the author of Lusk's letter, whom is clearly of the lowest order?'

'Did he have someone write it for him?'

'An amanuensis may have penned it on his behalf, of course. And I cannot ignore the fact that the handwriting bears little resemblance to the Goulston Street graffito, although chalked writing is rather more easily disguised. But when Mr Lawende's description is taken into consideration, it brings with it the possibility that I am wrong, and the killer is in fact a semi-literate sailor. But there is more than one man at work here, Watson. I am sure of it. Jack the Ripper may be a single assassin, but someone is assisting him. And what are we to deduce from the name of Lusk's companion?'

'Mr Aarons? Surely that must be the man to whom Kidney referred?'

'Almost certainly it is. But what connects Aarons to Kidney can only be guessed at. This is proving to be a case that simply won't tell.'

I observed Holmes as he cast a weary gaze upon the window. The sombre silence was broken by the entrance of Mrs Hudson, who passed a telegram to Holmes.

'Quickly, Watson!' he cried, leaping to his feet the instant he had read it. 'Put on your coat. We have an urgent engagement at Scotland Yard.'

'What has happened, Holmes?' I asked, as Holmes hurried to the door.

'I shall explain on the way, Watson,' he replied, disappearing from sight. 'Now hurry!'

I was barely sat in the hansom before Holmes passed me the telegram, which read as follows:

Michael Kidney has been arrested at the offices of The Star. Come at once to Scotland Yard. Lestrade.

'My word, Holmes!' I exclaimed. 'What can have happened?'

'That is what I wish to discover, Watson. Let us hope that whatever awaits us sheds some light upon this extraordinary business.'

We found Lestrade in his office, where he greeted us warmly before instructing us to accompany him downstairs.

'We arrested Kidney this afternoon,' he explained, as we followed him down to the cells. 'He managed to get himself into the offices of The Star and promptly punched the editor, Mr O'Connor. It's a straightforward case of assault and only aroused my interest because of your suspicions about Kidney.'

'I am indebted to your consideration, Lestrade,' said Holmes. 'Might Watson and I interview him alone?'

'I see no reason why not. We've managed to get nothing out of him beyond a sullen refusal to say anything.'

Lestrade showed us to Kidney's cell, where we found him lying perfectly still upon a rickety bench.

'We meet again, Mr Kidney,' said Holmes brightly. Kidney started at these words, springing to his feet with a wild look across his face.

'You?' he cried angrily. 'What do you want? Who is this?'

'This is my good friend and colleague, Dr Watson. And I wish to ask you some questions.'

'I'm saying nothing, Holmes,' he hissed.

'What has Joseph Aarons to do with Liz's death?' asked Holmes, his stern gaze fixed upon Kidney.'

'How do you know who he is?'

'Perhaps you cannot recall. You told me that he was connected with events while rather the worse for ale.'

Kidney cast Holmes a puzzled glance before sitting down wearily upon the bench.

'Curse my drunken tongue. I should never have accepted a drink from you. I have heard of your tricks.'

'I merely asked you some questions. What you decided to tell me was your own choice, Mr Kidney. I wish only to help you.'

'Help me? And why should you do that?'

'Because I believe you are caught up in the most mystifying case I have thus far encountered in my career. And because if you are honest with me, I may yet succeed in capturing Jack the Ripper and the man who murdered Liz Stride.'

Kidney rose to his feet and paced the narrow cell several times, appearing quite lost in his thoughts.

'Liz was employed by Aarons as a charwoman,' he said eventually. 'She worked for him now and then if his regulars let him down.'

'You fill me with intrigue, Mr Kidney,' said Holmes. 'Pray tell how this gentleman knows anything about her murder.'

'I think Liz always found him a regular enough sort. She was a touch above your average girl about Whitechapel and got on with the toffs better than most. She was a sharp woman and knew how to use her wits when need be. One day, about a week before she died, I came home and she tells me that I'd never guess what she has found out. That morning, she'd been charring for Aarons and heard voices coming from his front room. She was always of a curious nature and as the voices grew louder, she tiptoed across the hallway and found the door was ajar. Aarons was in conversation with a man whom she later found out to be George Lusk. They were discussing a man called McCarthy. Lusk was apparently worried about this fellow's business practices.

'It seems that this McCarthy had loaned money to Lusk, whose firm had been struggling. As Lusk was drawn into McCarthy's schemes more and more, he discovered that the man was involved in sending English girls to the continent as slaves, or so Liz said. Lusk didn't know what to do, so Aarons told him to confront McCarthy. According to Aarons, what McCarthy was doing could send him to prison.'

'McCarthy is involved in people trafficking!' I exclaimed.

'It would appear so, Watson. English girls have a curious charm across Europe. They are seduced with promises of money and fine living, only to end up enslaved in a life of misery. The practice is rife in the dark underbelly of London, where those of the least hope are more easily lured to their fate. Pray continue, Mr Kidney.'

'Like I said, Liz was sharp. She saw that she had in her possession information which might be used to her advantage. She'd learned from the conversation between Lusk and Aarons that McCarthy had a shop on Dorset Street, so we planned that she should go there and threaten to report him if he did not give her fifty pounds. When she did so, he refused and told her she couldn't prove anything. She persisted, but he merely laughed and challenged her to go to the police. She wanted to tell them, for she could be hot-headed when the mood took her. But I persuaded her it was not worth the trouble. Liz never had an enemy in the world. When she was found murdered, I was certain it must have had something to do with McCarthy. I went to Aarons, who was horrified when I told him what Liz had heard. He told me I was wrong, and that McCarthy had nothing to do with Liz's death. I wanted McCarthy to tell me himself, so I could know for sure. He promised to arrange a meeting, and so it was that I met them at Lusk's house. McCarthy seemed straight enough, saying how sorry he was for what happened and assuring me he'd had no hand in Liz's murder. It was Jack the Ripper who'd done it, he said. She was just unlucky.'

'And you believed him?' asked Holmes.

'I did. I put it down to coincidence. When I told you Aarons was to blame, I was drunk and upset. I blamed him in drink because I thought that if he had never employed her, Liz would still be alive. But I know it was not his fault.'

'I see. And how does this have any connection with you assaulting the editor of The Star earlier this afternoon?'

'I'd put the suspicions about Liz's death behind me. Then yesterday, I received a letter. It said that the editor of The Star, a Mr O'Connor, had murdered Liz.'

'Holmes!' I exclaimed.

'Do you still have the letter?' asked Holmes.

'It should be at my house, as best I remember.'

'And had it been sent through the post?'

'No. It had been pushed under the door.'

'And can you remember its exact wording?'

'It was very short.' said Kidney, nodding his head. 'It said: "I know who murdered Elizabeth Stride. It was T.P O'Connor, editor of The Star. He knows all."'

'It was not signed?'

'No. It was just as I said. Nothing more.'

'And this letter prompted you to take the earliest opportunity to visit O'Connor?'

'Of course. I had it out with him straight. He went as white as a sheet when I told him who I was. I asked him if he had murdered my Liz, but he denied it. I had him by the throat, but his cries attracted attention. I managed to strike him just before several people burst in and pulled me off him.'

'It certainly appears fortunate for O'Connor that they arrived when they did,' said Holmes with a wry smile.

'I believe I may have killed him if not for their interruption, Mr Holmes. I am certain that he did it.'

'I share your certainty, Mr Kidney. Although proving it will be quite a different matter. But I believe that what you have told me will be of enormous assistance to that end.'

'An incredible turn of events,' I said, as we returned to Lestrade's office.

147

'Quite extraordinary. This case continues to astound, Watson.'

'You were sincere in your belief that O'Connor murdered Stride?'

'I was. We have been wrong footed several times in this investigation, but I believe that we are finally on the fellow's trail.'

'And you still think he will lead us to Jack the Ripper?'

'I am more certain than ever, Watson.'

18.

A ring and a Duke

Barely had we returned to Baker Street when Mrs Hudson entered our
sitting room, brandishing a letter.

'This came for you while you were out, Mr Holmes,' she
announced.

'Thank you, Mrs Hudson,' said Holmes, eagerly taking the letter
from our landlady's hand.

Upon her departure, Holmes ripped open the envelope and
withdrew from it a sheet of paper. I watched with interest as he scanned
it several times, a look of bemused astonishment across his features as
he held it to the light.

'This is quite incredible, Watson,' said he, passing me the letter.
In rough capitals on a torn piece of paper, was the following message
written in crayon:

BE WARNED: JACK THE RIPPER WILL STRIKE
AGAIN ON 8th NOVEMBER

'But this is extraordinary, Holmes!' I cried. 'But can it possibly
be true?'

'It is entirely possible, Watson. In fact, I am certain that whoever
sent this letter believes that they have some foreknowledge of the next
murder.'

'Can you tell anything from it?' I asked, handing the curious
missive back to Holmes. He gazed at it in silence for some seconds
before responding.

'The envelope bears a central district postmark and was sent by a
middle-class man. He is slightly snobbish, lives with a family and,
although he is well-educated, he is not quite as affluent as he would
have people believe. His handwriting is known to me, or at least he
suspects that it may become so. I believe, therefore, that we have met.
He has recently discovered the identity of the murderer and lives in
morbid fear of the man, whom he believes may be following him. He

has, by means which I cannot fathom, discovered the date on which the murderer will next strike, although the killer is not aware that he possesses this information. At considerable risk to his own person, he has gone to great pains that I should believe this warning to be genuine. The letter was written with some haste in a public House of which he is not a regular. He was wearing gloves while he composed it.'

'I am sure I am being very stupid, Holmes, but I fail to see how you can possibly arrive at such fanciful conclusions.'

'Ha! Of course you do, my dear Watson. You have singularly failed to observe the obvious. That the man is middle class is evident from the quality of the paper. I should guess six pence a packet? He has torn the sheet in half, probably to save the remainder for future use, suggesting a necessary frugality. This is also evident in the envelope, which is of much inferior quality and, to judge from the faded lettering of the maker's name, had been in the possession of the sender for some time. From that I deduce that he finds the cheapest envelope his stationary cupboard provides, intending to create the illusion of a less affluent writer. But the only writing paper he can find is a new set of much better quality.

'He has no time to procure paper which might match the envelope, but he decides that this doesn't matter, just so long as there is no clue which might reveal his identity. Such alacrity suggests that he has only very recently become aware of the information which he so wishes to impart. He lives with a family, for who else other than a man with children would possess a crayon? He takes his collection of stationery with him, for he wishes to compose his letter in privacy. He writes in capitals, in order so that his own hand may go unnoticed. He is snobbish, for he assumes a working-class man should write a letter with so crude an instrument, when in fact a pencil is far more likely.

'He goes to a public house for, if you observe the underside of the paper, you shall see it is streaked with lines where it has been placed on a table which is exceedingly chipped and scored. Only a public house would possess such battered furniture. Our man is not a regular of the establishment, as he would not compose his letter anywhere in which he might be found by the killer, of whom he lives in fear. This point is evident from the shaky hand in which the letter has been written. There are no finger marks upon either paper or envelope, which leads me to believe that he wore the gloves purposely, in order that no fingerprints might be used to identify him. He is therefore educated, for only such a man would be aware of the advancement in the science of fingerprinting that would allow such identification. I admire the work of Henry Faulds in that particular field. He is in mortal terror that his actions should be discovered. If the killer was aware that our man knew when he would next strike, he would surely change the date of his next murder, thus rendering our correspondent's warning quite obsolete.

'Our letter writer therefore acquired the date surreptitiously and believes the murderer to be ignorant of this knowledge. I have met him, for the envelope addresses me not by title, but merely as Sherlock Holmes. It is a curious quirk of the English that a gentleman will only address a fellow in this fashion if he is known to him, thus dispensing with such formal nuances.'

'Quite astonishing, Holmes,' I said in wonderment. 'Although can you be sure it is not some bizarre hoax?'

'It is not a hoax, Watson,' said Holmes, leaning across towards me. 'How else could our man have sent this?'

Sherlock Holmes opened out his right hand. There, in his long, pale palm, was a brass ring.

'Good Heavens!' I ejaculated. 'You don't mean to say that this belonged to Annie Chapman?'

'There is, of course, no way to be certain. But I believe so, Watson. The ring has been cleaned, but it certainly corresponds with the description given by Eliza Cooper of those worn by Chapman.'

'Then whoever sent it must have some close association with her killer?'

'I believe he does, Watson. And he wishes us to catch the man.'

'Then why not tell us his name?'

'Because we would immediately attempt to apprehend the fellow. Were we to fail to procure evidence enough to detain him, which is probable, he would be free to exact his revenge upon the letter writer, upon whom his suspicions would undoubtedly fall.'

'I understand your logic, Holmes,' said I. 'But what shall we do to find this man?'

'I think we shall pay a visit to our old friend, Benjamin Bates, Watson,' said Holmes brightly. 'Only he can help us now.'

Sherlock Holmes was swift in procuring an audience with Benjamin Bates. Although The Star reporter flattered himself upon being the best-informed journalist in London, there were few men in the entire capital who rivalled my friend for the apparently limitless supply of contacts at his disposal. At times, it seemed as though Holmes had the entire spectrum of London life held on a string; one which he merely had to pull in order to summon those who could provide the required assistance.

The following day, Holmes was absent from Baker Street for some time after breakfast, returning with his thin features beaten to a light hue by the wind, but smiling nonetheless.

'I have discovered where Bates lives,' said he, removing his coat and scarf. 'It was quite an enterprise, in point of fact.'

'You are going to visit him?' I asked, surveying Holmes over the top of my newspaper.'

'We shall both visit him tonight, Watson. He lives in Stephen Street, just off Tottenham Court Road.'

'Could we not invite him here?' I asked, mindful of the awful fog in which London was presently enveloped.

'That would not do, Watson,' said Holmes, shaking his head. 'The stakes are considerably higher now that I feel the net is beginning to close in upon Jack the Ripper. I do not wish to converse with Bates in the public realm, while I fear his presence at Baker Street would be subject to equal scrutiny. And this miserable weather provides us with the perfect cover for such an adventure, does it not?'

Considering a hansom in such conditions as too hazardous, I followed Holmes through the numbing fog, quite unable to see little other than the tall outline of my friend as his hazy shadow marched ahead of me. The spires of Westminster cleaved through the yellow smog above me; the only vestige of our surroundings which was not laid victim to the impenetrable gloom. I heard the sharp clip of Holmes' step as I stumbled in his wake, his shrill cries echoing in the near distance to periodically assure me that I had not lost him. It was but seven o'clock, yet darkness had already descended. The hazy glow of the streetlamps cast a gauzy light upon the fog through which it struggled.

'Watson!' cried Holmes, gripping me firmly by the shoulder. 'There you are! I suggest we do not part from this point. I confess to being increasingly unsure of our destination with each step. But never fear, for I am certain we are close.'

The remarkable senses of Sherlock Holmes had often proved vital to his well-being, and they did not fail him on this occasion. He soon announced that we had passed onto Mortimer Street and, minutes later, following several unfathomable twists of direction, that we had reached Stephen Street. The dense fog had lightened enough for me to make out that we were in a wide thoroughfare, the tall buildings on either side a collection of businesses and gentrified dwellings.

'Here we are, Watson,' said Holmes. 'Number fifteen.'

It was a three-storied building, whose charming sash windows and frontage were stained and streaked by the yellowing fog.

'Good evening,' said Holmes, when his knock upon the door was answered by an elderly woman of stern visage and stooping posture.

'Evening,' she replied in a dull tone.

'I am here to call upon Mr Bates.'

'Are you now?' she asked, surveying us both with a narrowing of her hard, brown eyes. 'He's on the second floor. Mind your feet upon the carpets.'

Holmes thanked the woman, who continued to observe us as we ascended the narrow staircase.

'My word!' exclaimed Bates upon opening his door to us. 'Holmes and Dr Watson. Has there been another murder?'

'Not to my knowledge, Bates,' replied Holmes. 'Although it is that very matter which I wish to discuss with you. May we come in?'

'Certainly. Although I confess that I am quite astonished as to how you discovered where I live,' said he, as we entered his sitting room. 'I have few visitors and seldom let my address be known.'

'I have my own methods, as you have yours, Mr Bates.'

'I'm sure you do, Mr Holmes,' said Bates, with a wry smile. 'Please make yourselves comfortable.'

We sat down upon the sofa, while Bates drew up the armchair facing us. The sitting room was light and airy, reminding me somewhat of our own at Baker Street. Several bookcases of various heights were jammed against the furthest wall, with volumes squeezed into every inch of its expanse and spilling upon the floor.

'Forgive the jumble of books,' said Bates, observing my glance towards them. 'I am afraid that I am something of a bibliophile.'

'It is a most impressive collection,' I said.

'You live alone, I see?' asked Holmes, his eyes sweeping the room,

'I do, Holmes. You yourself know the joys of the bachelor life, of course.'

'Quite. Now, Bates, if you will excuse my impertinence, I have come on foot through the most ghastly fog in order to ask you questions which I consider to be of the utmost importance.'

'Please, be my guest.'

'I want to know who wrote the letters that were received by the Central News Agency and signed Jack the Ripper.'

'And what makes you think I should know that?' he asked with a faltering smile.

'Do not play games with me, Bates. Four women have died and on the eighth of November, I believe a fifth shall suffer an identical fate.'

'What?' cried Bates in astonishment. 'How can you possibly know that?'

'I have it on reliable information. I promise to share this with you in return for your assistance. Now, there are lives at stake upon the question I will again ask. Who wrote the letters?'

'It was Fred Best,' said Bates, his gaze fixed upon Holmes.

'A colleague at The Star, I presume?'

'Yes.'

'And he undertook this enterprise on the instructions of O'Connor?'

'That is correct.'

'Begin at the beginning, Bates. I implore you to tell me every detail about this business from its inception.'

'When I joined The Star, I could see from the first that O'Connor was a driven man. You will have noticed yourself that I have my own ambitions. It quickly became apparent that the two of us shared his vision of making the paper the talk of London. It was to be the first newspaper to cater for the new literate working class. I admired him and, for my part, proved to be a most able reporter. Yet I began to see a different side to him.'

'When the murders started?' asked Holmes.

'Precisely. O'Connor was convinced he could establish The Star on the strength of these crimes, just so long as he made its coverage more inventive than every other paper.'

'I believe he succeeded,' observed Holmes. 'Thanks in no small part to yourself.'

'I admit that no-one embraced his ethos greater than myself,' said Bates, almost apologetically. 'I spent countless hours interviewing the locals. In the process, I amassed notebooks full of gossip which I used to give O'Connor what he wanted.'

'Which was a long series of articles espousing, if not entirely inventing, a variety of unsubstantiated rumours that contained not the slightest regard for the truth?'

'That is a harsh judgement, Holmes. But not an unfair one.'

'Did anything strike you as unusual about O'Connor's approach?'

'Only his disregard for the facts.'

'I gathered as much. And what of Leather Apron? He was quite the lynchpin to the cause, was he not?'

'When some of the women I spoke to in Whitechapel mentioned Leather Apron, it seemed as though we could be onto something. Of course, I could find no evidence for his existence. It was all merely cobbled together from second-hand accounts. Other papers carried the story, but not with the same vigour as The Star. When it was discovered that Leather Apron was a man called Jack Pizer, and he subsequently proved to be entirely innocent, I expected O'Connor to be downcast. But he merely told us to continue our trawl of the streets and find out what we could.

'He was convinced that the murderer was local and instructed me to write articles to that end. I don't think his philosophy was to solve the crimes so much as perpetuate them.'

Holmes shot me a knowing glance, but otherwise remained transfixed upon Bates.

'Yet you were always amongst the first on the scene of the murders?'

'That is certainly true for both the Chapman murder and the double event.'

'And how was that so?'

'As I have explained before, Holmes, I have my contacts. They are my own and have nothing to do with O'Connor.'

'Very well. Apologies, Bates, if I have hurt your professional sensibilities. Yet the suggestion to form a connection with myself was O'Connor's idea, I take it?'

'Yes, it was. He felt it would provide The Star with credibility if we could claim a connection with Sherlock Holmes. Through Dr Watson's accounts, your name is all too valuable to a burgeoning newspaper. As our readership grew, so did the need to maintain the stories in order to sustain it. My instructions were to offer you a deal whereby we exchanged information. I was to let you know of any developments and request anything of interest from yourself in return.'

'I see. Primarily, I take it, in order that I might endorse the letters you brought to me as authentic?'

'O'Connor feared that people may suspect him as the author of the letters. He was anxious to deflect any suspicion away from The Star. If the great Sherlock Holmes was seen to believe them genuine, then who could possibly doubt their provenance?'

'Of course, I did nothing of the sort. For I saw them for the impudent fakes they were.'

'O'Connor suspected as much. I think perhaps he was curious to see if he could fool you.'

'Ha! A most unlikely prospect. Now, about the letters, Bates?'

'When the Leather Apron story died down, O'Connor felt we needed something bolder to keep up interest. He hit upon the idea of a letter from the murderer. O'Connor wrote the text and Best, being the best calligrapher at the paper, copied it out in the required straggling hand. When I arrived at your rooms with the letter, I thought it entirely genuine. It was only after I'd brought you the postcard that O'Connor confessed that it was he who had authored them.'

'That is how I supposed it. Did you ever suspect O'Connor's motives might extend beyond the desire to boost circulation of The Star?'

'I am not sure what you mean,' said Bates anxiously.

'I think you do, Bates.'

'Has this something to do with your knowledge of a fifth murder?'

Holmes studied the young reporter, his eyes unwavering upon the fellow as he contemplated his next words.

'I wish you to understand the importance of what I am about to say,' said he, in a low, deliberate voice. 'I shall be frank with you in the hope that the consequences of your divulging this intelligence to anyone may become apparent. I received a note yesterday which informed me that Jack the Ripper will strike again on the eighth of next month. I am certain that it is genuine. I am also certain that Jack the Ripper has an accomplice, one who may or may not prove to be T.P O'Connor. I believe that the murder of Elizabeth Stride was not committed by Jack the Ripper, but by someone who may have knowledge of the murders. That man was O'Connor.'

'O'Connor killed Stride?' gasped Bates.

'I have as yet no direct proof. But I consider it a certainty, nonetheless.'

'But he couldn't have,' he said, his features growing ashen.

'I am afraid Holmes is correct, Mr Bates,' I assured him.

'But this is too much!' cried the young man, rising to his feet. 'Why should he do such a thing?'

'I confess that at present, I do not know. I have yet to discover a link between he and Stride. She worked for a Mr Aarons. Does the name mean anything to you?'

'I've never heard of him, Holmes.'

'What about Jack McCarthy?' I asked,

'Yes, I know of him. He is a friend of O'Connor's.'

'A friend, you say?' asked Holmes.

'I have seen him at our offices on a few occasions; usually when I have been working late. How they came to know each other, I do not know.'

'Yet you have heard his name?'

'O'Connor mentioned it after I observed McCarthy leaving his office one evening. He said that he was just an acquaintance. This was some time ago and I have not seen him since. Do you think this man is also involved somehow?'

'I do. Now, is there anyone else whom you have observed in the company of O'Connor that may be of interest to me?

Bates pondered the question for several seconds.

'The Duke,' he said eventually.

'The Duke, Bates?'

'He came to the offices once, not long after the paper started. I heard a whisper that he had some financial interest in The Star. He was a Duke, I remember. I am not sure of his full title.'

'Was he of the middle height and possessed of a great beard and rather solemn features?'

'He was.'

'The Duke of Buckingham!' I exclaimed.

'The very same, Watson.'

'I'm afraid you have lost me, gentlemen,' said Bates in bewilderment. 'Is the Duke involved also?'

'That I shall have to establish,' said Holmes. 'In the meantime, remember what I have told you, Bates, and keep everything you have heard to yourself.'

'You have my word, Holmes. Is there anything else I can do to help?'

'I wish you to observe and report. I want to hear immediately of anything which may help me catch this man.'

'Consider it done.'

'Excellent, Bates. I was certain that you were to be relied upon. There is just one more thing I must ask of you,' said Holmes, as he rose to his feet. 'I want you to arrange for a guest article to appear in The Star.'

158

'Written by whom?'

'Why, myself of course.'

19.

The man who knows

'A most worthwhile exercise, would you not agree, Watson?' said Holmes brightly, once we had returned to the inviting warmth of Baker Street.

'It most certainly was, Holmes. I admit to not expecting you to tell Bates so fully of your suspicions.'

'He can be trusted,' said Holmes.' And, for once, I have been the recipient of as much information as I have myself imparted. Bates has proved a most unwitting informant. He may yet provide the final clue with which I can complete this sorry jigsaw of a case.'

'A link between O'Connor and McCarthy?'

'There are some cases, Watson, whose elements are so inextricably bound that one cannot see the whole for the layers which encompass it. Only once you have connected each thread in its correct place does the solution reveal itself.'

'And you have done that?' I asked eagerly.

'Not quite,' replied Holmes. 'But we are almost there. Now that we know O'Connor and McCarthy are confederates, we have but to discover what is binding them.'

'The killer is one of them?'

'Or perhaps both. Either one of them could also be assisting the actual murderer. I confess I am not yet in possession of all the pieces.'

'And what of the Duke?' I asked. 'Has he anything to do with matters?'

'I suspect not,' said Holmes, shaking his head. 'The most probable explanation is that O'Connor persuaded The Duke to enquire on his behalf as to what extent my investigations were succeeding. I suspect that my non-committal answers to Bates alerted O'Connor to the fact that I was being rather reticent on what I knew or suspected. He hoped that I would reveal to the Duke what I refused to tell his reporter, which of course I did not.'

Holmes smiled and took his violin from the table and began to play a rather mournful tune. Yet the alertness of his features as his long

161

fingers drew across the bow spoke of his hope that at last the case was beginning to unravel. He played for some time, his vacant gaze suggesting that he had drifted into some kind of reverie. Yet I knew this to be but a façade and that, like the whirring parts behind a slowly ticking clock-face, Holmes' mind was busy at work on the matter at hand. He continued playing long after I had retired to bed. My last thought before submitting to tiredness was that Sherlock Holmes appeared closer than ever to revealing the identity of Jack the Ripper.

The following morning, I entered the sitting room to find Holmes sat at his bureau. He was quite oblivious to my presence as he scribbled away furiously, muttering to himself as he did so.

'Ah, Watson!' he said, when he finally glanced up from his work. 'You will be pleased to know that the fog has lifted somewhat since last night.'

'You have been out already?' I asked, mindful of my friend's proclivity for late mornings.

'As you are aware, I abhor exercise for its own sake, Watson. But I took an extremely rare and rather brief constitutional as far as Marylebone Road some hours ago. The streets at that time, before the dirge of mankind has laid foot upon them, are quite extraordinary. The waves of watery sunlight pouring from the eves above and slowly bathing the London skyline are quite majestic.'

'The fresh air certainly seems to have invigorated you. I take it you are working on the article you propose to have published in The Star?'

'That is correct, Watson. I do not consider myself a wordsmith, as you know. Yet I confess to being rather happy that my offering will convey its intended message.'

'Which is?'

'I do not wish to spoil your enjoyment of reading it in its published form, Watson,' said Holmes with a smile.

In truth, I guessed that the purpose of the article was to give an entirely disingenuous account of Holmes' attempts at capturing the murderer, one with which he might procure some advantage. Although such an exercise suggested that the prose need be of an entirely perfunctory nature, Holmes took to the task with typical dogmatism. By late morning, he was surrounded by reams of discarded paper. It was lunchtime before he finally held up a collection of sheets, which I took from his satisfied expression to be the triumphant culmination of his efforts.

'Now, I'm afraid I must leave you to your own devices, Watson,' said Holmes, stuffing the foolscaps haphazardly into his coat pocket. 'I may be late in returning.'

With these words, he breezed past me and disappeared out of the door. I imagined that he was headed for the offices of The Star. Whatever his destination, he had not returned to Baker Street by early evening. At eight o'clock, Mrs Hudson entered the sitting room and passed me a telegram. It read:

I am on enquires and shall not return until tomorrow evening. Be sure to read tomorrow's edition of The Star. SH.

I raised a smile at the message and awaited Holmes' article with great interest. My chief concern, however, was the result of his enquires, and whether they had yet yielded a solution to the mystery.

The fog had returned the following morning, as a result of which I did not venture from the comfortable environs of Baker Street until late that afternoon. By this time, the choking mist had scattered into thin yellow wisps which swirled about the rooftops, merging in the sky above me with the shallow streaks of sunlight. I made my way to the newspaper vendor on the corner of Crawford Street and eagerly bought the early edition of The Star. I immediately found myself staring incredulously at the front page. There was the article which I had seen Holmes so studiously construct the previous day, introduced by a headline which could only have come from the pen of Benjamin Bates. It read as follows:

SHERLOCK HOLMES SEARCHES FOR JACK THE RIPPER

THE FAMOUS DETECTIVE ON HIS HUNT FOR MANIACAL

163

KILLER WHO STALKS LONDON'S EASTEND

Of the many cases which I have investigated in my career as a consulting detective, the one in which I find myself presently involved-the series of murders committed in Whitechapel- is by far the most baffling I have yet to encounter. Since the murder of Martha Tabram, I have believed that a lone killer was at large in Whitechapel. My fears were confirmed when he claimed a second victim on the last day of August. It became clear to me that this man would continue to kill until he was apprehended. I have since endeavoured, without success, to run him to ground. He has defied every attempt by both myself and the police to fathom his actions and reveal his identity. In the interest of the public well-being, I have decided to inform the readers of The Star what I know of Jack the Ripper.

I have been at each of the last four murder sites. On two occasions, the victim's corpse was still present while I searched in vain for a clue. On each occasion, I have been left baffled by the killer's ability to execute such a crime and disappear without a trace. What I do know of him is that he is right-handed, lives locally and that I believe the best description of him to be as follows:

Aged 30, height 5 ft 7 or 8 in, fair complexion and moustache, medium build and dressed in pepper-and–salt colour loose jacket, grey cloth peaked cap, red neckerchief tied in knot, appearance of a sailor.

The above was furnished to the police by a witness who saw a man of this description in Mitre Square just minutes the atrocity was committed. This man was in the company of a woman. When the witness was subsequently shown the body of the victim, he unhesitatingly identified her as the woman he had seen. Thus, the man he described is undoubtedly Jack the Ripper. To this end, I have searched the various docks about London. I have enquired with the masters of all ships as to any suspicious characters who may have absented themselves on the nights that the murders were committed. These investigations have been to no avail, and I can only conclude that he may not be a sailor, but a man who adopts their style of dress, either as a deliberate subterfuge or as part of his daily attire.

Opinion has been divided on the subject of the letter received by a news agency on 27th September, along with a postcard written in the same hand and received on 1st October. I was initially in disarray on the matter. Yet I am now certain that both communications were sent by the murderer. The letter received recently by the Chairman of the Whitechapel Vigilance Committee, containing what purported to be the kidney of Catherine Eddowes, appears to be a crude hoax.

When Jack the Ripper will strike next, I do not know. But I assure the readers of The Star that I am continuing my efforts to bring this elusive phantom to justice, however long it may take.

I completed reading Holmes' article just as I was turning onto Baker Street, giving a snort of laughter in approval at the words, for I saw in an instant their purpose.

'Splendid!' I cried, as I rolled up the newspaper and made my way home.

'I am pleased to see that you enjoyed it,' said a familiar voice from behind me.

'Holmes!' I exclaimed, spinning around to see my friend in front of me, a broad grin across his face.

'And what did you make of my foray into the world of journalism, Watson?'

'It is wonderful, Holmes,' I enthused. 'I could see what your game was from the first.'

'As I knew you would, Watson. But I would prefer to continue our discussion in the comfort of our sitting room.'

We returned to find that Mrs Hudson had lit the fire during my absence and were soon sitting back comfortably in our armchairs discussing Holmes' article.

'I hit upon the idea while we were in Bates' sitting room,' said Holmes, gesturing at the copy of The Star in front of me. 'It occurred to me that whoever had sent the letter forewarning of the next murder had almost certainly delivered the similarly brief message to Kidney. But what was this man's rationale? He would surely expect that upon receiving the letter, Kidney would seek out O'Connor and confront him about its allegation that it was he who had murdered Liz Stride? O'Connor would no doubt realise that our man was responsible for telling Kidney and immediately seek revenge.

Now, this leads me to the conclusion that the man who sent the letter to Kidney has no fear of O'Connor. He may, in fact, not even know the man directly. No, it is Jack the Ripper whom he fears. Kidney received the note on the evening of 17th October. That is the day after Lusk received the kidney, yet also the day before I received a message informing me of the date of the next murder. What do you make of that, Watson?'

'I am not sure what to think, Holmes.' I confessed.

'There is a chain to these letters, Watson. I refuse to believe it is mere coincidence that George Lusk received a kidney from Jack the Ripper the day before Kidney received his anonymous note. Taken with the letter we received the same day that Lusk presented the parcel to us, it presents a compelling case. Someone has discovered the identity of both Jack the Ripper and Elizabeth Stride's murderer, suggesting unequivocally that the two killers are somehow connected.'

'Assuming, of course that the man who murdered Stride is not Jack the Ripper,' I posited, much to the obvious annoyance of Holmes.

'I cannot see how the clumsy assault upon Stride was committed by the assured hand which slew the other women. No, the murders are distinct from each and yet they are somehow linked.'

'Can you be sure that the notes to yourself and Kidney are linked?'

'I can, Watson!' said Holmes. 'I went to see Kidney yesterday evening. He had been released from custody when O'Connor hadn't the audacity to formalise the charges against him. Kidney had had the foresight to keep the note. The paper is identical to that on which mine had been written, although the envelope differs. And it was written not in capitals, but in a man's hand.'

'Does that not raise the probability of a different author? I confess, Holmes, that you appear to have committed the cardinal sin of twisting the facts in order to fit a theory.'

166

'It fits my theory perfectly, Watson,' said Holmes, shaking his head dismissively. 'Our man writes a note to Kidney. He has very recently discovered the identity of Stride's murderer and, in his mortification, cares not a jot for the consequences of his actions. He unhesitatingly writes a note in his own hand, using his usual stock of writing paper and an accompanying envelope from the same set. He has no fear of being caught. When, however, he composes a similar letter to me two days later, he is infinitely more guarded. He is forced to use the same paper, but everything else about the missive betrays his great desire that he should not be suspected of authoring the communication.

'Between the first and second notes, therefore, I believe he made a further discovery. He realised the identity of Jack the Ripper. He was compelled to inform me of this fact, but in the interim had himself been the recipient of a letter which meant that he was now in fear of his life. It should all become clear to you now, Watson.'

'You do not mean-'

'I recognised the handwriting immediately. It was George Lusk's.'

20.

A disappearance

'Lusk!' I exclaimed. 'Do you mean to say that he was sat right here in our sitting room, all the while knowing the identity of the man for whom the entire country is searching?'

'I do, Watson.'

'Of course, that would explain his extreme agitation upon his arrival here with the parcel.'

'Exactly, Watson. Lusk was rather disingenuous when he said he considered it to be a hoax. In truth, I believe he *hoped* this to be the case, and that I would tell him as much upon examining it. Of course, I deduced immediately that it was genuine. My pronouncement of this fact left him in no doubt that the killer had sent it to him as a warning. Later that afternoon, once he had presented the parcel to the police, he pondered his next move. He decided that the best course of action was to deliver a note to me without delay advising, in lieu of the murderer's name, when he would strike next. How he came to know this, I cannot fathom. Nor can I imagine how he came to be in possession of Annie Chapman's ring.'

'Could it be that he is playing a very clever game, Holmes?'

'Some elaborate subterfuge, you mean?'

'It has occurred me that if, as you say, the murderer of Elizabeth Stride wished to have his foul deed attributed to Jack the Ripper, could not the reverse be possible? Could not the killer have sent the notes linking the murders together in the hope that if O'Connor was found to have murdered Stride, he would inevitably be suspected of having committed the other murders. Jack the Ripper would thus escape detection?'

'I commend you, Watson. I always find myself enthralled by your occasional dazzling bursts of lateral thinking. I of course considered the possibility that I was viewing events from entirely the wrong angle. My instincts told me that Lusk was up to something from the moment he first set foot in our sitting room. He subsequently proved

169

to be involved in an unseemly affair with Mary Kelly. Could he also be embroiled in the infinitely darker matter of murder? I do not think so.'

'But you admit to suspicions immediately upon meeting him,' I protested.

'For which, I recall, you admonished me at the time,' said Holmes with a wry smile. 'No, Lusk's terror when I assured him that the kidney had been sent by Jack the Ripper was undoubtedly genuine.'

'Then surely suspicion must fall upon Jack McCarthy?' said I.

'Precisely, Watson. I was sure to make enquires about the man during my absence yesterday.'

'Did you discover anything?' I asked eagerly.

'Jack McCarthy is as big a scoundrel as you may ever wish to meet. Those of whose opinion I sought were quite unanimous on that point. He has proved to be quite as interesting a character as I have encountered in some time. Of whether he is also a murderer, however, I am far less certain. Tomorrow, Watson, you and I shall pay a visit to Millers Court.'

The following morning, I entered the sitting room to find Sherlock Holmes had yet to rise and set about reading the morning papers which Mrs Hudson had left upon the table. A glance at The Telegraph, which was atop the thick stack of periodicals, revealed a headline which caused me to shudder.

'Holmes! Holmes!' I cried, racing to his bedroom door. I was met some seconds later by a wild-eyed and gaunt Holmes, whose dishevelled appearance and weary expression served notice that I had awoken him from his slumber.

'Watson! What on earth is the matter?' he asked in sleepy astonishment.

I placed the newspaper in his hands by way of response and waited as he scanned the front page, his eyes focusing on the gaudy print of the headline.

'Good Heavens, Watson!' he bellowed.

'What shall we do now?' I asked, gazing at his horrified countenance.

'I haven't the first idea, Watson,' said he, handing the paper back to me.

I again surveyed the front page. The headline which had so shocked me read as follows:

VIGILANCE COMMITTEE MAN LUSK MISSING

RIPPER KIDNEY CHAIRMAN NOT SEEN IN DAYS

George Lusk reported missing by housekeeper–
Received kidney from Jack the Ripper just days before.

The accompanying story provided details of how Lusk had not returned home the previous evening and then failed to attend a committee meeting at The Crown Public House. The alarm had been raised by his housekeeper and no trace of him could be found. His possessions had apparently been untouched, and no sign could be found that he had deliberately absconded.

'We must go to Alderney Road at once, Watson,' said Holmes. 'I expect you at the street door in five minutes.'

We were duly clattering east in a matter of minutes, Holmes still adjusting his attire as we turned along Marylebone Road.

It was a fresh morning, my breath casting smoky trails which merged with the wind swirling around us. What could have happened to George Lusk, and whether it was somehow connected to his apparent involvement with Jack the Ripper, I hadn't the least idea. But it appeared beyond the realms of coincidence that the man had vanished just as his role in the affair had come to our attention. As we arrived at our destination, a row of respectable three-story townhouses, we saw Inspector Lestrade outside one such dwelling. The Inspector appeared downcast as he skulked about the doorway chatting to a Constable. Yet his hard features eased into something of a smile when he observed us approach.

'Holmes! Dr Watson!' he greeted, offering his outstretched hand. 'You have read of this business, then?'

'A little more than twenty minutes ago,' said Holmes brusquely. 'A man receives a kidney from Jack the Ripper, yet you do not deem it important enough to inform me when he subsequently disappears? You disappoint me, Lestrade.'

'Don't you start, Holmes. I've already had that Bates fellow from The Star hunting around for a story. Is he a friend of yours?'

'We are acquainted,' said Holmes, casting me a knowing look. 'Now, what can you tell me?'

'Very little, Holmes. Mr Lusk left a renovation job at four o' clock yesterday afternoon and hasn't been seen since.'

'And where was this renovation taking place?' asked Holmes.

'Commercial Street. A place called the Royal Cambridge,' replied Lestrade, consulting his notebook.

'I see. The telegraph states that there was no sign he had taken any belongings with him. Is that the case?'

'The housekeeper has confirmed that his clothes and belongings are untouched, yes. She was here all afternoon and is positive that no-one could have entered the house without her knowing. Do you wish to see inside?'

'There is little point if he never returned home,' said Holmes. 'But please let me know immediately if you discover anything at all of interest.'

'Holmes,' said Lestrade, drawing closer to my friend. 'Is Lusk's disappearance connected with the kidney he received?'

'I believe it is, Lestrade. This business is darker than I ever imagined.'

'God Lord!' exclaimed the Inspector. 'What is going on, Holmes? Is Lusk dead?'

'I cannot rule out that prospect,' said Holmes. 'I shall be in touch.'

'Do you have any idea where Lusk might have gone, Holmes?' I asked as we made our way back to the hansom.

'We shall head to Millers Court, Watson,' he said. 'Halloa! And here is Bates himself.

'Holmes! Watson!' cried the reporter as he caught sight of us. 'I imagined you may turn up.'

'Was everyone informed of George Lusk's disappearance before us, Watson?' asked Holmes.

'Apologies for failing to pass on a tip this time,' replied Bates, having overheard Holmes' remark. 'For once, my contacts proved ineffectual in placing me ahead of the game.'

'Not to worry, Bates. Have you discovered anything of interest?'

'Nothing from next door. Of course, your Inspector Lestrade refused to tell me anything.'

'I assure you that he knows nothing of importance, Bates. Now, I take it that you have grasped the significance of Lusk's disappearance?'

'Of course,' replied Bates, looking about shiftily. 'But O'Connor's acting just the same, Holmes. I'll keep an eye on him, of course.'

'Good. Keep me informed. Watson and I are off to Millers Court.'

We arrived at Dorset Street from the Commercial Street end and made the short walk to McCarthy's shop. The light blue sky and wandering wisps of cloud above served only to make the dark shadows of the narrow street appear more foreboding as we passed the crumbling arch of Millers Court. When we arrived at the door to McCarthy's shop, Holmes peered in through the window before signalling for me to follow him inside.

The shop was little more than a small rectangular room, the floor of which was stuffed haphazardly with rough sacks containing various foodstuffs. The walls were adorned with several uneven shelves on which were placed dozens of dusty jars, each labelled with its contents. Our entrance attracted the attention of a young man, who entered through the back door and assumed a position behind the ancient wooden counter.

'Can I help you, Sirs? he asked cheerfully.

'I wish to see Mr McCarthy,' said Holmes, in an equally agreeable tone.

'He is upstairs. Are you friends of his?'

'That is correct. Might you be able to fetch him for us?'

'Of course. Whom shall I say is calling?'

'My name is Mr Kidney.'

'Just a moment, Mr Kidney.'

The youthful shop assistant disappeared through the back door and Holmes shot me a knowing smile as he surveyed my astonished expression. The young man presently re-emerged. He was followed closely by McCarthy, whose look of complete bewilderment must surely have eclipsed my own.

'What? What on earth?' he stammered.

'Good morning, Mr McCarthy,' said Holmes brightly.

'Tom, out the back with you. There's a good lad,' ordered McCarthy. The young man offered his employer a quizzical glance before obeying. 'Now, what do mean by this?'

'I was led to believe that this establishment was open to the public,' said Holmes.

'You're not Mr Kidney.' he rasped.

'I confess I am not. The young chap must have misheard me.'

'A likely story.'

'Nevertheless, I have to enquiry of the whereabouts of Mr George Lusk.'

'I don't know him.'

'You must surely be aware by now that I have knowledge to the contrary.'

'I advise you not to play games with me, Holmes.'

'Nor you with I, Mr McCarthy. You are aware that Mr Lusk has disappeared?'

'I read something of it this morning, yes.'

'You are not troubled by your friend's disappearance?'

'I am of course concerned for his safety.'

'You admit, then, to knowing him?'

McCarthy eyed Holmes narrowly, his countenance growing ever more sullen as he pondered the question.

'I was not truthful with you, Mr Holmes, when you visited here last. I'll not deny that. You know, of course, that George had become intimate with Mary. I merely wished to protect the reputation of my friend.'

'Highly commendable, Mr McCarthy. You have been a true friend to Mr Lusk. Would you happen to know of his present whereabouts?'

'I do not, Mr Holmes. I have not seen him for several days.'

'And he has not contacted you in that time? Today, perhaps?'

'I had not been downstairs yet this morning until my shop boy called me a few minutes ago. I have heard nothing from him, nor have I any idea where he might be.'

'Thank you, Mr McCarthy,' said Holmes brightly. 'I do not wish to take up any more of your time and shall bid you good morning.'

Holmes paused as we passed Millers Court, peering in through the gloom of the narrow archway. He signalled for me to wait as he walked along the passageway and into the court, surveying it for several seconds before shaking his head.

'There is nothing more we can do here, Watson,' he said.

'Do you have any clue where Lusk is?'

'I do not, Watson. But I do know that Jack McCarthy is an inveterate liar.'

'How can you tell?'

'His hands, Watson. His hands.'

For several days following the disappearance of George Lusk, Sherlock Holmes began to keep the irregular hours which became his hallmark when on the scent of a solution. The scattering of newspapers across out sitting room floor and crumbs of food upon the dining table became the only evidence that he been at Baker Street at all. During those brief moments when he was to be found in our rooms, he appeared bedraggled of dress and weary of senses. He would take a long bath, no doubt to reinvigorate his exhausted frame, before departing again at an ungodly hour without so much as a word. I never troubled him for a report on his progress, although each day that passed without the discovery of George Lusk made me ever more curious as to what could have happened to the man.

The papers failed to suspect that Lusk's disappearance was in any way associated with Jack the Ripper. My own knowledge of affairs convinced me that either the poor man had suffered for what he knew of the murderer's identity, or else had perpetrated the crimes himself and fled London. There seemed little doubt that T.P O'Connor had killed Elizabeth Stride and knew, therefore, something of the other murders. Yet Holmes had chosen not to inform Lestrade of this or run the man to ground himself. Perhaps he hoped that The Star editor would unwittingly lead him to Jack the Ripper, or would himself prove to be the murderer. I had no doubt that Holmes would capture this man, whoever he proved to be. Yet, as the eighth day of November drew ever closer, it seemed that his efforts were against the clock as much as the killer.

The third day of November, a Saturday, found me returning home from my practice in the late morning. A desultory number of clients and the ensuing boredom led me to idling about my consulting room with only my medical journals for stimulation. At eleven o'clock, I decided to close early and make my way to Baker Street to read the morning papers. As I reached the top of our staircase, I was surprised to hear the voice of Sherlock Holmes emanating from our sitting room. As I drew closer, I also heard the lighter tones of a woman, whom I assumed to be a client. Although Holmes had undertaken little other work since he began investigating the Jack the Ripper murders, he was often persuaded by those of a more wretched disposition to offer his assistance.

I knocked before entering, casting my head around the door and observing a young woman of some beauty sitting upon the sofa.

'Ah, Watson!' said Holmes, rising from his chair and clapping his hands together.

'Apologies if I am interrupting,' said I, glancing at his visitor, who met my gaze with a smile.

'Nonsense, Watson. I should be most grateful if you would be good enough to listen to this young lady's remarkable story.'

'Certainly, Holmes.'

Our visitor had soft blue eyes and a narrow, expressive face whose open features spoke of a keen intelligence which seemed quite at odds with her delicate, pale skin.

'This is Miss Mary Kelly,' announced Holmes, gesturing to the woman before me. I shot him an incredulous glance, recognising her at once as the lady whom we had seen in the company of George Lusk.

'Yes, Watson,' he said with a wry smile. '*The* Mary Kelly. Forgive my friend's startled countenance, Miss Kelly, for he has met Mr Lusk and is well acquainted with your story. Allow me to introduce Dr John Watson.'

'Good morning to you, Doctor,' said Mary Kelly brightly, in a broad Irish lilt.

'Miss Kelly has visited us upon the matter of George Lusk's continued disappearance.'

'I am aware from the papers that he has yet to be found,' said I. 'Have you any hope of finding him, Holmes?'

'Alas, the whereabouts of George Lusk are proving beyond my usual methods, Watson. If Miss Kelly had not been so forceful in her dismissal of the possibility, I should think the most likely scenario would be that he had purposely absented himself and wished not to be found. It is notoriously difficult to locate a man once he has it in his head to escape the public gaze and vanish from sight.'

'But you do not believe that this is the case, Miss Kelly?' I asked.

'It cannot be, Doctor. I had arranged to meet him on the night of his disappearance. He did turn up and I have heard nothing of him since. He would never leave his children or me without a word as to his whereabouts. Something must have happened to him.'

'It is certainly a puzzle, Holmes,' said I. 'Could someone not have kidnapped him?'

'Why should anyone wish to do that?' asked Mary Kelly, before my friend could answer. I glanced at Holmes, whose expression made it evident that he had yet to inform Kelly of her lover's apparent connection with the murders.

'Miss Kelly, there is something which I must now tell you that I feel may have a direct bearing upon the current disappearance of Mr Lusk.'

Holmes recounted the suspicions which had caused him to investigate Lusk's activities. He explained that the kidney which Lusk had received was probably a warning from the murderer. That Lusk had subsequently sent letters to both Holmes and Michael Kidney proved that he was somehow connected with events. Mary Kelly's incredulity as Holmes recounted what must have appeared a most unlikely sequence of events, quickly became replaced by unbridled anger. She of course declined to accept the notion that George Lusk had had any involvement with the matter. Only when Holmes showed her the letter which Lusk had sent to Michael Kidney did Mary Kelly grow silent in mute astonishment, evidently recognising her lover's hand.

'But I don't understand,' she stammered. 'Why did he not say anything?'

'If I am correct, Miss Kelly, George Lusk did not discover until several days before his disappearance the information which he then conveyed in the letters he sent to both myself and Michael Kidney. By the time he composed the latter, he was in fear of his life and did not, I imagine, wish to endanger your own by involving you in the business in which he had suddenly found himself.'

'But where is he?' she cried, tears coursing her pale cheeks.

Holmes, who was not often responsive to such showings of feminine sensibilities, surveyed Mary Kelly with a rather quizzical expression.

'I believe that Jack McCarthy may know the answer to that question,' said he.

'Jack McCarthy?' she asked in disbelief. 'You are saying he is Jack the Ripper?'

'I do not necessarily suggest that, Miss Kelly. But I do believe that he knows something of the murders and, I should imagine, what has become of Mr Lusk.'

'You have visited him, I take it?'

'I have. He has denied any knowledge of the matter, of course.'

'It is preposterous to suggest that Mr McCarthy has kidnapped George or harmed him in any way. They are friends.'

'I confess to having observed McCarthy over the last few days, only to find that he has barely ventured beyond Dorset Street. I am certain that he has not visited Mr Lusk, wherever he may be, during that time.'

'You see?' said Miss Kelly. 'He can have had nothing to do with the matter.'

'May I ask, Miss Kelly, if each of the rooms in Millers Court is currently occupied?'

'Yes, they are,' she replied, appearing puzzled by Holmes' question. I confess that I myself was unsure as to its purpose.

'Thank you, Miss Kelly,' said Holmes.

Holmes concluded the interview with Mary Kelly with the promise that he would devote the full extent of his energies to finding George Lusk. He implored Miss Kelly to contact him the moment she heard anything which may assist in this endeavour.

'Are you hopeful, Holmes?'

'I confess that this case perplexes me, Watson. I had hoped that Miss Kelly may bring with her some avenues of enquiry which I had not yet considered. Instead, she has closed several existing ones. I fear that the disappearance of George Lusk may yet defeat me.'

21.

8th November

In the days following Mary Kelly's visit to Baker Street, Sherlock Holmes was in turn as baffled, vexed and yet unwaveringly focused as I had ever seen him. Never a man to whom the conventions of conversation and cordiality were something to be given any particular regard, Holmes became quite insufferable as 8th November approached. He stomped about our rooms with the vilest of tempers, quite oblivious to my presence as he fretted and fussed over the whereabouts of George Lusk and the enigmatic letter which he had sent Holmes shortly before his disappearance. Often in those dark days, I observed Holmes clutching the offending missive, gazing at the scrawled capitals with a look of utter despair. What was evidently meant as a warning by Lusk became an impenetrable challenge.to my friend's professional sensibilities. I could see from his inexorable expression that Holmes had become taunted by the words, his very being appearing weighted with the prospect of defeat.

The morning of the eighth began with a heavy rain which awoke me with its ferocity as it lashed against the windowpanes. At ten o'clock, I found myself reading the morning papers in the sitting room. Holmes had yet to rise and Mrs Hudson again expressed concern at his recent refusal to eat nought but the most meagre of morsels. Her frustration at his ingratitude became replaced with anxiety for his health upon Holmes refusing even his most favoured of our landlady's dishes. I had also become anxious for my friend's well-being, for it appeared that every fibre of Holmes' being was alerted to capturing Jack the Ripper.

It was not until approaching the hour of eleven that Holmes finally emerged from his bedroom.

'Morning, Watson,' he said cheerfully, sweeping into the room with alacrity. 'It is a most miserable day.'

'Indeed it is, Holmes,' I agreed, observing the heavy streaks of rain smeared across the windows.

'I sincerely hope that such foul elements are not a portent of more sinister events to follow, Watson. You know, of course, that today is when George Lusk believed Jack the Ripper would next strike?'

'I could not possibly fail to notice these last few days, Holmes.'

'Forgive me, my dear Watson. I fear I have proved quite intolerable of late.'

'Think nothing of it, Holmes. I only hope that you can effect an end to these murders.'

'Thank you, Watson. It shall certainly not be for want of effort were Jack the Ripper to escape our clutches tonight. I fear it is time I acquired some help to that end. Can you be ready in a quarter of an hour?'

'Most certainly.'

Minutes later, with Holmes forsaking the sustenance offered him by our landlady, we were in a hansom on our way to visit Scotland Yard.

'I fear that the time has come when I must reveal matters to Lestrade,' said Holmes, his voice barely audible above the howl of the rain. 'I dread to think how he will react to such intelligence.'

Holmes' consternation was proved correct, for Lestrade met the belated news of George Lusk's letters with the utmost apoplexy.

'And you did not think to tell me of these before?' asked Lestrade incredulously.

'I felt it best to conduct my own enquires before troubling you.'

'Did you now?' seethed Lestrade, his thin frame shaking with anger. 'And where have these enquires taken you? Here, where you should have delivered them in the first place. I could arrest you for withholding evidence, Holmes.'

'We both know you will not do that, Lestrade,' said Holmes calmly, ignoring the Inspector's rage. 'The fact of the matter is that you would have dismissed the letters as unconnected hoaxes and failed to grasp their importance. I am here now because my own efforts to capture this man have resulted in failure. The only person I feel could have assisted me to that end has disappeared. I believe that George Lusk knew something of the murders, Lestrade, and that tonight there will be another one.'

182

'And what do you wish me to do?' he sighed, a look of exasperation swept across his features.

'I wish you to place every officer at your disposal on duty tonight in Whitechapel. When he strikes, there must be a policeman within seconds of the crime ready to catch him in the act. There is nothing else for it.'

'You are sure he will strike tonight?'

'George Lusk sent his message to me at what he considered to be great personal risk. That he has subsequently disappeared, apparently against his own will, speaks for the importance of his communication. I would not wish his efforts to be in vain, Lestrade. Tonight, you have a chance to capture Jack the Ripper.'

'Very well, Holmes,' said the Inspector. 'I will place as many extra men on duty tonight as I can, although I dread to think how I shall explain it to the Commissioner. Do you have any idea where the man will commit his deed?'

'Alas I do not, Lestrade. It is evident that the victims lead their killer to the place where they are then slain. I therefore suggest that your men search the darkest alleyways and quietest thoroughfares, for it is in these that Jack the Ripper plies his trade.'

'I shall trust your judgement, Holmes,' said Lestrade. 'Let us hope that we meet with some success for our efforts.'

'Thank you, Lestrade,' said Holmes solemnly.

The morning rain failed to abate as evening drew, appearing only to have worsened as the last strains of light faded into blackness. I surveyed the wild conditions through the sitting room window, grateful for the warmth of Baker Street on such a night.

'The weather has taken a turn for the worse, Watson. I fear we shall get quite wet this evening,' said Holmes.

'You do not propose to venture out in such a storm, surely?' I asked in astonishment.

'I'm afraid that we have no choice, Watson. I should not like to think of a single courtyard or passage going unobserved tonight.'

'You mean to assist the police efforts?'

'Most certainly, Watson. If George Lusk can risk his life in order to impart such a warning, we cannot let a little rain dissuade us from acting upon it.'

I could provide no argument to such a noble sentiment and once suitably attired, joined Holmes as we waited on a rain-soaked Baker Street for a cab. Minutes later, we were heading east, the wheels of our hansom sloshing noisily through the mud and puddles. Where Holmes planned to begin his search, I did not know. Yet he instructed our driver to stop along Whitechapel High Street, just on the corner of Commercial Street.

'The axis of Whitechapel, Watson,' he said, gesturing ahead of us. Commercial Street is the main artery which must provide our starting point. We shall scour the alleyways which branch off it in the hope of capturing our man.'

'But it will be like searching for a needle in a haystack, Holmes' I lamented, mindful of the warren of thoroughfares with which the area was littered. 'Even you cannot possibly know them all.'

'Indeed, I do not,' said Holmes. 'I daresay there is not a man alive who does. We can but hope to stumble across him through sheer good fortune. It is regrettable that we find ourselves reduced to such a haphazard pursuit, Watson. But I confess to seeing little more that can be achieved tonight.'

It struck me at that moment that for all his deductive powers and intuitive genius, Sherlock Holmes was possessed also of the most tireless energies of any man I had ever known.

We trudged about the side streets and thoroughfares, the slight easing of the rain doing little to raise our spirits as we inspected the foulest, darkest corners of the metropolis. There we were amongst the urchins and idlers; those downtrodden souls whose snarling visage and loathsome aspect spoke of mortals stripped bare of the last vestiges of humanity. They were huddled in the doorways of dilapidated houses, their hardened faces twisted grimly against the miserable elements and appearing as though mere imperfect effigies of the human form. Yet their eyes, as soft and searching as any I had seen, told their own miserable stories with unspoken eloquence. That these poor creatures lived lives of such unbridled misery and wanton hardship mere miles from the snug comfort of Baker Street made their appalling struggle yet more unpalatable.

Yet amongst these woeful alleyways, we could discover no sign of Jack the Ripper. At approaching one o'clock, we emerged purblind from one such lane onto Commercial Street into the hazy glow of a streetlamp, thoroughly soaked and defeated. Holmes' determined countenance had remained throughout our grim task, as though scarcely affected by either the battering elements or the futile nature of our search.

'You look quite the picture of misery, Watson!' he declared, surveying me in the flickering streaks of gaslight.

'I am fine, Holmes,' I protested. 'I have suffered far worse hardships in Afghanistan.'

'Yet I would wager you have never before laid eyes upon such squalor as that of Whitechapel when its vilest quarters are veiled in darkness.'

'I confess that I have not, Holmes. It seems quite impossible that we are so close to home and yet seemingly in another world entirely.'

'It is a remarkable yet little-observed fact, Watson, that London is possessed of the most microcosmic kaleidoscope of humanity in the known world. A distance of five miles might be judged as five thousand if measured by the salubrity of one's surroundings. Such is the violence to be found in Flower and Dean, to provide but one example, that even during the hours of daylight no policeman would dare to enter it unaccompanied. Yet, from so unspeakable a spot, one might hear the clatter of carriages upon the cobbles of Westminster.'

'Well, I am certainly glad that tonight's adventure is a solitary escapade,' said I, rubbing my hands in the chill.

'Let us hope that proves to be the case, Watson. Although I fear it is not yet over. We shall head north towards Spitalfields. There, the lodging houses are rife. Our man might have his pick of those women who haven't the required pennies to seek shelter.'

Thus, we made our way slowly along Commercial Street, arriving on Dorset Street some minutes later as the rain returned fiercer than ever, pounding spitefully against the black walls either side of us. I followed Holmes as he ran across to Millers Court, seeking refuge from the downpour in the narrow passage.

'It is quite the thunderstorm,' said he, brushing rivulets of water from his sodden coat. 'We shall take refuge here until it eases a little.'

I peered into the court, which was illuminated only by the faint glow of a gas lamp. We waited in silence for several minutes until at last the downpour abated and we made our way out of the passage. Holmes surveyed the windows above McCarthy's shop and I followed his gaze, observing the light visible through the curtained windows.

'Our friend is not out tonight at any rate, Watson,' said Holmes, staring up at the window.

'This weather might keep anyone indoors,' I said, immediately drawing Holmes' gaze upon me.

'It is entirely possible, of course, that the murderer will have been persuaded to forego his efforts in consequence of the atrocious weather. In which case, our efforts this evening have been quite wasted.'

As we walked to the opposite end of Dorset Street, I noticed that the tireless spirits of Holmes appeared to have at last dampened. He would carry out his thankless task to the end, of course. Yet his zest for the endeavour seemed extinguished as he trudged ahead of me. I would have dared not suggest it at that moment, but I questioned whether he believed he had been tricked into this fruitless labour. As he stared at the blackness ahead of him, it must have seemed to Sherlock Holmes as though Jack the Ripper was a mere phantom who would never be caught.

We turned onto Crispin Street, Holmes nearly colliding with a portly figure walking in the opposite direction. As my eyes focused upon the man, I saw to my astonishment that it was Inspector Abberline.

'My goodness!' he said upon recognising us. 'Mr Holmes and Dr Watson! I hardly expected to bump into you here.'

'The surprise is mutual, Inspector,' said Holmes. 'It is quite a night to be strolling about Spitalfields.'

'I confess that these murders have quite taken a hold of me, Mr Holmes. My daily work has ceased to quell my desire for catching the man responsible. Of late, I have found myself traversing these streets until very nearly dawn in the hope of laying my hands upon the fiend. I have yet to find the slightest trace, of course. But I cannot rest in bed with the knowledge that he may be out here somewhere, seeking yet poor another victim. Might I ask what brings you here in such inclement weather?'

'I believe we are possessed of the same instincts, Inspector Abberline. Lestrade has no doubt informed you that I received a warning of a further murder tonight.'

'I am aware of his deploying extra men on your say so. Although I confess that I hardly expected you to join the hunt yourself, Mr Holmes. Have you any success to show for your efforts?'

'Alas, I have found nothing,' said Holmes.

'Not to worry, Mr Holmes. The man has defeated us all. At least we can say we tried, if nothing else.'

'I hope to do more than that,' said Holmes, casting the Inspector a withering look. We bade the Inspector goodnight and continued on our way.

We began a gradual descent back to the southern end of Commercial Street, our spirits dissipating only further as each rookery yielded not the slightest prospect of finding our quarry. It was well past two o' clock when Holmes finally admitted defeat and we made our way to Leman Street Police Station. From the duty sergeant, we learned that no wire had been received that evening to report the discovery of a murder. It had, by all accounts, been an unusually quiet night in consequence of the appalling weather. The sergeant arranged for a cab and minutes later we were heading back to Baker Street in dejected silence.

Upon our return, Holmes flung his sodden coat angrily across an armchair. He stood for some time with his arms folded, peering vacantly through the window at the quiet street below. Eventually he turned to me with as solemn an expression as I had ever known him to possess.

'I have been defeated, Watson,' said he. 'Tonight belongs to Jack the Ripper, whoever he is.'

'But he has not killed, Holmes,' I replied. 'You have failed at nothing.'

'At nothing?' bellowed Holmes, his face contorted in rage. 'He has reduced me to wandering the soaked streets of Whitechapel in the

187

blind hope of capturing him. He has played a game with me, Watson. And he has defeated me.'

'You will catch him, Holmes,' I said, attempting to quell my friend's temper. 'I have no doubt.'

'But when, Watson? That is the question I ask myself. How many more women must be slain before he is unmasked? Confound the man! The clues have run to nought. I cannot fathom it at all.'

'No-one could have done more to catch him, Holmes,' I said at last, breaking the dreadful silence of our sitting room. 'I will say again that you have failed at nothing.'

'I did not succeed, Watson,' he said in a low voice. 'Therefore, I have failed. That is the only remaining possibility.'

'You did the only thing you could possibly have done, Holmes. You could not ignore the note warning of another murder.'

'Ah, the note!' said Holmes, turning around and meeting my gaze with a grim smile. 'Of course, I could not ignore it. I have been played for a fool, Watson, and I confess that I do not like it.'

'You think it was a hoax?'

'I do not know what to think,' he said wearily. 'I shall attempt to put this evening's disaster behind me and think upon it tomorrow.'

Without another word, Holmes retired to his bedroom, appearing every inch the defeated man as he brushed past me. Despite the fatigue of our ill-fated adventure, I slept little that night. Several times I heard the footsteps of Holmes wandering about our sitting room, his wounded sensibilities evidently disallowing slumber.

The following morning, I awoke in rather a stupor, exhausted by both the exploits of the previous night and my inability to obtain more than a fitful sleep by way of recovery. By a little before eleven o'clock, sufficiently fortified by one of Mrs Hudson's cooked breakfasts and having extinguished the last pernicious effects of my exertions, I decided to go out in search of the morning papers. Upon my return, I found Holmes standing at the window in his dressing gown, idly observing the comings and goings of Baker Street.

'I am always in wonder at nature when a nightly storm presages so gentle a morning sun. I cannot observe the glistening sheen upon the pavements retreat at the advancing yellow rays without a thought for the fact that we are but all victims of the same natural order. Good morning, Watson,' said Holmes, turning to greet me. 'I am pleased to see that one of us at least has shaken off the spectre of so ghastly a night.'

'I feel better for the mild morning,' said I, placing the newspapers upon the table.

'A fresh start, shall we say, Watson?' said Holmes. 'I shall be thankful for a bath and some breakfast before I consider what our next move may be.'

Before I could reply, Mrs Hudson appeared in the doorway, struggling to hold back an urchin-faced youth who was attempting to free himself from her grasp.

'I am sorry, Mr Holmes, Dr Watson. This young imp barged his way past me as I opened the front door. I told him you would not be up to receiving visitors.'

'It is quite alright, Mrs Hudson,' I said, observing the young boy wriggling furiously in an attempt to free himself. 'Let him speak.'

The poor lad collected his breath as he glanced between Holmes and I, as though unsure of whom to address.'

'I was told to ask for Mr Holmes,' he said uncertainly.

'You are addressing him,' said Holmes. 'What is the matter, young man?'

'Mr Bates said to bring this to you and make sure I put it into your hands and yours only,' said the boy haltingly, as though reciting a script. He held out a folded piece of paper in his small, filthy hands. Holmes, with a quizzical glance towards myself, took the paper and began to read. In an instant, my friend's pale features convulsed into a look of thunderstruck terror as he stared at the message in his hands.

'There has been another murder, Watson,' he said eventually.

'What?' I cried. 'But that is impossible!'

'It is not, Watson,' said Holmes darkly. 'Bates is there now.'

'Where?'

'Millers Court. They already have a name for the poor woman.'

'Who is it, Holmes?'

'It is Mary Kelly, Watson.'

22.

Millers Court

Such was my astonishment at these words that our journey to Dorset Street appeared but a hazy dream. It seemed extraordinary that the pretty young woman who had been in our sitting room mere days before had fallen victim to Jack the Ripper. Bates' messenger explained to Holmes what scant details he knew of the murder. It appeared that Mary Kelly had been discovered earlier that morning in her room at Millers Court. The young boy had been attracted by the commotion and Bates had offered him a shilling and his first ride in a hansom to send word of the deed to Baker Street. When pressed by Holmes, our companion recalled that everyone at the scene was astonished by the horror to which they had borne witness.

'An older man with a beard said it was the worst of the lot,' he assured us.

'Abberline,' said Holmes, nodding his head.

As we approached the western end of Dorset Street, I observed the furore of which the boy had spoken. The entrance to Millers Court was obscured by dozens of policemen guarding the passage against a great throng of sightseers. I saw Bates amongst the rabble, eagerly scribbling away as several people around him competed for his attention. As we got closer, I observed that every face was quite aghast as they discussed the murder. Holmes barged his way through the crowd, telling one of the policemen that he wished to see Inspector Lestrade. The Constable viewed Holmes dubiously before disappearing into the court, duly returning some minutes later with the vexed Inspector.

'You have heard then,' said Lestrade solemnly, as he emerged through the passage to greet us. 'Come with me.'

We hurried through a gap made for us by the obliging officers and followed Lestrade up the passage.

'What can you tell me, Lestrade?' asked Holmes. The Inspector stopped and turned to my friend.

'It is worse than you could imagine,' he said, shaking his head.

The small yard was packed with policemen, none of whom acknowledged us as we entered. I nudged Holmes upon seeing McCarthy standing at the back of his shop, his hands covering his face in horror.

'There is nothing left of her,' he murmured as we approached. 'It looked more like the work of a devil than a man.'

'Tell me everything that you know, Lestrade,' implored Holmes as the Inspector drew beside us.

'Thomas Bowyer, Mr McCarthy's assistant, knocked on the door at about a quarter to eleven. Mary Kelly was behind in the rent and he wanted to catch her before she went to the Lord Mayor's show. He got no reply, so went around the side there and peered in through the window. He saw the remains of the poor woman lying on her bed.'

'May we see her?' asked Holmes.

'You may, Holmes. But I warn both of you that even the doctors drew aghast when they first saw her. Poor Bowyer is quite delirious with shock.'

We followed Lestrade, who received the muttered permission of Inspector Abberline before ushering us around the corner. There were two windows, the nearest of which had a broken pane.

'The door is bolted shut. But if you just place your hand through the pane and pull the curtain back, you shall see her.'

Holmes stooped down and followed the Inspector's instructions. He made no sound, but drew himself back upright seconds later, his face so white and terrified that I feared he was about to collapse into my arms.

'Dear God!' he cried, reeling back in horror. 'Prepare yourself, Watson.'

I steeled myself for a moment before slowly pulling back the curtain and peering inside. When my eyes had become accustomed to the dim light, I saw before me on an ancient bedstead the grotesque remains of Mary Kelly. Her torso and lower extremities had been hacked so frenziedly that they had become mere ragged mounds of flesh, while the poor woman's left arm had been placed by her killer into the cavity of her eviscerated stomach. The legs had been skinned so savagely that the bone was quite visible, while such was the wound to the poor woman's throat that I could scarcely be certain her head had not been entirely cut off.

On the bedside table was a pile of flesh which had been plundered from the body and placed there by her murderer. Yet I found myself gazing upon the face of Mary Kelly, which had been hacked into an unrecognisable map of gashes. So complete was the evisceration of her pretty features that it was impossible to see where the flesh ended and the cuts began. Only her soft blue eyes remained as a vestige of the woman who had once existed. They stared peacefully at me, oblivious to the surrounding horror. I recoiled in disgust at the awful spectacle, gasping for breath as though the unspeakable sight had caused me some momentary apoplexy.

'Are you alright, Watson?' asked Holmes, observing my distress.

'I am fine, Holmes,' I replied, steadying myself against the wall. 'It is quite the most appalling thing I have ever seen.'

'It is a most ghastly sight. I shudder to think any man capable of so furious a rage that he might do that to a young woman,' said Holmes. 'This is not crime, Watson. This is the darkest extremities of the human condition laid manifest before us. We are searching for a monster, not a man.'

We stood in silence at these words for some time before Inspector Abberline approached us.

'It is an awful affair, gentlemen,' he said softly. 'How we catch a fellow like this, I cannot imagine.'

'Surely the killer's conduct must betray his madness?' said Lestrade. 'No man could commit such an atrocity without effect upon his own condition.'

'I believe you are right, Lestrade,' said Abberline in agreement.

'I fear that you are both wrong,' said Holmes, drawing the curious gaze of both Inspectors. 'From the first, I have believed that the man we sought was an assassin of quite remarkable calm and cunning. He is perfectly able to detach the abominable sensibilities which cause such frenzied attacks from his daily aspect. If he were to appear here at this very moment, we would be amazed to discover that he was the perpetrator of the grotesque sight which lays beyond this window.'

'And do you have any clue as to who this mysterious man is, Mr Holmes?' asked Abberline.

'I have several, Inspector. But the ordinariness of the man is his greatest deterrent against capture.'

'Well, we shall soon see if he has left us a clue amongst the carnage of Mary Kelly's room,' said Lestrade. 'He surely cannot have committed such an act without leaving some trace of himself.'

Yet we were required to wait in order to test Inspector Lestrade's theory. Amongst the many ideas which had abounded in newspaper correspondence pages since the outset of the murders, an enterprising bloodhound breeder from Scarborough had suggested the use of that same canine in the capture of the killer. Trials were conducted in Hyde Park, with no less an illustrious personage than Sir Charles Warren used as appropriate 'bait'. When these proved successful, it was a common belief that the dogs were to be domiciled in London, ready to pounce upon the scene of the next tragedy. Thus, Abberline had received intimation that the bloodhounds were to be brought to Millers Court and, at Dr Phillips' request, did not order the door to be broken in until their arrival. It was not until half past one that Superintendent Arnold arrived with the news that the dogs were unavailable. He immediately ordered that the door be forced open.

McCarthy, still rather shaken, but having been fortified with a brandy, obliged by obtaining an axe from the back of his shop and breaking down the door himself.

We followed Abberline as he and Lestrade led the way into the tiny room, treading slowly across the filthy bare floorboards. The four of us squeezed just inside the doorway and surveyed the scene, careful to avert our eyes from the mutilated remains of Mary Kelly. There was a rickety old table and two accompanying chairs in the centre of the room, while a disused washstand slung in the corner completed her meagre furnishings.

Holmes' interest immediately focused on the fireplace opposite the door. I observed it to contain the ashes of a rather large fire. Holmes knelt to inspect it, pulling from the grate what appeared to be the charred rim and wirework of a hat.

'What have you there, Holmes?' asked Lestrade.

'The remains of a lady's hat, Lestrade,' said Holmes. 'There is also a piece of burned velvet, which I believe came from a woman's jacket.'

'Do you think they belonged to Mary Kelly?' asked Lestrade.

'I have no idea, Lestrade,' said Holmes. 'Although the fire was certainly recent.'

'It evidently raged rather fiercely,' said Lestrade, drawing besides Holmes and examining a kettle placed beside the fire. 'To judge from this melted kettle spout. I suppose you overlooked that, Holmes?'

'I did nothing of the sort. And what, my dear Lestrade, makes you so certain that the fire, whose ashes we can still observe, caused the melted spout? The kettle may have stood in its damaged state for many months before this morning. No, it is the fire which intrigues me.'

'Did the killer use it to destroy something?' I asked.

'Perhaps,' said Holmes. 'Although I cannot fathom what.'

'He evidently burned the clothing in order to provide the light by which he might work,' said Lestrade, glancing triumphantly between Holmes and I.

'Again, you grasp blindly at the obvious, Inspector,' replied Holmes, hardly averting his gaze from the fireplace. 'What do we know of our man? That he can operate in the darkest, most hazardous conditions and with the most dazzling disregard of capture. I fail to see that the darkness of the room would cause him to light so raging a blaze by which to illuminate his grisly task.

'Consider the broken window, not to mention how cold it was last night. I would guess that Mary Kelly herself lit the fire, and that it was already burning when her killer entered the room. I suggest that he merely stoked the blaze by the meagre addition of the clothing, whose remnants are still evident in the grate.'

'I see,' blustered Lestrade, turning away from the fire. 'Well, I suppose that is certainly a workable theory.'

'And what of this overcoat?' I asked, following the Inspector to the centre of the tiny room.

On the back of a chair was a man's black overcoat, which Holmes began to examine.

'It smells of smoke,' he said presently. 'But more strongly on the side facing the fire. It evidently remained undisturbed while the murder took place. In all probability, it belongs to Miss Kelly's erstwhile paramour.'

'The Barnett fellow? He walked out after an argument with Kelly some days ago,' said Lestrade. 'We haven't yet found him.'

'You intrigue me, Inspector,' said Holmes. 'But I doubt that Barnett would leave his coat behind on so foul a night. I'm afraid we must hope Dr Phillips here finds something more tangible from his examination of the body.'

At mention of his name, Dr Phillips availed us of his preliminary findings. He was of the opinion that Mary Kelly had died between the hours of five and six that morning. Aside from this fact, Dr Phillips could only confirm the unbridled fury evident upon the corpse. He desisted from any other further examination of the body until it had been taken to the mortuary. Holmes inspected the remainder of the room, yet found nothing which afforded him the least clue.

At four o'clock, a carrier's cart arrived to remove the tortured remains of Mary Kelly into a filthy shell. The crowd outside Millers Court swelled as word spread of this event. I observed many of them attempting to break the cordon of police in order to catch a glimpse of proceedings. Yet as the shell was taken to the awaiting van, the crowd stood in respectful silence. Men doffed their caps while women could be observed shedding tears for the poor woman. We departed Dorset Street shortly after Kelly's remains had been removed, our hansom slowed by the crowds of people who remained for some time after that solemn event.

'What do you make it all, Watson?' asked Holmes, when we were back in our sitting room that evening.

'It was awful, Holmes. I have never seen anything like it.'

'And of the fact that it was Mary Kelly who was slain in so appalling a manner? Do you not find it beyond coincidence?'

'It did strike me as incredible that a woman who was sat in this very room not more than a matter of days ago has fallen victim to the murderer. But Mary Kelly was a woman accustomed to the streets of

Whitechapel at night. I suppose it could have been her as much as any of her sort.'

'Yet she was not killed in the street, Watson,' said Holmes. 'She was murdered in her own bed. That fact alone surely marks the circumstances of her death as somewhat unique to the previous killings. Mary Kelly was involved in an affair with George Lusk. He has gone missing and now his lover is found ripped to pieces in her bed. Something is not right, Watson.'

'I confess that I see your point, Holmes. It appears as though they are each at the centre of this mystery. And what of Jack McCarthy? The door to the room was locked. If anyone had a key to it, surely it was him?'

'My ears pricked up when Lestrade mentioned a locked room,' said Holmes. 'But I quickly realised it was of no actual importance. I am, as you are aware, something of an expert on the matter of locks. I saw immediately that Mary Kelly's door was possessed of a spring-lock. It is a type which cannot be opened without a key once the door has been closed. Anyone, therefore, could have left the room and effectively locked the door simply by pulling it behind them.

'The broken window also provided a clue. Judging by the numerous finger marks upon the outer side of the curtain, today was not the first time that it had been handled by someone reaching in through the window. The matter thus appears simply that the key had been lost by either Kelly or Barnett. They were loath to seek a replacement from McCarthy in consequence of their rent arrears. He did not have a spare key at any rate, to judge from his assault upon the door this afternoon.'

'That would appear to explain matters,' I said. 'But why then did you allow McCarthy to destroy his own property with an axe?'

'I wished to observe if he was aware of Kelly's method of entering the room. He was not.'

'Do you suspect him?' I asked.

'He did not murder Mary Kelly. Of that I am quite certain. I observed him closely, Watson. Everything from his horror when recounting his viewing of the body, to his trembling hand when wielding his axe spoke unmistakeably of a man in the midst of some great shock.

I believe he has something to hide, but not the murder committed on his own property this morning.'

'Is there not a chance that we have viewed this affair quite erroneously, Holmes? Could not Lusk be the killer and McCarthy the man charged with shielding him?'

'I must confess that the same theory formed itself in my own mind on our way back to Baker Street. I certainly cannot discount the possibility. His disappearance, of course, may be of his own manufacture. And the date which he gave for the next murder was certainly prophetic. If he is not the murderer, then he is certainly involved in these atrocities to some degree. Yet he surely would not have sent me the note had he something to hide? I confess that this business grows ever more puzzling, Watson.'

'And what about the boyfriend?'

'Barnett? Yet another twist in the tale. He would have known McCarthy, of course, and may have somehow become embroiled in events. Is it yet another coincidence that he left Millers Court just days before Kelly's murder?'

'He may have discovered Mary's affair with Lusk.'

'Precisely, Watson! What is there to say that he did not first dispose of Lusk before murdering Kelly? Perhaps during an argument about her infidelity?'

'I am beginning to favour that conclusion, Holmes.'

'It has much to recommend it, Watson. Although it must remain a mere theory until we can procure evidence to support it. Barnett may be found tomorrow and proved entirely innocent. For now, we must await Lestrade's enquires and hope that he turns up something of value. I also hold out expectations of Bates to keep us updated with the rumours which will no doubt be abounding the streets of Whitechapel in the wake of the murder. At present, we are held hostage to the vagaries of fate.'

The words of Holmes proved curiously prophetic, for Lestrade paid us a visit late the following afternoon. I was unusually pleased to see the Inspector, for the police had padlocked Mary Kelly's room, with Holmes being denied by Lestrade's superiors from gaining access to Millers Court whatsoever. I spent a long morning watching Holmes pacing up and down our sitting room, wondering aloud what was happening, while lamenting the fact that he was not there to observe proceedings. Lestrade had promised to update him on matters as soon as he was able to absent himself from his enquires.

Thus, Holmes was constantly peering out of the window, hoping to see the Inspector making his way along Baker Street. Upon his eventual arrival, Holmes quickly ushered Lestrade into a seat, waiting impatiently for him to remove his coat and make himself comfortable so that the Inspector could commence his account.

'It has been quite a day, Holmes,' sighed the Inspector. 'Firstly, I have just had the post-mortem report from Dr Phillips and Dr Bond. They disagree on the time of death, but it looks as though Mary Kelly died earlier than Dr Phillips initially believed. Dr Bond opted for a time of one or two o'clock in the morning based on the body temperature. But he admitted that the body may have cooled more rapidly due to the extremity of the mutilations. The time, in any case, appears to have been settled by two witnesses.'

'Witnesses, Lestrade?' asked Holmes eagerly.

'A Mrs Prater lives in the room above Mary's. She was awoken during the night by her kitten calling across her neck. Minutes later she heard a woman cry "Oh! Murder!" Such cries are common in the area, so she paid it scant regard. She estimated the time as being half past three to four 'o clock. She was quite an excitable woman, and I was not impressed by her account of the matter. Yet she seems to have been corroborated by a Mrs Sarah Lewis. Mrs Lewis had come to stay with friends of hers at number two Miller Court, just about opposite Mary's room.

'She dozed fitfully in a chair for much of the night. From half past three until almost five o'clock, she was sat wide awake. She heard a single loud scream of 'Murder!' just before she heard the clock strike half past three. The cry was that of a young woman and seemed to come from close by, although Mrs Lewis did not trouble to look out of the window. We are certain that both women described the same event, having heard what must have been the last mortal cries of the dead woman.'

'Undoubtedly, Lestrade,' enthused Holmes. 'The attack was evidently sudden. Yet she had allowed the man into the room. I suspect that he was someone whom she knew.'

'Possibly. But she certainly put up a fight, whoever he was. The post-mortem found a small incision on her right thumb and cuts to the back of her hands.'

'No doubt from the desperate struggle which accompanied her cry for help,' observed Holmes.

'There is something else you should know, Holmes. The killer again took a portion of his victim's anatomy with him as a souvenir.'

'What?' gasped Holmes.

'Which part of her was missing, Inspector?' I asked.

'Her heart, Dr Watson,' said Lestrade. 'He had taken her heart.'

23.

Bates brings a visitor

'This is utterly appalling, Holmes,' I cried, quite aghast at the notion.
        'The devilment of the man knows no bounds,' agreed Holmes.
        'We have little hope, of course, that this organ will turn up and lead us to the killer,' lamented Lestrade. 'But you may find something else Mrs Lewis observed to be of interest.'
        'Please proceed, Lestrade,' said Holmes.
        'She arrived at Millers Court at half past two. As she entered the court, she noticed a man standing outside the lodging house on the opposite side of the road. She could give no description of the man, but it appeared to Mrs Lewis that he was looking up the court, as though waiting for someone.'
        'A lookout? I asked Holmes, mindful of the man with the pipe whom Schwartz had observed at the scene of Elizabeth Stride's murder.
        'I think so, Watson,' said Holmes. 'Is there anything else of interest that has occurred, Lestrade?'
        'We managed to find Joe Barnett. He stayed at Buller's Lodging House, Bishopsgate, on the night of the murder. He called upon Mary that evening and a Miss Lizzie Allbrook, who was there during the visit, observed that he left on good terms. It wasn't his jacket that was found in the room, either. It belonged to the husband of a Mrs Harvey. We've interviewed Barnett and are satisfied that he had nothing whatsoever to do with the murder. He was playing cards with fellow residents until late in the evening before retiring to bed. He identified Mary's body and was very much affected. It was only by her eyes and ears that he could be sure it was her.'
        'I see,' said Holmes thoughtfully. 'Most interesting, Lestrade.'

'Tomorrow, I shall visit Bates,' said Holmes brightly after supper that evening. 'I am hopeful that he may have turned up something which may provide a clue. We are getting there, Watson. We shall beat him.'
        'You appear rather buoyant this evening, Holmes,' I remarked.

'I have failed Mary Kelly,' said Holmes solemnly. 'She came to me for help which I could not provide. However this case concludes, Watson, I shall consider it to be a failure. I owe it to Mary to discover her murderer. I have felt frustration and confusion as I have never before known these two emotions and confess that I have misdirected them. I must not feel resentment towards Jack the Ripper, for he is responsible for five murders, not my failure to prevent them. I feel a certain thrill, Watson, for I am in the midst of my greatest case. This man has tested my powers like none before him. Were he to defeat me, my career, despite its innumerable successes, must be judged a failure. I must not fail, Watson.'

Sherlock Holmes set out the following morning to locate Benjamin Bates, returning some time later that afternoon possessed of an exuberance which I had not observed in him for some time. As he entered our sitting room, he appeared a man to whom the prospect of failure had been rendered obsolete.

'The weather has taken a remarkable turn, Watson,' said Holmes, removing his coat and placing it on the stand. 'It has become rather mild, while the air has about it a crisp wind which I found to be quite invigorating.'

'I observed through the window that the sky no longer holds the threat of rain. Was your meeting with Bates fruitful?'

'Meeting may be too formal a description, Watson. I had to hunt the young man down while he was tramping about the streets of Whitechapel, earnestly collecting his daily quota of gossip. This was no easy task in the wake of so sensational a murder. The streets are quite choked with crowds who have gathered, it appears, merely in order to express their horror at the latest outrage. But I eventually ran him to ground in Osborn Street. From there I took him to a coffee shop in Spectacle Alley for some badly need fortification.'

'Did he have anything of importance to tell you?'

'He certainly did, Watson,' said Holmes. 'Of course, much of what he had gleaned was already known to me courtesy of Lestrade. 'But he did provide me with a rather interesting account of O'Connor's behaviour on the night of the murder. It appears that both Bates and O'Connor worked in the offices of The Star until almost midnight that night. O'Connor appeared rather anxious about something, constantly surveying the clock and growing increasingly agitated as the hour drew later. When O'Connor left the offices at approaching twelve o' clock, Bates observed him to be positively panic stricken. He appeared to be in the throes of some great apprehension, as Bates described it, as though fearfully nervous of something.'

'That would appear to be significant in light of the murder.'

'It would indeed, Watson. Nor can we forget that Lusk knew the date on which the killer would next strike. It would seem probable, therefore, that others knew of it too. I suspect that O'Connor was one of them. He is involved somehow, Watson. Mark my words.'

'But you do not suspect him of being the actual murderer?'

'I am certain that he killed Elizabeth Stride, although I would struggle at present to convince a jury of that fact. But there is compelling evidence that he is not Jack the Ripper. Bates checked through O'Connor's appointment book and discovered that on the night of Annie Chapman's murder, he was at a dinner at the house of John Murray, the publishing magnate who sponsors The Star. Bates had it confirmed by a young maid at the house that O'Connor spent the night there on account of his being rather drunk. It is beyond question that he was in any state to have murdered Annie Chapman and, therefore, cannot be Jack the Ripper.'

'And you have ruled out Jack McCarthy?' I asked, frowning as I considered the diminishing list of suspects.

'I certainly do not believe him to be Jack the Ripper,' said Holmes. 'Yet I still suspect he knows something of the matter.'

'Is it not curious, Holmes, that McCarthy seemed in complete shock at the murder of Mary Kelly, whereas O'Connor's actions suggest that he anticipated it?'

'Bravo, Watson,' said Holmes. 'I myself had considered how their respective behaviour appears incongruous to the notion that they are working as confederates. It is growing increasingly difficult to ascribe all five murders to the same hand. The idea of several lone killers is, of course, quite absurd. If Jack the Ripper is more than one man, then logic dictates that there is something which binds them to one another. But what is it? And what has Lusk to do with all of this? Every answer we find is merely replaced with yet a further question. When we eventually unravel the solution to this mystery, Watson, I am certain that the truth shall astonish us.'

On Monday, 12th November, Holmes and I attended the inquest into Mary Kelly's death at Shoreditch Town Hall. It proved to be an odd affair, with my notes from that grim day recording some petty dispute over whose jurisdiction the inquest was to be conducted. It was eventually determined that as the body presently laid in Shoreditch, the coroner for that district, Roderick McDonald, would oversee proceedings. We arrived early for the inquest, yet the pavement outside the grand building was already streaming with sightseers. They milled about and chatted with a great deal of excitement in anticipation of the event.

When the inquest commenced at eleven o'clock, a great sea of people surged forward in an attempt to enter the building. We managed to dash in amongst the rabble and inch through the door before it was besieged completely. Yet the entrance hall itself became choked by a massive throng of sightseers, who proceeded to follow us up the narrow staircase and threatened to overwhelm the coroner's office. We eventually managed to obtain seats in the packed room, an Inspector locking the door behind us and remaining outside to prevent any interruptions.

Once sworn in, the jury was escorted out of the building to view the body at Shoreditch mortuary, before proceeding to the scene of the ghastly murder at Millers Court. We awaited their return impatiently, yet hardly daring to vacate our precious seats. It was close on twelve when at last the evidence began to be taken. Jack McCarthy took the stand first, still evidently distressed by Mary's death as he recounted how Thomas Bowyer had first alerted him to the murder. Dr Phillips gave only the tersest account of Kelly's injuries. This reticence was prompted, I later discovered, by the fear that relaying the full details might hinder the police investigation.

A wretched-looking woman named Mrs Mary Ann Cox described seeing Kelly at about a quarter to midnight in the company of a man of blotchy complexion and carroty moustache. Although she gave her evidence convincingly, Holmes shook his head, muttering that this event had happened far too early for the man to have been Kelly's murderer. He tapped his leg idly while she gave her evidence, yet became attentive when Mrs Sarah Lewis took to the stand.

I recognised the name as that of the woman whom Lestrade had mentioned having observed a man standing opposite Millers Court. She had originally told the police that she was unable to provide any description of the man. Her memory had evidently improved since, for she proceeded to give a modest account of the man's appearance. He was not tall, but rather stout and wore a black wideawake hat. It seemed to me that this man was surely the killer's lookout, for why else would he have been waiting outside Millers Court?

What promised to be a drawn-out affair became something of a truncated farce when Dr MacDonald drew the inquest to a sudden close that same afternoon. The jury had decided that they had heard enough evidence by which to return a verdict of wilful murder by some person or persons unknown. We had heard testimony which abounded with dubious characters, although it appeared that we had learned far less of the actual murderer than might have been hoped.

Whether Holmes had some unfathomable inkling that events at Millers Court would yet yield more clues, I could not tell. But his cheerful dismissal of the desultory inquest as we departed the Town Hall appeared well-placed, for early the following morning, Benjamin Bates arrived at Baker Street in the company of a man whom he claimed had seen the Millers Court murderer.

As luck would have it, Holmes had risen uncommonly early that morning, and we had already breakfasted by the time Mrs Hudson announced that we had visitors. Holmes eyed Bates' companion curiously as he bade them to take a seat upon the sofa. He was aged about thirty, of rather short stature and solid build. From his dress, I thought him a labourer, for his coat was shabby and his boats much worn and caked with dirt. Yet his strong, clean-shaven features and alert blue eyes hinted at an intelligence beyond his station.

'This is Mr George Hutchinson,' announced Bates, gesturing to the man next to him on the sofa, who greeted us in a deep, polite voice. 'He saw Mary Kelly on the night of the murder in the company of a man. What is more, Mr Hutchinson can describe the fellow in detail enough that he is sure he would recognise him again.'

'I see,' said Holmes dubiously. 'And why is it that Mr Hutchinson was not called before the inquest with such startling information?'

'I heard of the murder on the Saturday, Mr Holmes, although all I discovered was that it had been committed in Dorset Street,' said our mysterious visitor, his gaze fixed upon Holmes. I did not, therefore, trouble to question anyone upon the matter, nor did I have a penny to spare in order to buy a newspaper. It was not until yesterday, while I was drinking in The Commercial, that I discovered to my horror that it was Mary who had been murdered,' said Hutchinson. 'I at once realised the importance of what I had seen. Yesterday evening, I presented myself at Commercial Street Station to tell them all that I knew.'

'Most commendable, Mr Hutchinson,' said Holmes. 'You mention Miss Kelly by her first name. Might I assume that she was known to you?'

'For some years, Mr Holmes.'

'I see. I think perhaps it would be best if you commence from the beginning, Mr Hutchinson.'

George Hutchinson leaned forward and proceeded to give one of the most remarkable narratives that I had ever heard recounted at Baker Street.

'I am a casual labourer and presently live at Victoria Working Men's Home in Commercial Street. I had known Mary Kelly for three years and occasionally gave her the odd shilling. On Thursday last, the night of the murder, I was walking along Thrawl Street at about two o clock in the morning. Just before I got to Flower and Dean Street, I saw Mary and she asked me for a shilling. I told her I had spent all my money going to Romford, which was the truth. She said in that case, she would have to go and find some money elsewhere. She then turned back along Thrawl Street. A man coming in the opposite direction tapped her on the shoulder and said something to her, which caused them both to burst out laughing. I heard her say "Alright" to the man, who said she would be alright for what he had told her. He put his right hand around her shoulders while in his left he carried a small parcel with a kind of strap around it. I stood against the lamp of the Queen's Head pub and watched them. They walked past me and the man hung his head down with his hat over his eyes. I stooped down and looked him hard in the face. He replied with a stern glance.

'I followed them as they went to Dorset Street and stood outside Millers Court for a few minutes. He said something to her and she said "Alright, my dear, come along. You will be comfortable." He placed her arm on his shoulder and gave her a kiss. She remarked how she had lost her handkerchief. He promptly pulled out a red handkerchief from his jacket and gave it to her. Then they went up into the court. I looked up the passageway, but they had gone inside. I waited opposite the entrance for about three quarters of an hour. They did not come out, so I went away.'

'A most remarkable story, Mr Hutchinson,' said Holmes. 'You have relayed what you observed so precisely that I have no questions as to the events you witnessed.'

'Thank you, Mr Holmes.'

'Although I could not help but be struck by the fact that you have hardly presented yourself as a disinterested party. You have chronicled your attempt to follow Mary and her companion expertly, yet without explaining what prompted so concerted an effort. I observed Mary in this very room where you now sit, Mr Hutchinson, and she was a woman of great personal attractions. While the matter of a man's heart is his own affair, might I be correct in suggesting that you yourself held designs upon Mary Kelly, and thus viewed her companion with a degree of jealousy?'

'Your reputation is well-deserved, Mr Holmes,' said Hutchinson, clearly astonished by my friend's powers of deduction. 'I admit that I had feelings for Mary. If you met her as you say, then you no doubt realised that she was a very special woman. She had few close friends, but I knew that she was fond of me. But she was with Joe Barnett and I am not one to take another man's girl. I was used to seeing Mary in the company of other men, but this one was different. He was something of a toff and, to tell the truth, I was jealous of his affections towards Mary. If he had emerged from Millers Court, I meant to have it out with him straight.'

'I appreciate your frankness on so delicate a matter, Mr Hutchinson. Mary was indeed a most handsome figure of womanhood. Now, Mr Bates has informed us that the description you have given of this man is nothing short of first rate.'

'I have something of a faculty for detail, Mr Holmes,' said Hutchinson. 'And as I have explained, I took a special interest in this fellow.'

'I have taken down Mr Hutchinson's description, Holmes,' said Bates. 'It is a fuller one than that which he gave last night to the police.'

Bates produced a large sheet of paper on which was written in his own hand a copy of Hutchinson's statement. He handed it to Holmes, who raised an eyebrow before passing it to me. It was as follows:

The man was about 5 ft. 6 in. in height, and 34 or 35 years of age, with dark complexion and dark moustache, turned up at the ends. He was wearing a long dark coat, trimmed with astrakhan, a white collar with black necktie in which was affixed a horseshoe pin. He wore a pair of dark 'spats' with light buttons over button boots and displayed from his waistcoat a massive gold chain. His watch chain had a big seal, with a red stone hanging from it. He had a heavy moustache curled up and dark eyes and eyelashes. He had no side whiskers, and his chin was clean shaven. He looked like a foreigner.

'Your skills at observation perhaps exceed that of my own, Mr Hutchinson,' said Holmes wryly. 'I confess that I do not believe I could swear to such a wealth of detail from a momentary glance in the dark, with the man illuminated only by the single lamp of a public house.'

'That is what I saw,' said Hutchinson matter-of-factly. 'Inspector Abberline questioned me on the same point, and I told him that I can picture the man now the same as I can see you.'

'Very well, Mr Hutchinson. I shall believe that what you have given me is no less than an exact description of the man you observed.'

'Thank you, Mr Holmes.'

'Right. Well, if you have no further questions for Mr Hutchinson, I shall not detain you any longer,' said Bates, rising to leave.

'That is quite alright, Bates. I believe I have everything I need.'

'Do you believe him, Holmes?' I asked, when our visitors had departed.

'Hutchinson? Undoubtedly, Watson. He has seen the killer. We can only be thankful that his powers of recollection match the earnestness of his affections for the late Miss Kelly.'

'I confess to finding his story rather fanciful. Could he not be an attention seeker? This case has already attracted enough of those.' Holmes shook his head.

'Attention seekers appear at inquests in order to have their names appear in the papers, thus gaining a fleeting modicum of fame, Watson,' he said. 'They do not tell a story which places them at the scene of the crime with questionable motives, and with no means of proving that their role in the matter was merely that of an observer. If he wished to simply gain some notoriety, he would have presented himself to the police immediately, armed with a far less incriminating tale to tell. No, his account was thoroughly genuine, Watson. I am sure of it. And of course, you must remember what Sarah Lewis claims she saw on the night of the murder.'

'Of course!' I exclaimed. 'She saw a man standing outside the court, as though waiting for someone.'

'Exactly. The times tally precisely. There can be absolutely no doubt that Hutchinson was the man whom Mrs Lewis observed. He saw the killer, Watson. George Hutchinson saw Jack the Ripper lead Mary Kelly to her death. We shall have him, Watson. I know we shall have him.'

24.

Jack the Ripper

Several evenings after the visit of George Hutchinson, Sherlock Holmes entered our sitting room attired in his finest evening dress.

'Ah, Watson,' he cried, as I sat up from the sofa in surprise. 'It is far too precious a night to waste lounging about Baker Street. Would you care to accompany me to dinner? There is a charming Italian in town of which Bates speaks most highly.'

'Why, I'd be delighted, Holmes,' said I. 'It has been far too long since we last dined out of an evening.'

'That was also my reasoning, Watson. I fear that my devotion to capturing Jack the Ripper has been to the detriment of my palate. It is high time I took a hiatus in order to reacquaint myself with the finer points of dining.'

We took a hansom to the West End and alighted at Leicester Square, from where I followed Holmes as he led us through several side streets off the main road, halting at the entrance to a quaint-looking restaurant. We took a table towards the back, with Holmes insisting upon a seat which afforded him a view of the door.

'Now, Watson. I confess that this evening's sojourn is something of a pre-emptive celebration. I almost have him.'

'The Ripper?' I asked in a whisper, leaning across the table.

'The very same, Watson,' said he. 'I have spent the last few days placing the pieces of this puzzle together. It has been the most ardent investigation of my career. But we are almost at an end.'

'You know who the killer is?' I gasped. Holmes nodded.

'I am certain, Watson. But there was far more to unravel than simply identifying Jack the Ripper. For I was proved correct: this is quite the most fiendishly intricate web I have yet untangled.'

'But Holmes, if you have uncovered the identity of the murderer, then why on earth are we here instead of apprehending him at this very moment?' I asked incredulously.

'Ha! If only things were so simple, Watson. I could lay my hands upon Jack the Ripper within the hour. But within that same time again he would be a free man, for I cannot yet prove it. This is a case whose conclusion will not be rushed, lest it be ruined all together.'

'I understand, Holmes,' I said. 'Would I be correct in thinking that George Hutchinson's evidence has enabled you to reach this delicate conclusion?'

'Entirely, Watson. His observations baffled me at first, but it soon became clear that they in fact explained almost everything that remained of the mystery. I require just one final piece of the puzzle and the picture shall be complete. But what have we here?'

I turned around as Holmes peered over my shoulder and saw, much to my astonishment, T.P O'Connor and Benjamin Bates enter the restaurant. The latter waved as he recognised us, although O'Connor's face grimaced at the sight of Holmes and I.

'Holmes! Dr Watson!' greeted Bates as he approached us, followed gingerly by O'Connor. 'What a surprise.'

'Good evening to you both,' replied Holmes brightly. 'Won't you join us?'

O'Connor met this suggestion with a contemptuous look, yet acquiesced and took the seat next to mine.

'Wine, gentlemen?' asked Holmes, pouring two new glasses.

'I must say, Mr Holmes, that I hardly expected such conviviality from a man who accused me of murder,' said O'Connor gruffly.

'I confess that I owe you a great apology, Mr O'Connor. I hope you will understand that the letters which Mr Bates here kindly brought to my attention sent me quite down the wrong path. I have since revised my opinion on the matter entirely.'

'I read your article, of course,' he blustered. 'And are you any the wiser on the matter now?'

'I'm afraid that the trail has grown only colder since I penned my trifling account of the matter. Admitting publicly to one's ignorance is quite foreign to my nature, Mr O'Connor. But I felt it better to be frank if it meant bringing this depraved man to justice.'

'A most noble sentiment,' said O'Connor. 'Yet I fear your misgivings may prove correct. Jack the Ripper appears to be beyond capture.'

'Well, perhaps you are right, Mr O'Connor,' said Holmes with a mischievous smile. 'But let us forget the matter for now. Talk of murder is not quite fitting of such a charming ambience.'

One of the many contradictions which I had observed in Sherlock Holmes was that despite his abhorrence at seeking the company of others for its own sake, he could on occasion be as charming a host as one could wish to meet. Thus, he skilfully managed to divert the conversation away from any topic which might circumvent its way back to the darker business of Jack the Ripper. At times as he spoke, I could do little but wonder how he sustained such an act in the company of a man who had committed murder and might yet prove complicit in several more. It seemed obvious that our casual dinner was nothing of the sort, and had no doubt been arranged by Holmes and Bates in order to fulfil some purpose which at present escaped me.

The evening ended in a wave of wine-induced conviviality, with O'Connor particularly the worse for drink as he sloped off towards a hansom, clutching a bewildered Bates as a means of steadying himself.

'You will forgive the subterfuge, I hope, Watson,' said Holmes, once we were in a cab on our way back to Baker Street. 'I could see your astonishment as Bates and I played out our parts.'

'I admit to being unable to fathom what the exact meaning of tonight was, Holmes,' I said. 'Was it so important to have O'Connor believe you still ignorant of events?'

'My dear, Watson, I suspect you resent my not allowing you into my confidence. I promise that all shall very soon become clear.'

On Monday, 19th November, the funeral of Mary Jane Kelly took place at St Leonard's Church, Shoreditch. That morning found Holmes dressed in readiness for that sombre event, yet with his thoughts clearly elsewhere as he paced up and down our sitting room in a state of great anxiety.

'What is the matter, Holmes?' I asked. 'Have you lost something?'

'I have lost nothing, Watson,' he replied testily. 'But I fear that I may yet lose everything. Confound it!'

'What on earth do you mean, Holmes?'

213

'I almost have it, Watson,' he said, drawing to a halt in front of me. 'We are almost at the end. But this is unlike any case I have yet known. If I strike too soon, then we may yet fail. I have just to recall one more detail before I shall know all. Yet I am running out of time. What is it that I have forgotten?'

He resumed his pacing and began glancing out of the window periodically, as if in some futile attempt to spur a memory which might assist him. Yet this proved to no avail and he eventually settled down upon the armchair in apparent defeat.

'I promised myself that I would have everything resolved before Mary's funeral,' said Holmes in disgust. 'If only I could remember.'

'I have never known you to make an empty promise, Holmes. I am certain you shall succeed.'

At these words, Holmes sprang up from his seat with a wild look upon his face.

'What did you say, Watson?' he asked eagerly.

'I said that I had never known you to make an empty promise,' I replied, quite shocked by my friend's unfathomable manner.

'That is it, Watson!' he cried, gripping me euphorically by the shoulders. 'I have it!'

'Holmes?'

He grabbed his coat, turning to me as he reached the door.

'There is no time to explain. I shall meet you at St Leonard's,' he said breathlessly. 'I have several urgent things I must do before then. We are almost there, Watson.'

At midday, the ancient church bell of St Leonard's, known locally as Shoreditch Church, rang as a signal to the restless masses that the funeral of Mary Kelly was about to commence. A great many people began to gather at the main gate. I had arrived there in expectation of a sizeable contingent of mourners. Yet I confess to being overwhelmed by the size of the solemn crowd, which was several thousand strong. When four men carrying a handsome coffin of elm and oak appeared at the gate, it sparked a scene of great emotion. The entire crowd became alive with grief, men removing their caps while comforting their women, many of whom convulsed into tears at the sombre sight. There were shouts and cries from those nearest the coffin as it passed through the crowd. A great swell of mourners surrounded the open car brought to transport the coffin, jostling each other in their struggle to touch it.

As the procession departed the church on its way to the cemetery, the crowd duly followed: a great sea of humanity sweeping along the thoroughfare and resisting any attempts to disperse it. As I followed them at a distance, I scanned the crowd in the hope of seeing the tall figure of Holmes. Yet he was nowhere to be seen, and I arrived at St Patrick's Cemetery doubtful that I would see him at all until I had returned home to Baker Street. I stood at the back of the crowd as it hustled past me, followed by the cortège. Jack McCarthy, his head bowed, was in the final carriage, while amongst the police I observed Inspectors Abberline and Lestrade.

'It has proved to be quite the event, Watson,' said a familiar voice from behind me.

'Holmes!' I exclaimed, turning around to see my friend standing nonchalantly behind me. 'I thought you wouldn't make it.'

'As you rightly pointed out, Watson, I abhor empty promises.'

'Was your morning successful?'

'It was, Watson. Within half an hour, I shall introduce you to Jack the Ripper.'

'My goodness, Holmes. This business is finally at an end?'

At that moment, a great cry came up from the crowd as Mary Kelly's savaged remains were committed to the earth. Women wept uncontrollably and appeared for all the world as though they had lost a cherished loved one, while men lamented her passing as though they had been intimately acquainted with the girl from Millers Court.

'Quite the display of grief,' said Holmes sardonically. 'And yes, Watson. I have effected a solution to the point where I have but to announce it to the relevant parties before I consider the affair closed forever.'

We left the proceedings shortly before they concluded, thus exiting prior to the roads becoming crushed by the departing throng. Holmes instructed our driver to take us to Dorset Street, meeting my quizzical glance at this instruction with a flashing smile. When we alighted outside Millers Court, I duly followed Holmes into McCarthy's shop. To my surprise, there were several police officers stationed inside. Holmes greeted them cheerfully as he swept past, beckoning me to follow him into the back parlour. There I saw the unmistakeable figure of Squibby, who was holding a cup to the lips of what appeared to be an elderly man sat on a chair with an old, mottled coat thrown over his shoulders.

'Ah, Squibby. I see you are doing an admirable job of attending to our patient,' said Holmes.

'He's eaten some of the stew, Mr Holmes. And I'm giving him some beef tea.'

'Splendid. Watson, I can see that you are quite confused by the scene before you. Allow me to introduce an old friend of ours, Mr George Lusk.'

I gasped in utter astonishment as Squibby stepped aside and the man on the chair raised up his head. It was indeed George Lusk whose countenance I gazed upon. Yet so dishevelled and haggard was his appearance, that I might have passed him in the street without recognising the man.

'My God!' I exclaimed. 'Mr Lusk?'

'Good afternoon to you, Dr Watson,' he said hoarsely.

'Holmes?' What has happened?'

'Mr Lusk has been held against his will for some time and is far from the best of health, Watson. But he has been examined thoroughly by a Doctor, who assures us that he shall be quite fine once he has had the required rest and nourishment.'

'But Holmes!' I stammered incredulously.

'Patience, Watson. All shall be revealed shortly.'

I heard the shop door opening at that moment, followed by the sound of approaching footsteps. Moments later, the figure of Lestrade appeared in the doorway.

'We have him, Holmes,' he said. 'Good afternoon, Dr Watson.'

'The others should be here at any minute,' said Holmes, before I could return the Inspector's salutation.

'Excellent. The men are ready and know their task, Holmes.'

Lestrade joined us in the parlour and closed the door behind him as Holmes bade us all to remain silent. A few minutes later, an audible commotion came from the shop. Presently, amidst many cries of protest, the door swung open and two burly constables escorted a livid T.P O'Connor into the room.

'Ah, Mr O'Connor,' said Holmes calmly. 'How pleasant to see you again. Do please sit down.'

'What do you mean by this?' he protested, as one of the constables placed him forcibly into a wooden chair. His features contorted into incredulity upon recognising Lusk, who glared at him fiercely.

O'Connor's features drew visibly pale as he pondered his predicament and shot Holmes a pitiable glance. Mere minutes later, the handcuffed figure of Jack McCarthy was escorted into the room. In contrast to O'Connor, he had evidently accepted his fate. He sat down meekly in a chair next to The Star editor when instructed to do so by Lestrade. He said nothing, yet eyed O'Connor with a bewildered expression as Holmes surveyed them both with a look of grim satisfaction.

'And now we await the finale, Watson,' said Holmes, checking his pocket watch. 'He should be here at any moment.'

'Who?' I asked.

'I imagine that our two guests here have an idea,' said Holmes, casting O'Connor and McCarthy a withering glance.

There was a knock upon the door and in peered Benjamin Bates.

'Ah! Do come in, Bates,' said Holmes. 'You are just in time.'

Bates duly stepped into the parlour, his gaze sweeping the room with a look of increasing amazement.

'What is the meaning of this, Holmes?' asked Lestrade angrily. 'He is a journalist. I cannot allow him to stay here.'

'Bates is a personal friend who has been instrumental at various key points of this investigation, Lestrade. He deserves to hear the whole truth and I wish him to remain.'

Lestrade eyed my friend narrowly before reluctantly agreeing to Holmes' request. Bates nodded in gratitude and stood to the left of the doorway avoiding, I noticed, the fierce glare of his employer.

Minutes later, I heard the distinctive clatter of hoofs upon the cobbles outside, followed by the sound of the shop door opening. A loud exclamation of surprise was audible and, amidst an almighty uproar, the door opened. Two constables ushered in a struggling, well-dressed figure whom I recognised immediately.

'Ah, good afternoon, your Grace,' said Holmes pleasantly.

'Holmes?' asked Lestrade, as he studied the noble figure presently attempting to free itself from the clutches of several policemen.

'Lestrade, the illustrious person before you is the third Duke of Buckingham and Chandos. His full name, which includes, I believe, the longest running non-repetitive surname in the entire kingdom is Richard Plantagenet Campbell Temple-Nugent-Brydges-Chandos-Grenville. You may, however, refer to him simply as Jack the Ripper.'

'What do you mean by this outrage?' cried the Duke.

'What?' gasped Lestrade. 'You are sure of this, Holmes?'

'I am certain, Lestrade,' said Holmes. 'Please take a seat, your Grace. I have provided a chair especially.'

The Duke eyed Holmes sullenly as he sat down on the chair positioned just inside the door.

'Please explain what has happened here, Holmes,' said Lestrade.

'Forgive me, Lestrade. My instructions to you were unfortunately absent of any great detail. If you would be kind enough to close the door, I shall explain everything from the beginning.

'I confess that the solution to this extraordinary case has unquestionably proved to be the most perplexing I have yet encountered. There were times when events left me entirely baffled and Jack the Ripper seemed destined to forever remain a nebulous phantom. I realised from the first that the man who had murdered Martha Tabram was to be an exceptional adversary. So frenzied an attack spoke of a madman, yet the stealth with which he went about his murderous business suggested an assassin of quite remarkable nerve. I realised that it was neither a domestic dispute nor robbery which had been the cause of the attack, for no-one had heard a struggle. The killer and his victim had entered the seclusion of George Yard on apparently amicable terms.

'Yet he proceeded to attack her so suddenly that she had not time to utter a single cry. There seemed to be no motivation to the crime other than murder for its own sake. Such a man seemed certain to strike again and, upon the murder of Mary Ann Nicholls, I felt certain that a maniacal killer was at large upon the streets of Whitechapel. The ferocity of this second attack, which included the slit throat and disembowelment that was to become the grisly hallmark of these murders, confirmed this suspicion. The killer had grown in confidence and his modus operandi evidently matured accordingly. Again, the silence of the attack impressed me. There were several families within earshot, yet they heard nothing until the police arrived upon the scene. The killer had left no clue which I could discern and, as with the Tabram murder, there appeared to be no apparent motive.

'The murder of Annie Chapman, however, afforded me rather more to consider. Given the circumstances of this attack, our man displayed perhaps the most remarkable composure of any criminal I have ever known. For he committed his grisly work in broad daylight and in a yard possessed of but a single means of egress. Yet he not only mutilated his victim, but paused to wrench the rings from her fingers and arrange the trumpery contents of her pockets neatly beside her body. In addition, he took part of Annie Chapman's viscera away with him as a souvenir.

'The killer, however, began to reveal himself, as I was sure he would if he continued such daring assaults. A man in the adjoining yard heard what was undoubtedly Annie Chapman stumbling against the fence as her murderer seized her by the throat. The killer evidently strangled his victim before turning his knife upon her, thus explaining both the absence of any cry and the lack of blood at the scene. In a patch of earth exposed by the removal of a flagstone, I observed a footprint which I was sure had been left by the killer. It was a size eight. Yet of far more interest, I deduced that it had been made by a John Lobb. Immediately, I felt certain that the killer was not a local man, but one evidently of some wealth. By this time, Dr Phillips had pronounced the killer to have exhibited a certain amount of anatomical knowledge. I was therefore certain that our man was not to be found in a common lodging house. Yet beyond this fact, I could tell extremely little of this elusive killer.

'The next twist in this horrid saga came in the form of a letter sent to the Central News Agency and purporting to have been written by the murderer. I of course deduced immediately that it was merely a hoax. I suspected it had been manufactured by Mr O'Connor, principally to sustain interest in the case once the Leather Apron story had run its course. Besides giving us the name Jack the Ripper, an ingenious sobriquet under which I am certain history shall remember these crimes, I had little interest in the letter. Yet it appeared that someone was using these murders to their own advantage. Shortly before receiving this curious missive, I received a visit from Mr Lusk in his capacity as chairman of The Whitechapel Vigilance Committee.

'I confess that I immediately questioned his motives. I set Squibby here to join his group and report back to me. It became evident that Mr Lusk absented himself from his nightly patrols in order to carry out an affair with one Mary Kelly. Upon confronting him about this matter, Mr Lusk provided me with a quite comprehensive, not to say emotive, account of his dalliance with the late Miss Kelly. I was left utterly convinced that he had had no hand in the Whitechapel slayings. His explanation of how Jack McCarthy had first introduced him to Miss Kelly, however, was entirely at odds with McCarthy's own assertion that he did not know George Lusk. This immediately alerted me to the fact that Jack McCarthy had something to hide, although there was nothing in his manner to suggest that it had anything whatsoever to do with the murders.

'By this time, Jack the Ripper had apparently killed twice more in a single night, allowing me to tear away at least part of his mask. But let us consider the first murder of the so-called double event. Even at the scene, I was struck by the dissimilarity to the previous murders when Dr Blackwell described Stride's injuries. While I was still considering the atrocity in Dutfield's Yard, we were alerted to the discovery of a further outrage in Mitre Square. On arriving at the scene, it became clear that our man had exceeded his own limits of depravity, for I had never observed such a controlled frenzy upon a body as that which I witnessed in that grim square. Yet the fellow had again left no clue by which I might trace him. While I was left to merely marvel at his guile, it became clear that we were not, after all, dealing with a phantom. For he had left behind evidence of his presence at Mitre Square that night.

'The enigmatic chalked message discovered in Goulston Street gave us little clue as to the killer's motives, yet it was undoubtedly he who had written it. Commissioner Warren's inexcusable decision to erase the message obscured the fact that the words themselves were of little use in catching their author. Of far greater importance was the accompanying rag, which the man had evidently ripped from Catherine Eddowes' apron in order to prove his communication genuine. It spoke of a quite startling foresight and dare which appeared scarcely credible. I could only hope that this man had been observed by a witness who would ultimately come forward to throw some much-needed light upon matters.

'My hopes were met by Israel Schwartz and Joseph Lawende. The former's statement confirmed my theory that the attack upon Elizabeth Stride was not committed by the same hand that would strike later that night in Mitre Square. It appeared impossible to equate the protracted assault in Dutfield's Yard with the calculating assassin who would later slay Catherine Eddowes that very night. While Schwartz's account told me nothing of Jack the Ripper himself, it alerted me to the fact that this business ran far deeper than I had feared.

'Murder, as I have explained to Watson, is surprisingly rare in Whitechapel. To have it effected by the slitting of the throat is rarer still. It occurred to me that what Schwartz witnessed was a crude attempt at attributing a murder to those of Jack the Ripper, so that its own motives would never be investigated. That Schwartz spoke of a second man, clearly a lookout, filled me with interest. Yet of greater consideration was the fact that the murder took place on the same night as that of Eddowes. As astonishing as it appeared, I was forced to conclude that the men Schwartz observed had some foreknowledge of a murder later that night. They therefore choose that date in order that their own attack would be more readily attributed to Jack the Ripper. They struck early, thus ensuring theirs would be the first attack of the evening. They were sure to inflict upon her the throat wound which would immediately mark at as a Ripper murder. A different weapon was used to that carried by Jack the Ripper of course, while the assassin had not the same devil in his work as the man he was imitating. While the cut to Stride's throat ultimately proved fatal, it lacked the ferocity which had become Jack's hallmark. Although of great interest, Mr Israel Schwartz was witness to a mere botched emulation of the man I sought.

'Then in one dramatic moment, the affair became much clearer to me when Benjamin Bates arrived at Baker Street the day following the murders. He had outdone himself on this occasion, for he brought with him both a witness from Mitre Square and a postcard allegedly from the murderer. I had no doubt that Joseph Lawende had observed the killer luring his victim to her unspeakable fate. Yet his description vexed me, for it bore no resemblance to the higher-class man that I took the killer to be. Of equal interest was the postcard, again received by The Central News Agency and in the same handwriting as the letter. Its author took responsibility for what it termed 'the double event'. It also corrected stated that Elizabeth Stride had screamed out; a detail that had thus far gone unreported in the newspapers.

'It seemed apparent that someone was playing a very clever game. By apparently having Jack the Ripper himself claim to have committed the murder in Dutfield's Yard, it would ensure Stride's death was viewed as just another motiveless assault in this grotesque series. I therefore became certain that whoever had murdered Stride had also authored the postcard. This led me to believe that Mr O'Connor was somehow involved in events, for it was he whom I had suspected of having written the first letter. Of course, he denied any part in the murders, but my suspicions of him remained.

'These grew to be certainties when I became acquainted with Elizabeth Stride's lover, Michael Kidney. He cast vague aspersions about a man called Aaron, whom I eventually identified as referring to Mr Joseph Aarons, the treasurer of the Whitechapel vigilance committee. I followed Kidney to Mr Lusk's house, where I also observed Jack McCarthy to be present. It seemed that I was about to discover the real reason that Elizabeth Stride had been murdered. Yet it was a telegram from Lestrade that provided the key to solving the riddle. Kidney had been arrested at the offices of The Star and his story began to unravel. Elizabeth Stride, it emerged, had worked as a charlady for Mr Aarons. In this capacity, she had stumbled upon a private conversation between Aarons and Mr Lusk regarding Jack McCarthy. Mr Lusk had discovered that McCarthy was involved in unethical business practices, one of which was people trafficking, no less. Stride, realising the value of this information, set about blackmailing McCarthy. He in turn steadfastly refused to buckle under her demands. When Stride was murdered, Kidney naturally thought it to be the work of McCarthy. He went to Mr Aarons, who promised to arrange a meeting with McCarthy in order to gain his assurance that he had had nothing to do with Stride's death. Kidney's suspicions were thus assuaged, so that he put her murder down to the vagaries of chance. Yet he then received a note claiming that the man who had murdered his lover was in fact T.P O'Connor. I had no doubts that this was indeed the case, although who sent the note and how they came to know this information was another matter entirely. And now, if he feels able to convey himself, I think the story is best continued by Mr Lusk.'

All eyes fell upon George Lusk, who straightened himself in his chair and gazed about the room. He barely seemed possessed of the strength to perform Holmes' request, yet proceeded to speak in a low, raspy voice.

'Thank you, Mr Holmes. For you have brought these terrible events to an end. I can only hope that you receive a fitting reward for your efforts from those who have the power to grant them.'

Holmes ignored this sentiment as Lusk began to explain what part he had played in this extraordinary case.

'Only a few hours ago, Mr Holmes informed me that the woman I loved, Mary Kelly, was slain in her room just yards from where I now sit. I shall follow his lead, however, and explain events from the beginning. What Elizabeth Stride overheard was entirely true. Jack McCarthy loaned me money to assist my ailing business and I thought him a friend. Indeed, in many respects he was. But I began to see a darker side to him. I learned of his people trafficking exploits one day when he was rather the worse for drink. He seemed boastful of the fact and I was horrified to think that I was an associate of his. I told Mr Aarons of my concerns and he advised me to confront McCarthy, or else go to the police. I confess that I was reluctant to do either. But then events transpired of an even darker nature. I had visited upon McCarthy at his shop, only to be informed by the shop boy that he had gone out. The lad had an errand to run and, as he knew me to be a friend of

223

McCarthy's, asked me to oversee the shop for the short time he would be away.

'While he was gone, I took a position behind the counter. I had often marvelled at the eclectic range of items which the shop stocked. To pass the time, I idly searched the shelf behind the counter. There was nothing of interest save for a small metal box. I confess that my curiosity got the better of me. I took the box and placed it upon the counter. When I opened it, I found to my surprise that it contained a series of letters. I would have closed the box the moment I realised it contained personal correspondence. Yet to my great shock, I saw my own name upon one of the pages. I read in horror as their importance became evident. They were from the Duke of Buckingham and Chandos, whom I knew was acquainted with McCarthy. They referred to certain 'events' in which McCarthy was to assist.

'To my utmost terror, I began to realise that they referred to the Whitechapel murders. It became clear that the Duke was the perpetrator of these awful crimes and had enlisted McCarthy to assist him. There was the mention of dates on which these atrocities were to take place, for it appeared that the Duke was able to absent himself only on particular occasions. McCarthy had evidently informed The Duke of the incident involving Michael Kidney, for he voiced his extreme displeasure upon the matter in the strongest possible terms.

'It appeared that McCarthy and O'Connor had committed the murder of the Stride woman. The Duke was angry that they might have been caught and risk the whole story being uncovered. McCarthy was asked to help the Duke at Mitre Square that night. A later letter confirmed that he did just this. I was mortified at this intelligence, dropping the box upon the floor in shock. A brass ring rolled out upon the floor. I heard the shop lad approaching the door and stuffed the ring into my pocket, having just time to replace the box before he saw it. I made an excuse and hurried out of the shop. This occurred the day before Mr Holmes observed me with Mary in The Horn of Plenty. Whether someone had reported this fact to McCarthy, or the brass ring had been discovered missing, I do not know. But McCarthy visited me and the second I saw him, I realised that he knew I had uncovered his terrible secret. He hissed at me to keep quiet about it, warning me that I would die for what I knew if I were to tell anyone of what I had discovered.

'I was at my wits' end. I was compelled to do something, yet I feared for my life and of what would become of my children were I to ignore McCarthy's warning. A few days later, I received a parcel containing part of a kidney. I tried to convince myself that it was merely a macabre hoax, although in my heart I was certain that it was a warning from the Duke. When Mr Holmes confirmed my suspicions, I was unsure of what to do. I decided to send Kidney a note informing him who had murdered Elizabeth Stride. The letters I'd seen had made it clear that O'Connor had slain her while McCarthy kept watch. I wanted to tell Mr Holmes of what I knew. Yet I lived in fear of the Duke discovering that I had divulged this information. Eventually, I decided to inform Mr Holmes anonymously. When he confirmed that the kidney must have been sent by the murderer, I returned to Baker Street that afternoon and left a note. The final letter mentioned the 8th November as the date of the next murder. I feared my letter would be dismissed as a hoax, but then remembered the brass ring. I was certain that it had been taken from one of the victims. I placed it in the envelope, hoping that Mr Holmes would recognise its importance and take my warning as genuine.

'I lived in fear for the days that followed. Yet I heard nothing from McCarthy. Then one afternoon, I was making my way along Commercial Street. A carriage drew up and two large men accosted me and bundled me inside. We travelled for about half an hour, although I knew not where. When I was presently dragged out of the carriage, I was taken into what appeared to be a warehouse. The Duke was present and told me that he knew of my visit to Sherlock Holmes. I denied it, yet he did not believe me. When night-time came, I was placed back in the carriage with my head covered. I was transferred to a tiny, filthy room and chained to a pipe. There, I was kept for days on end and brought food and water twice a day by a hooded figure. I have learned only this morning from Mr Holmes that this hooded figure was Jack McCarthy. I am only grateful that Mr Holmes discovered me, although to be greeted by the awful news of Mary's death was worse than spending a lifetime kept prisoner. Yet how Mr Holmes knew where I was at all is beyond me.'

The attention of the cramped room rested upon my friend, who surveyed his audience before continuing the extraordinary narrative.

'I was sure that Jack McCarthy knew what had befallen Mr Lusk. I could not be sure that he hadn't been done away with entirely, but was certain that if Mr Lusk were still alive, McCarthy was the man who would lead him to me. Yet I observed McCarthy for days upon end, only to find that he rarely left the confines of Millers Court. When I visited McCarthy in his shop, he claimed that he had not yet set foot outside that day, yet his hands were stained from having handled something rusty. Why he had lied, I could not be sure. When Mary Kelly visited me, I asked her if any of the buildings were unoccupied. She told me that they were not. That extinguished the possibility that Mr Lusk was being held in Millers Court, which was the only place he could be if McCarthy was his captor.

'But Mary was mistaken. Bates casually mentioned that one of the women who had heard a scream of murder on the night of Mary's demise had lived above an empty room. I confess that I failed to realise the importance of this remark. Yet I was also certain that I'd overlooked something. An unwitting prompt from Watson allowed me to realise my glaring omission. I raced to Millers Court, aware that McCarthy would be at Mary's funeral. Mr Lusk relayed to me the story which you have just heard, confirming the conclusions of my own investigations. I sent bogus telegrams to The Duke and Mr O'Connor on behalf of McCarthy, informing them of an emergency which required their presence at Millers Court this afternoon. The results of this subterfuge you see before you.'

'This is quite unbelievable, Holmes,' gasped Lestrade. 'I have heard you recount some fanciful explanations in your time, but this exceeds them all.'

'I believe that it does, Lestrade,' said Holmes. 'It is quite the most extraordinary affair I have yet to encounter.'

Lestrade surveyed the Duke who, along with his cohorts, had remained in stoic silence as their foul deeds were recounted. It appeared as though the Inspector could scarcely comprehend that the pompous man in front of him was in fact Jack the Ripper.

'Do you wish to say anything?' he asked the Duke.

'I believe Mr Holmes has already provided you with an adequate account of events,' said the Duke sullenly. 'I have little to add to his narrative. I congratulate you, Mr Holmes. Your brother has on many occasions spoke glowingly of your abilities. Yet I confess to believing myself clever enough to avoid your notice.'

'And you very nearly succeeded, your Grace,' replied Holmes. 'Were it not for the tell-tale John Lobb print at Hanbury Street, I may never have suspected you. It may be scant consolation, but it was your subordinates who gradually revealed themselves. Were it not for them, I do not believe you would be sitting here now.'

'Bunglers!' bellowed The Duke, glaring at O'Connor and McCarthy.

'Were it not for us helping you at every turn, you would have been caught long ago.' hissed McCarthy.

The Duke said nothing in response, merely holding his contemptuous stare upon the two men.

'I confess, your Grace, that I am still yet to fathom what enabled you to acquire two such loyal assistants for so unspeakable an enterprise,' said Holmes.

'The secret to gaining the obedience of one's underlings, Mr Holmes, is culpability,' said the Duke, smiling grimly at my friend. 'If you ensure that they are responsible for some vital role in one's schemes, you thus guarantee their continued assistance. The more involved they became, the more escape became an impossibility. They grew to hate their work, but of course by then it was too late.'

'And just what part did you two have in these murders?' asked Lestrade, glancing between McCarthy and O'Connor.

'I never murdered anyone,' said McCarthy in faltering tones. 'That's the truth, with God as my witness. Listen, the Duke owns a lot of property in Whitechapel. I reckon he must own forty houses in the Old Nichol alone. Through a friend of a friend, shall we say, I ended up meeting him. He offered me a deal whereby he would put money into buying the most derelict properties I could find, while I would be responsible for finding tenants and collecting their rents. He didn't want his name to be involved, you see. Of course, I was impressed to be talking with a Duke and unhesitatingly agreed. He told me I was just the man he'd been looking for. This went on for a while and everything was fine. We split the money and I did pretty well out of it. Then one day, he says he needs a favour. He needs somewhere he can stay in Whitechapel. I couldn't understand why, but again I didn't want to refuse the request of a Duke. He said he had some business to take care of and that it might be dangerous. I agreed to go with him and took a dagger with me. It was just an old thing that I had lying around the shop.

'Something didn't seem quite right, though. We wandered about for a bit and I thought he had simply got lost. Then he saw some woman and went over and started talking to her. When he signalled for me to follow him, I began to wonder what it was all about. I followed him into a doorway and up the stairs onto the landing. I just thought he was after some bit of rough. But he started choking her, saying that she was trying to rob him. He told me to stab her; that she was going to kill him. I didn't know what was going on. I hesitated before drawing out my dagger and he kept telling me to kill her. By that time, she was insensible. I stabbed her just the once, in the breastbone. I recoiled in horror as I saw the blood run down her front. But the Duke just grinned and went into a mad frenzy, stabbing her over and over again. I have never seen a man in such a rage. I hadn't the nerve to do anything, such was my horror. At last he stopped and appeared quite calm, telling me that I had done well. I took him back to Millers Court, where he spent the night in this very room. I didn't know what could have happened to cause such an astonishing attack. Yet I dared not breathe a word, for I had had a hand in the poor woman's murder.

'And he continued to use you,' said Holmes. 'It was you who penned the letter which accompanied the kidney sent to Mr Lusk. It was also you whom Joseph Lawende saw in Mitre Square. You were the man who persuaded Catherine Eddowes to enter the square, knowing that the Duke was lying in wait for her. And the man whom Hutchinson saw was Mr O'Connor, of course.'

'It was,' said O'Connor bitterly. 'I regret the day that I ever met this cursed fellow. It was Jack who introduced us. It was the Duke who

228

persuaded John Murray to sponsor The Star. I thought him a godsend, before I realised that he was the devil. He asked for my assistance on a private matter in return, to which I of course agreed. It was I who assisted him in escaping from Hanbury street after he had hideously butchered that poor woman. I wondered, of course, what business he could have had in such a house at that hour, but I did not dare ask. Like Jack, I suspected that he had a penchant for women of the lower order. By the time I'd realised just what he had been doing in that back yard, I had become his unwitting accomplice. He told me that he would see to it that Murray withdrew his funding if I told anyone of what I knew. He also reminded me that I would be judged as an accessory.

'From that point on, he had me trapped. I had met Mary Kelly on several previous occasions. It was I who took her back to her room that night in the knowledge, I confess, that the Duke was sitting in wait for her. It broke my heart to take her to her death, but I had no choice. He had decided to punish George by slaying her. He had by now become increasingly erratic and both Jack and I lived in fear of him. Yes, I murdered Elizabeth Stride. I concocted the plan with Jack, so that we struck on the same night as the Duke. The plan was to try and cover our tracks by making it look like a ripper attack. We murdered her earlier in the night, for Jack had to meet the Duke later on in order to assist him in finding a girl.'

'I have never heard such an appalling story,' said Lestrade in horror. 'I think it is time that we took these men into custody.'

'I agree, Lestrade,' said Holmes. But with your permission, I wish to ask the Duke something in the last moments he has at liberty.'

'Very well, Holmes. As you have brought this ghastly affair to its conclusion, I cannot deny you that request.'

'Thank you, Lestrade. Your Grace, the deeds which you have performed shall forever remain in my memory and that, I suspect, of the entire country. You have abused your position in the most unspeakable manner. I wish merely to ask what could have caused you to commit the most monstrous desecration of the human form I could imagine possible.'

The Duke surveyed Holmes for several seconds before his face creased into a hideous smile.

'You ask the impossible of me, Mr Holmes,' he said, shaking his head. 'I am quite certain that no man walking the earth could understand what compelled me to do what I have done. I took comfort one evening many years ago in the arms of a gutter whore. It was only this year that I was told I had tertiary syphilis. How long I have left, I do not know. But I can already feel that my body is shutting down. I felt enraged when I discovered my illness, as though I was the victim of some sort of contamination. There was no hope, of course, of tracking down the woman who had afflicted me. But I became obsessed with extracting revenge upon women of her ilk; those dregs of humanity who betray the sanctity of womanhood. I was unsure as to whether I would kill the Tabram woman, or merely frighten her. But when Jack plunged the dagger into her chest, it awoke every carnal desire I had ever possessed. On the next occasion, I was more adventurous. She opened like a pig at the market. I had learnt something of anatomy and dissection while in India. I flatter myself that I advanced rather quickly in my technique.'

'You feel no shame? No remorse for your actions?' asked Holmes in disgust.

'I do not, Mr Holmes,' he said flatly, and without a flicker of emotion. 'For it gave me what every man must possess: a purpose. I could never rid the streets of every one of those ghastly specimens, but I could atone for the existence of that one woman who had corrupted me. Each of those women became part of my sacrifice.'

'I have heard quite enough from this wretched man, Lestrade,' said Holmes. 'You may take him away.'

'You imagine it to be as simple as that, do you not, Mr Holmes?' sneered the Duke, rising from his seat and fixing a cruel stare upon my friend. 'You imagine that your victory can pass unchallenged?'

Without warning, the Duke gave an almighty shove to the Constable to his right and made for the door. Bates made to grab him but, with a flash of steel, was laid stricken by a stab to his chest. He collapsed instantly, just as the Duke disappeared through the door and up the passage.

'My goodness, Watson! Bates!' cried Holmes, as he observed the young man laying quite still in a widening arc of crimson.

'Get after him!' bellowed Lestrade at two policemen, who promptly ignored their winded colleague and raced out of the room after the Duke. With equal speed, I made for the injured reporter, although I had little hope that I might be able to save him.

'He is dead, Holmes,' I said, following the most cursory of examinations. 'The wound was close to the heart. It was quite instantaneous.'

'Curse the man!' he cried. 'Come, Watson, there is little more we can do here.'

I followed Holmes as he ran through McCarthy's shop and out onto Dorset Street, to be met by quite a bewildering scene. Our hansom had disappeared, the driver standing in a state of considerable shock as a policeman held him up by his shoulders.

'What has happened?' asked Holmes.

'The Duke pulled him from his cab and threatened him with a knife. He was speeding off towards Commercial Street before we could stop him.'

'God Lord!' I exclaimed.

'Quickly, Watson!' cried Holmes. 'We must catch him!'

Holmes jumped upon Lestrade's cab and ordered the driver to start after the Duke. I barely managed to clamber up beside him as we sped off along Dorset Street.

'He has a head start, Watson. We must hope that our driver proves superior.'

We caught sight of the hansom as we turned onto Commercial Street, watching as it careered across the road some distance away. Holmes implored our driver to go faster as the Duke's vehicle lurched violently from side to side some distance ahead of us.

'He is evidently something of an inexpert driver, Holmes,' said I.

'It would certainly appear so. I believe we shall have him eventually.'

Yet we lost sight of the Duke as he merged with the traffic and disappearing from view. Holmes further lambasted our poor driver, who responded with a protestation I could barely hear above the clattering of wheels. Yet a crack of his whip sent us lurching ever faster along Commercial Street. I clutched the side of the carriage in terror as we weaved between carts and omnibuses at a ferocious pace, eventually catching sight of the Duke's errant vehicle as we approached the junction of Whitechapel High Street.

'Confound the man, Watson!' cried Holmes. 'He must falter soon.'

We gained upon our quarry as we passed through the junction, racing along Commercial Road until we at last drew alongside the Duke.

'I must get him somehow, Watson,' said Holmes, rising to his feet and leaning out of the carriage.

Holmes leapt out of his seat and jumped upon the side of the speeding cab, managing to clutch the roof to prevent himself from falling under its wheels.

'Holmes!' I cried, as he struggled to maintain his hold upon the rushing vehicle. 'For God's sake, be careful!'

I watched transfixed as Holmes raised himself up upon the roof and began grappling with the Duke, who aimed several blows at my friend in an attempt to fend him off. Holmes manoeuvred himself alongside the Duke on the driver's seat, somehow managing to take command of the vehicle and bring it almost to a halt. Yet a blow from the Duke caused them both to topple from the vehicle, Holmes bearing the brunt of the fall as they crashed upon the cobbled road.

When our driver had brought us to a halt, I raced across the road to attend to my stricken friend. The Duke had already begun his escape, making his way back along Commercial Road through the growing crowd of onlookers. Holmes was rather shaken as I assisted him to his feet, his arm hanging limply by his side and a streak of blood flowing from the back of his head.

'Come, Watson,' he insisted, making light of his injuries. 'We must stop him before he kills somebody.'

We ran after the Duke, whose mania had evidently endowed him with great vigour, for he ran ahead of us with surprising speed. Yet we eventually gained on him, Holmes hollering at him to desist as we had him almost in our grasp.

The Duke spun around and met us with an inexorable gaze, holding in his hands a long knife.

'You see, Mr Holmes, that I am not quite so easy to defeat,' he said, quite possessed with rage. 'Admit that you would never have caught me if that miserable pair had not given the game away.'

'You have proved a most worthy adversary,' said Holmes. 'I confess, your Grace, that you resisted my most determined efforts in capturing you. But the game is surely at an end.'

'There may be time for me to yet claim a final victim,' replied the Duke, his face creased in a defiant sneer.

'Mr Holmes!' cried a familiar voice. I turned to see a cab draw to a halt, from which both Lestrade and Squibby emerged. Several policemen in a four-wheeler followed just behind them.

'It is too late,' said Holmes. 'You must know all is lost.'

'It is never too late, Mr Holmes.'

With that, the Duke lunged towards my friend, brandishing his knife as Holmes fought to disarm him. I rushed to assist, yet our adversary swept me aside and I watched in horror as he struggled free from Holmes' injured grip, poised to aim a fatal blow upon his person. Yet the next moment, a great arm enveloped the Duke's torso and threw him with great force to the ground.

'Squibby!' cried Holmes in astonishment, as the Duke was hauled to his feet, now quite secure in Squibby's iron grip.

'He will not escape me, Mr Holmes,' said he.

'Thank you, Squibby.' said Holmes, surveying the helpless Duke. 'Indeed, I believe he shall not. Watson, our nightmare is finally over.'

25.

The public good

Sherlock Holmes was laid upon the sofa in our sitting room a couple of days after our adventure, his head bandaged and his arm still affording him some discomfort from his struggle with the Duke. Holmes had talked little upon the matter while he convalesced, until I at last ventured to steer the conversation in the direction of his vanquished nemesis.

'It appears remarkable,' said I, peering over that morning's copy of the Times. 'That the papers have yet to announce that Jack the Ripper has been caught. Nor have they reported the death of Benjamin Bates. What game do you suppose that Lestrade and his lot are playing?'

'It is no concern of ours, Watson,' said Holmes dismissively. 'I have provided Scotland Yard with the solution to the crimes. It is now their task to conclude matters in accordance with the law.'

'Yet there is one aspect of the case which still puzzles me, Holmes.'

'And what might that be, Watson?'

'After meeting Bates and O'Connor in the restaurant, you claimed to have gained the final piece of the puzzle. Yet I confess to being unable to fathom what this apparently conclusive clue might have been.'

'Ah! You were quite bewildered at proceedings, as I seem to recall,' said Holmes, with a mischievous grin. 'I had, of course, arranged with Bates that he and O'Connor would be there that evening, as you have no doubt fathomed. The question which remained concerned the identity of the man whom Hutchinson had seen with Kelly. I was certain that it was O'Connor, yet I wished to prove myself correct. You perhaps did not notice the tell-tale slivers of dried wax upon his moustache? It is a remarkable fact that traces of its application might remain visible many days after its user believes himself relived of its effects. I confess that I might have failed to observe such minute particles upon O'Connor's whiskers had I not purposely looked for them.'

'You expected to find wax upon O'Connor's moustache?' I asked in wonderment.

'I did, Watson. It seemed obvious that he applied this in order to achieve the curled appearance to his moustache of which Hutchinson spoke. Why he did so, I cannot be sure. But I suspect he adopted such a distinguished feature as part of a modest attempt at a disguise. Bates attested to the man's nerves upon the night of the murder. I would guess that O'Connor sought any conceivable means of disguising his identity before venturing out into the night. It appears to have been successful, for Hutchinson spoke of the man he saw as being some years younger than O'Connor.'

'Extraordinary,' I exclaimed.

'It is nothing of the sort, Watson. I was also able to deduce that it was he who had assisted the Duke during the murder of Mary Kelly. Do not look so astonished, Watson. It took only a casual glance at O'Connor's hands for me to observe that his fingers were punctured with cuts which could only been inflicted by fingernails. They were evidence of Kelly's last struggle as her life ebbed away. O'Connor was present when the Duke struck. Her desperate cries alarmed him, so he assisted the Duke as she clutched at the knife that was to slay her. Our visit to the restaurant enabled me to complete my understanding of the precise order of events.'

As I absorbed this intelligence, my thoughts were interrupted by Mrs Hudson's arrival at the door.

'Gentleman to see you, Mr Holmes,' she said. Before she could announce our visitor's name, the enormous figure of Mycroft Holmes framed our doorway.

'Thank you, Mrs Hudson,' said Holmes.

Mycroft Holmes observed our landlady as she departed, waiting until the door was safely closed before turning to us with a grim expression across his face.

'I need to speak to you, Sherlock,' he said gruffly. 'You too, Dr Watson.'

'My dear Mycroft, if the rarity of your visits is proportionate to their importance, then this is indeed a matter of the utmost seriousness.'

Mycroft ignored Holmes' brusque tone and eased himself into an armchair.

'I am here on the order of the Queen,' said he.

'The Queen?' I gasped.

'You have spoken to Her Majesty?' asked Holmes dubiously.

'Her representatives have contacted me. I warn you, Sherlock, that both of you are at the heart of a great constitutional crisis.'

'Crisis, brother?'

'The unfortunate matter of the Duke of Buckingham and Chandos.'

'You are referring to his murder of five women, I presume?'

'This is a most delicate matter, Sherlock,' implored Mycroft, leaning forward in his chair. 'The Government wished me to speak to you. They and Her Majesty's advisors are most keen to gain your assurances of silence.'

'Silence, Mycroft?'

'You must understand the predicament in which we find ourselves, Sherlock. The Duke's indiscretions have caused a great deal of embarrassment to the Establishment. Were it to emerge that Jack the Ripper was a member of the British nobility, incalculable damage to the monarchy would be incurred.'

'Surely they do not propose to cover-up these awful crimes?' I protested. 'The man is guilty.'

'That is regrettably correct, Dr Watson. But he also a Duke. It is felt that more harm than good would result from his denouncement as a murderer.'

'But this is outrageous!' I cried in horror. 'The man sent those poor women and young Bates to their deaths. Holmes, you cannot possibly condone such action?'

'In truth, Watson, the moment I discovered the identity of Jack the Ripper, I expected such a conclusion to the affair.'

'I am astounded, Holmes!' I thundered, rising to my feet.

'Calm yourself, Watson,' said he. 'Your principles are admirable but, I regret to say, misguided. There can be no hope of bringing such a man to justice without the most unsightly of scandals.'

'My brother is correct, Doctor,' said Mycroft. 'We would face a crisis that would rock the British Empire to its foundations were the Duke to stand trial.'

'So, he will be free to kill again?' I asked incredulously.

237

'Rest assured that the Duke shall claim no further victims,' said Mycroft solemnly. 'His exertions of a few days ago have caused a stroke from which he will never recover. The Doctors have informed me that he is not expected to live much longer.'

'I am sorry, but I find it intolerable that a man possessed of such evil may go unpunished.'

'He was a sick man, Doctor. The syphilis had taken a hold of him. Apparently, it can cause a form of madness, of which I am sure you are aware.'

'It is true that some sufferers can develop generalised paralysis of the insane,' I conceded. 'It can alter their personality quite completely.'

'You see, Dr Watson? He was a good man before falling victim to this unfortunate mania. During his tenure as Governor of Madras, he organised relief for hundreds of thousands of people. The people there called him the 'saving Duke'. But his laudable attributes aside, he is, of course, a peer of the realm and descended from a former Prime Minister. Heavens, if the vagaries of history had fallen more kindly, his family might have acceded to the Throne. We must think of the public good before we consider what is right or wrong. The Crown requires your assistance, Dr Watson.'

'Then it appears that I have no choice. You have my word, Mycroft. I shall not reveal anything of the matter whatsoever.'

'Thank you, Dr Watson. Sherlock?'

'I shall be the soul of discretion, my dear brother.'

A smile of satisfaction flickered across the face of Mycroft Holmes as he lifted his great frame from his seat and made his way to the door.

'And what of O'Connor and McCarthy?' I asked. 'Are they to also escape justice?'

'Dr Watson, you must understand that the government must place the national interest above the prosecution of these two men. It is regrettable that they must remain unpunished, yet the simple fact is that their prosecution would inevitably lead to exposing the Duke's role in the matter. We have, however, curtailed Mr McCarthy's rather sordid business upon the continent. Rest assured that his actions shall remain under scrutiny for some time. But his and O'Connor's role in these murders can never be revealed.'

'It just seems so unjust,' I remonstrated.

'The public good, Doctor,' said Mycroft, turning to me as he departed. 'I have your word.'

'I do not know what to make of it all, Holmes,' I said when we were alone.

'This affair has certainly left a bitter taste as none before it, Watson,' replied Holmes. 'Capturing the Duke was one thing. Bringing him to justice was another matter entirely. As unpalatable as it may appear, my brother is entirely correct. No good could arise now from exposing the truth.'

'Perhaps you are right, Holmes,' I said. 'But I confess that I do not like it.'

'We have had quite an adventure, Watson,' said Holmes. 'Let us merely be thankful that it is finally at an end.'

Sherlock Holmes took his violin from the side-table and began to play a rather euphonious melody. From my room, I could hear the dulcet tones of his playing until late into the afternoon.

Epilogue

It was not in the nature of Sherlock Holmes to retain an interest in a case once his part in the matter had concluded. Never had I heard him contemplate what had become of those involved in his investigations, no matter how extraordinary their stories had proved. I applied Holmes' detached approach to my chronicles, my notes thus containing remarkably few mentions of what became of the clients in even his most famous cases. Due to the unique nature of the Whitechapel murders, however, I followed the lives of those involved for many years after the passing of events.

The Duke of Buckingham and Chandos died on 26th March 1889. The official cause of his death was recorded as unknown, with prostatitis being cited as the most probable.

George Lusk was able to put the awful events of 1888 behind him, his business flourishing over the ensuing years. He never re-married and died earlier this year, still resident at Alderney Road.

Holmes managed to have Squibby rewarded with a job at the Royal Mews. He proved to be exceedingly hard-working, eventually gaining a position of considerable responsibility before dying in the great influenza epidemic of 1918. It was only from a notice of his death in the Evening Standard that I discovered his real name to be George Cullen. It is pleasing to note that Squibby's improved finances enabled him to educate his young nephew, who had once appeared at Baker Street as nothing but a straggling youth. Edward Buckley is presently a successful blacksmith with his own premises in Bethnal green.

T.P O'Connor was editor of several newspapers in the years following the Whitechapel murders. He is presently an M.P for Liverpool and remains a well-known figure amongst the luminaries of Fleet Street.

Jack McCarthy expanded his Dorset Street empire, purchasing huge tracts of the street before his retirement in 1914 following the death of his wife. He still commands great respect in the area as both a landlord and businessman.

The later and continued successes of both O'Connor and McCarthy serve only to exacerbate my dismay at the conclusion of this extraordinary case. I record these vile fellows here, merely as amongst that diminishing body of men still living who know the true story of Jack the Ripper.

Dr John H. Watson

March 1919

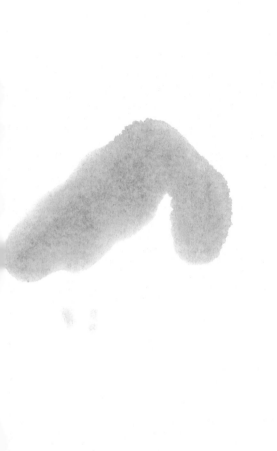

Printed in Great Britain
by Amazon

81889122R00144